HOLMES IS MISSING

For a preview of upcoming books and information about the author, visit JamesPatterson.com or find him on Facebook, X, or Instagram.

HOLMES IS MISSING

A HOLMES, MARGARET & POE MYSTERY

JAMES
PATTERSON
and BRIAN SITTS

Little, Brown and Company
New York Boston London

Copyright © 2025 by James Patterson
Excerpts from *The Writer* and *Paranoia* copyright © 2025 by James Patterson

Little, Brown and Company
Hachette Book Group
1290 Avenue of the Americas, New York, NY 10104
littlebrown.com

First Edition: January 2025

Little, Brown and Company is a division of Hachette Book Group, Inc. The Little, Brown name and logo are trademarks of Hachette Book Group, Inc.

The publisher is not responsible for websites (or their content) that are not owned by the publisher.

The Hachette Speakers Bureau provides a wide range of authors for speaking events. To find out more, go to hachettespeakersbureau.com or email hachettespeakers@hbgusa.com.

Little, Brown and Company books may be purchased in bulk for business, educational, or promotional use. For information, please contact your local bookseller or the Hachette Book Group Special Markets Department at special.markets@hbgusa.com.

ISBN 9780316569972 (hc) / 9780316584463 (large print)
LCCN 2024941730

Printing 1, 2024

LSC-C

Printed in the United States of America

HOLMES IS MISSING

CHAPTER 1

IT WAS 2 a.m. The posted speed limit on the Williamsburg Bridge into Manhattan was 35 miles per hour. But Auguste Poe was abiding by his personal driving code: Go as fast as possible, whenever possible. For short stretches, the needle on his vintage Shelby Charger was touching 60. The hum of the tires bounced off the concrete side barriers. Margaret Marple sat beside him in the front passenger seat, gritting her teeth — and biting her tongue.

"I know what you're thinking, so keep it to yourself," said Poe. "Helene said to get there in a hurry."

"And hopefully, still among the living," Marple replied, watching the bridge struts whiz by in a blur.

The call had come in on Poe's personal cell phone barely half an hour ago — not on the main line at their private detective agency, Holmes, Marple & Poe Investigations. Marple was usually the one with connections, so it irked her just a little that in this case Poe was the one with the inside line to an NYPD homicide detective, but she knew why. And a case was a case.

"Helene said this was a big one. That's about all she had time to say," Poe had told Marple after he'd knocked on her apartment door, down the hallway from his own.

Now fully awake, Marple took in the glittering lights of Manhattan, its towers and spires glowing like party ornaments. They crossed the bridge and sped west across the city. Even at two in the morning, there was traffic along Delancey. Poe downshifted through a yellow light and made an illegal screeching left turn onto Ludlow, heading south.

Marple rocked hard to the right. *"Bus!"* she shouted.

Poe swerved just in time to avoid clipping the thirty-ton brute.

"I wish Holmes was here," she said.

Poe shot her a quizzical look. "Why would you miss him right now?" he asked. "Brendan is a terrible driver."

"That makes two of you," said Marple.

Their destination was St. Michael's Hospital, but the police barricade stopped them a block short. Poe pulled the Charger to the right and double-parked, effectively blocking two NYPD patrol cars. He turned off the ignition and opened the driver-side door, ignoring the "Hey, asshole!" shouts from cops nearby. Marple could barely squeeze out between the passenger door and the police vehicle to her right. Poe met her on the sidewalk. He put both hands on her shoulders.

"Look, Margaret. It goes without saying that I miss Brendan too," he said. "Don't worry. He'll send us a sign when he's ready."

They both turned and hurried to the end of the street, where St. Michael's loomed—a ten-story hunk of granite with small, narrow windows. It had been a fixture in the neighborhood since the late 1800s, when the Sisters of Charity convinced a group of rich Upper East Siders that the Lower East Side needed help. The nuns were long gone, but the hospital had evolved into one of the city's most prestigious private medical centers.

As Marple and Poe got closer to the hospital entrance, they

saw cops running in the same direction, flowing from a nearby precinct house, shoulder radios squawking. The street was lined with small businesses, most closed and shuttered for the night. One glowing exception was Cops & Docs, a worn-looking bar sitting kitty-corner from the hospital.

"There's Helene!" Poe called out. Marple spotted her at the same time.

Detective Lieutenant Helene Grey was waiting near a stone pillar in front of the hospital. She wore dark trousers and a matching jacket, with a telltale bulge from the gun belt at her hip. Her badge was suspended around her neck, dangling over her crisp white blouse.

As they got closer, Marple noted there was no overt acknowledgment between Grey and Poe that they'd been lovers for months. There were no pleasantries at all, just cursory nods all around. Helene's face looked drawn—as grim as Marple had ever seen her. And they had been together in some very tough situations.

"What is it?" asked Poe. "What's going on?"

"It's a kidnapping," said Grey. "But not just that. Honestly, I've never seen anything like it. Nobody at NYPD has." She turned to lead the way past a hospital security booth and into the main lobby. Grey walked quickly, blowing past other detectives and plainclothes teams. Uniformed cops gave her room as she powered toward the first-floor elevator bank.

"Where are we headed?" asked Marple.

Grey jabbed the Up button with her thumb. Her expression turned even darker.

"Maternity," she said.

CHAPTER 2

POE ALWAYS FELT a tingle in Helene's presence—an enlivened state of being. Even when she was all business. Even when the circumstances were bleak. Like now. Standing a few inches behind her in the elevator, Poe fixated on the clip that held her blond hair in a tight bun above her jacket collar. It was a small circular disk the color of a blood moon. As omens go, it was far from good.

Marple squeezed his arm. "Please behave yourself when we get there," she whispered.

"When have I not?" asked Poe.

A second later, the elevator door opened onto total chaos.

Poe could hear women crying even before he saw them. He followed Grey and Marple toward the nurses' station in the center of the unit. Cops and nurses and detectives were milling around the hallways. Hospital security honchos paced the floor in dark suits while floor guards in short-sleeved shirts gripped their walkies and tried to appear useful.

Poe looked toward a small glass-fronted room off the main

unit. The crying was coming from there, from where half a dozen women in shapeless hospital gowns were sobbing and wailing and clinging to one another like condemned prisoners. Suddenly, Poe felt a hard shoulder against his chest. An athletic man in a bulky grey suit was blocking the way. Like Helene, he wore a detective badge around his neck.

"What are these assholes doing here?" he asked. The question was directed at Grey, as was the follow-up: "Who the hell invited PIs to an active crime scene?"

"Back off, Vail," said Helene. "I brought them in. My call."

Poe was fully aware of the friction between his firm and the NYPD in general. The reason for it was simple. Holmes, Marple & Poe Investigations had recently solved some very big cases—right under the noses of the police department. Those noses were still out of joint. But Poe didn't care. He poked Detective Vail in the chest. "Haven't you heard? There's been a kidnapping."

"That's not possible," said Vail. "This place has security up the ass. You couldn't steal a goddamn Band-Aid from this floor."

Before Poe could respond, Marple yanked him aside. "Stop it, Auguste! You won't make any friends with that attitude."

"I'm not here to make friends," Poe replied. "I'm here to get answers."

A nurse in burgundy scrubs walked up and handed Grey a sheet of paper.

"Is this the list?" Grey asked.

The nurse nodded grimly. She had the look of a woman at the end of a very long shift—maybe two.

Grey tapped the page. "Six," she said. "Six missing newborn babies."

Poe looked at Marple. Helene had not exaggerated. This was a huge case. Too bad their firm was not at full strength. He leaned over and whispered in Marple's ear. "Of all the times to be one brain short!"

CHAPTER 3

MARPLE TURNED TOWARD the roomful of sobbing women in hospital gowns. She realized that she was looking at the frantic mothers—the ones whose babies had been stolen from the nursery in the middle of the night. Had they been gathered together in the same room by the cops or had they found one another in their fear?

As she watched through the glass, Marple saw a detective slip into the room with them, her pen and notepad ready. The women lurched forward, almost engulfing her. Their faces were streaked with tears, their expressions haunted.

Marple felt Poe at her elbow. "Best day of their lives," he said. "Now the worst."

Suddenly, an elevator door opened and a whole new group burst into the unit.

"Brace yourself," said Marple. "I think the dads just arrived."

The partners emerged as a single mass, wild-eyed and panicky. Marple counted five men and one woman. A big guy in expensive slacks and a blue dress shirt was in the lead. *A Master of the Universe type,* thought Marple, *looking to take control.*

"Where's my wife?" he shouted. "Christine!" He moved like a rugby player, bumping cops and nurses aside. When he spotted the room full of distraught women, he waved frantically. One of the women waved back. A young cop stepped up to ask for ID. The big guy pushed past him like he wasn't even there.

Marple watched as the other five followed him into the glass-fronted room, finding their partners and embracing them tightly.

The keening inside the room intensified, now accompanied by curses and angry mutters. The man in the dress shirt turned on the young detective. "What happened here? What are you doing about this? Where are our babies?"

Marple saw the detective try to assert her command, but it was no use. The furious father towered over her. A couple of hospital security guards hustled over, but the angry dads shoved them out of the room. The detective backed out too, clearly flustered.

Helene Grey walked over to Marple and Poe. "What a shit show," she muttered.

"What else do we know?" asked Poe.

"It was clean. It was quick. It was professional."

"How many babies were in the nursery at the time?"

"Eight. We're keeping the remaining two babies there for the moment—under close watch—but we've isolated the mothers and moved all other patients off this floor."

"Inside job?" asked Marple.

"No doubt," said Helene.

"Everybody listen up, please!" The voice had come from the nurses' station in the center of the floor. Marple turned to see a tall woman in a knee-length lab coat standing in front of the curved countertop. Her posture was perfect and her greying chestnut hair was pulled into a severe ponytail. Through piercing eyes, she looked out over the turmoil and commanded silence.

"I'm Dr. Revell Schulte," she said, her voice clear and firm. "I'm head of the maternity unit. I know what's happened here is terrible. But we need order. And we need calm. This is a birthing center, not a police station. The women down this hallway have just given birth. They've all undergone massive physical trauma and are in need of medical care. So if you don't absolutely need to be here, please leave."

"You heard the doctor," a tall, bookish-looking man in a dark suit said to Grey. He'd walked up during Dr. Schulte's speech. "I don't understand what a homicide detective is doing at a kidnapping scene in the first place."

"Good to see you, Captain," said Grey.

Marple decided this must be Captain Graham Duff, the newly arrived head of the Major Case Squad. She had heard about Duff but hadn't yet met him in person. Her first impression: he was every inch the prick she'd expected.

Marple could tell Grey wasn't a fan of her new boss either. It was clear now that she was unsettled by his intrusion, but she quickly regained her composure. "I figured it was all hands on deck on a call like this, Captain. I know it's not my case to catch. I'm just here to help."

"So what's with the spectators?" he asked, jerking his head toward Marple and Poe.

Marple cleared her throat. "Captain Duff, I'm Margaret Marple, and this is my partner Auguste Poe. We're private investigators from Brooklyn. You may have heard about—"

"I know who you are," said Duff, cutting her off. "And like the good doctor said, you don't need to be here."

"Look! It's *them*!" The shout had come from the roomful of parents. Marple glanced over to see the frantic mothers and fathers looking their way. "It's Poe! And Marple!" one of the women shouted. "Thank *God*!" another mom sobbed. The parents spilled out of the tiny room and headed across the floor.

Marple smiled at Duff, her British accent adding an extra dab of sweetness. "See that, Captain? I believe we might be wanted after all."

CHAPTER 4

POE AND MARPLE held their ground as the parents swarmed around them. Grey and Duff took a step back to avoid being run over. It was almost an assault — the desperate parents clamoring for answers, all talking at once. *"What's going on?"* *"Can't you do something?"* *"Why is everybody just standing around?"*

Poe held out his hands and pressed them gently downward, as if calming the waters. "One at a time, please. We're here to help." He glanced at Helene. "We're *all* here to help."

One of the mothers spoke up, her voice shaking. "You were the ones who found those killers this summer."

"Yes," said Poe. "We are."

"Is this a murder case?" wailed another mom. "Is my baby dead?"

Her husband wrapped his arm tightly around her shoulders. "Nobody's dead!" he said firmly.

"Nobody knows anything yet," said Duff, stepping in front of the throng, "but it's important we move quickly."

The parents totally ignored him. The man in the dress shirt reached past Duff to grasp Poe's hand. "I'm Sterling Cade," he

13

said. "I'd like to hire your firm." He looked around at the other parents. "I think we'd *all* like to hire you." The others mumbled and nodded their assent. "I promise you," Cade went on, "money is not an issue. Whatever you need from us, you've got it."

"We'd be honored to take the case," said Poe.

"Hold on a goddamn minute!" Duff called out, a sharp edge to his voice. "This is a New York Police Department investigation. And if it turns out to be an abduction, as it appears to be, we'll be calling in resources from around the country." Looking at the desperate faces in front of him, he softened his tone slightly. "Please, folks. I know this is a bad time. I know you're scared. But we have this investigation under control."

"We hear you," said a woman in a maternity gown, standing with her wife. She pointed firmly toward Marple and Poe. "But we want *them*."

"You're making a mistake, ma'am," said Duff, suddenly icy again. He held up his bony index finger and jabbed it in the air three times for emphasis. "We need *one* investigation, *one* central task force, *one* coordinated effort. That's how crimes like this get solved. By professionals doing their jobs. Not by amateurs playing cops and robbers for a fee."

Poe had a sharp retort ready, but he had a feeling he wouldn't need it. And he was right. Another mother piped up from the back of the crowd. She stared directly at Duff.

"So why didn't *you* catch those murderers this summer on your own? Why did you need help from Holmes, Marple, and Poe? It was all over the news."

Duff's mouth tightened. Poe glanced at Helene, reading her expression. Her look said, *Don't push it.* Then he heard the question he knew was coming.

"Hey," one of the dads said, "where's the other guy? Where the hell is Holmes?"

Poe looked over at Marple. He knew she'd been expecting the question too. She had an answer ready.

"Mr. Holmes is working on a private case of his own at the moment," said Marple. "But he's not far, I promise."

Poe nodded with a tight smile. Nothing Marple had said was strictly untrue. Their partner, Brendan Holmes, was indeed hard at work. At a private facility in upstate New York. Kicking his decades-long addiction to heroin.

Grey was aware of the situation. Duff, thank God, was not.

"If I know Holmes," said Poe, "he'll be helping out any way he can."

Duff's cell phone rang. He turned away to answer it. Grey stepped up and faced the group of distraught parents. She lifted her badge on its lanyard. "I'm Detective Lieutenant Helene Grey, NYPD." She nodded toward Poe and Marple. "I've worked with these investigators before. I trust them. And if you want their help, that's your decision. We're all on the same team here. What *all* of us want is to find your children. Your babies. So right now what we need is to get your statements. One at a time. In your own words. Everything you can remember about the last twenty-four hours. Can we please start there?"

Poe watched as the crowd melted into acceptance. Even the wannabe-alpha Sterling Cade was nodding. Grey had gotten to them. Poe had seen her play tough cop plenty of times. But what this crowd needed was empathy. Grey clearly sensed it, and she'd delivered. She'd also given his firm a solid endorsement. Poe felt like reaching out to hug her, which he knew would be wildly inappropriate. He looked to his right.

Marple was gone.

For a second, Poe was nervous. Then he realized that his partner was probably off doing what she did best.

She was snooping.

CHAPTER 5

IN CHARGED SITUATIONS like this, Margaret Marple found that flashing her private investigator's official license card opened as many doors as a bona fide police shield. The trick was to wave it quickly for effect and then tuck it away. Her British charm and no-nonsense attitude usually did the rest.

That's how she got nurse Ellie Tellman to lead her to the actual crime scene—the hospital nursery—after they first slipped into a small staff anteroom to don pale yellow PPE outfits. Tellman was in her early twenties, with neat, beaded cornrows that spilled across her shoulders. Marple had detected a musical lilt to her accent, now slightly muted by the N95 mask.

"You're Jamaican," said Marple.

The nurse nodded. "Montego Bay."

"How do you like working here?"

"I love working with babies," said the nurse, her eyes wide and expressive. "Until tonight."

Tellman led the way from the anteroom down a short corridor to an imposing metal door. A sign below a small window in the center read, STAFF ONLY BEYOND THIS POINT. Tellman pushed through. Marple followed.

Inside, everything felt jarringly wrong.

The nursery, designed as an oasis of comfort and quiet, was now occupied by sturdy cops in gowns and masks. Marple's stomach dropped at the sight of crime-scene tape on six empty bassinets in the center of the room. On one side of the brightly lit space, two new arrivals to the world lay in clear plastic bassinets, wrapped like burritos in hospital blankets. Marple scanned the room from one side to the other. It looked sound and secure. Other than the door they had entered, the only exit was at the back, leading to a side corridor.

This nursery was nothing like the old viewing galleries from the last century, where new parents stood tapping at a picture window, trying to pick their baby out from a roomful of newborns. This was more like a bank vault, designed to protect precious gems.

"Hey! Who let you in here?" It was a man's voice. Stern and irritated. Marple looked over to see a hospital security guard looming in the doorway, his PPE gown stretched tightly across his broad chest.

"It's okay, Santo," said Tellman in her charming lilt. "This is Miss Marple. She's investigating."

Marple was ready to whip out her ID card again, but Santo seemed willing to give her the benefit of the doubt. He let the door close behind him and walked over. He peeked at one of the new babies, whose tiny foot had slipped free of the blanket. Marple looked over. The little ankle was encircled by a bright green band, the same hue as the leaves of a neon pothos plant.

"I don't know how they beat it," said Santo, shaking his head.

"Beat what?" asked Marple.

Santo pointed at the tiny band. "Every baby has this band. Matched to a band on the mother. The band has a chip inside. A sensor. You know what I mean?"

Marple nodded. "I do."

"If that band comes anywhere near an exit," said the guard, "alarms go off." He pointed at a small monitor on the wall. "Here. At the nurses' desk. At the security station. Everybody knows." He made a scissors motion with two fingers. "You clip the band, same thing. Alarm."

Marple walked over and looked above the exit door. Sure enough, there was the sensor plate, right alongside a security camera. She walked slowly back across the room until she was standing with Santo and the young nurse next to one of the occupied bassinets. Suddenly, she placed her hands on the top and started wheeling the baby across the room.

"Hey!" said the guard, starting after her.

"Miss!" yelled Tellman. "What are you doing?"

"Making a point," said Marple, moving in smooth, gliding steps. She pushed the bassinet quickly toward the exit door and stopped one inch short as Santo caught up to her, scowling and furious.

"Just wait," said Marple, holding up one hand.

She stared at the door sensor. Listened for a couple seconds. Looked over at Santo.

No alarm.

"Your little green loops are counterfeit," said Marple, looking down at the sleeping baby. "They might as well be wristbands at Coachella."

CHAPTER 6

DOWN THE HALL, Poe was battling a touch of claustrophobia. The maternity unit's security annex was way too small for the dozens of law enforcement personnel inside — cops, detectives, and a couple of newly arrived agents from the local FBI office. Squeezed up against a wall between two overweight uniforms, Poe couldn't shake the image of a clown car.

"Quiet, dammit! I can't think!" The assistant head of security held up one hand for silence. He was sweating like a weight lifter as he ran through footage from the surveillance cameras. The audience was riveted. But there wasn't much to see.

Poe was not at all shocked to learn that the nursery cams had been disabled for two minutes — exactly the amount of time it apparently took to walk from the nursery to the supply elevator, then go down five floors to street level. He and Helene had timed the route themselves.

"How many cameras in the system?" Poe called out, still pressed against the wall.

"Hundreds," said the security guy. "Interior. Exterior. Everywhere."

"They disabled as few as possible," said Poe. "Surgical."

"What the hell are you doing in here?" It was Detective Vail. The room was so packed that Poe hadn't noticed him.

"I'm trying to solve the case," said Poe. "You?"

"Shit! *Look!*" said the security guy. Like the nursery cams, the loading dock views were all distorted with static. Except one. The view from this camera linked to an older CCTV setup. The image was grainy and the angle was not all that helpful. It showed a partial side view of a box truck, parked so that no driver or tags were visible. At 01:00:01 on the time code, the truck was there. By 01:00:15, it was gone.

"It's a Ford E-Series," said Poe, "2014 or '15."

Helene immediately pulled out her phone and put out an APB on the vehicle, but Poe knew there were probably thousands like it in the tri-state area. And he also knew that operatives this slick wouldn't be using the truck for long. If the babies were still alive, they were probably tucked away in a soundproof room by now.

A perimeter had already been set up around Manhattan. Highways. Bridges. Tunnels. A diligent step but probably worthless. Poe realized that even without breaking any speed limits, the kidnappers could already be in Connecticut, Massachusetts, or downstate New Jersey. Not to mention at any of the area's airports.

He needed air. He exited the windowless room the only way he could, by backing out, squeezing past police and security personnel as he went. Loosening his collar in the bright, antiseptic-scented hallway, he felt Helene's shoulder against his. She let out a long breath.

"We need to talk," she said. "You and me."

"Something you couldn't say in there?" asked Poe, nodding back toward the security room.

"Correct," said Helene. "It's private. Your ears only."

CHAPTER 7

THE ELEVATOR DOOR opened onto the hospital lobby. At ground level, the police presence was still thick, mixed with doctors and nurses moving around on their wee-hours shifts. Poe walked with Helene across the polished floor and through the revolving door to the sidewalk.

When they stepped outside, Helene nodded across the street to the Cops & Docs bar. "Over there," she said. They wound their way past idling police cars and entered through the weathered wooden front door.

The place was new to Poe, off the beaten path from his typical drinking establishments in the city. The décor was exactly as the name suggested: walls festooned with vintage photographs of New York police officers and white-coated physicians, and an eclectic collection of memorabilia: nightsticks, badges, wooden crutches, rusted handcuffs, and antique stethoscopes. A large plaque read, SERVING THOSE WHO SERVE SINCE 1885. Poe looked around. Even at this hour the place was doing a solid business. Clearly, building a neighborhood bar around two 24/7 professions was a pretty smart business model, especially when both jobs required a lot of decompression and commiseration.

Poe spotted a booth occupied by a team of uniformed cops and a couple of detectives. Helene steered him toward the bar instead. A plastic candleholder with a fake flame sat in the middle of the bar's worn wooden surface, marred by tiny scratches and stained with water rings from thousands of glasses.

"Eighteen eighty-five," said Poe, nodding toward the wall plaque. "Looks like some of this stuff has been here since they opened."

He was just trying to make conversation. Inside, he was anxious. *What is this about?* He was worried that he'd offended Helene with one or more of his odd habits. Or maybe she'd found out something about his past. As close as they'd become over the past few months, there were still a lot of things Poe didn't want her to know. Not yet.

Maybe never.

"Hi. What can I get you?" The black-clad bartender spoke in a monotone that seemed perfectly suited to the hour. It matched her jet-black hair and hollow-eyed expression.

"Bourbon. Neat," said Poe.

"Ginger ale for me," said Helene.

The bartender nodded and shuffled off.

"You're still on duty?" Poe asked Helene.

She nodded, then lowered her eyes. "Funny, right? Just when you need a drink the most, you can't have one."

"You can have a sip of mine," said Poe. "I won't tell."

Helene drew a deep breath then and exhaled slowly. She rested a hand on the bar and leaned toward Poe, looking him directly in the eye. "Auguste, I'm pregnant."

Poe sat up straight on his stool, his heart racing. He blinked.

It took a few seconds for the words to register completely. He reached over and grabbed Helene's hand.

She flicked her eyes around the room and pulled away. "I know this isn't what you were expecting," she said softly. "Believe me, neither was I."

"You're sure?" asked Poe. Stupid question. Stalling for time.

"I'm a pretty sharp detective," said Helene. "I think I can tell two lines from one."

"What are you...? What can I...?" Poe was fumbling for words. Fumbling for thoughts. "I mean, are you...happy...or...?"

"Detective Grey!" A uniformed cop was shouting from the doorway. Helene looked back. The cop took two steps into the room and jerked his thumb toward the hospital. "Duff wants you to get back up there. *Now!*"

Helene stared at Poe for a second, then abruptly stood up. She gave him a quick pat on the shoulder. "Stay," she said.

Poe turned to watch Helene leave, the uniform right behind her. A moment later, the bartender reappeared and set down the drinks, placing the ginger ale in front of Helene's now-empty seat. She turned and started shuffling back toward the other end of the bar. Poe glanced at his watch and then called after her. "Excuse me!"

"Something wrong with your drink?"

Poe shook his head. "I'm sure it's fine. I haven't even started on it. But seeing as you're busy and it's getting close to last call, I wanted to let you know that I'll definitely need another."

CHAPTER 8

FOUR HOURS LATER, Poe was still reeling over Helene's news and nursing a significant hangover besides. He'd tried texting Grey several times before dawn but had gotten no response. Either she was tied up with the case or she was avoiding him. When he came downstairs at 8 a.m. after barely two hours of sleep, he kept the pregnancy news to himself, as if telling somebody else would make it too real.

He sat down next to Marple at the island in the chef's kitchen that adjoined their office space on the first floor of their shared building, a two-story brick structure originally built as a bakery in the 1800s. Poe and his partners had had the space gut-renovated shortly after joining forces to establish Holmes, Marple & Poe Investigations, installing three private apartments and a personal library for themselves on the second floor, with interior balconies overlooking the lower level's open-plan workspace and an elegant staircase linking the two levels.

It was a perfect live-work situation, if a bit unconventional. What it lacked in privacy, it made up for in convenience. On mornings like this, Poe truly appreciated the one-story commute.

"Where did you disappear to last night?" asked Marple, sipping from a mug of tea.

"I could ask you the same thing."

"I was in the St. Michael's nursery investigating the security, which was supposed to be foolproof. Where were you?"

"Thinking," said Poe.

"And drinking?" asked Marple.

"I don't need a babysitter, Margaret."

Virginia, the investigation firm's young assistant-slash-housekeeper, was busy at the stove, the griddle sizzling. The twenty-four-year-old had been Poe's first hire, and one of his best management decisions. Everybody agreed on that. Virginia had immediately brought order to the firm's files, accounting practices, and contact lists. She'd even updated their security system. She had an uncanny knack for knowing what was needed at any particular moment. *An absolute gem,* Marple called her.

Virginia's dark hair was newly tinted—orange today. The light glinted off the hoop in her nostril. Baskerville, her huge white mastiff, was hunkered down at her side, waiting expectantly for scraps. Marple's black cat, Annabel, sat poised across the room, clocking each of Virginia's movements.

"Who wants pancakes?" Virginia asked, spooning golden batter into the sizzling skillet.

Poe raised his hand. "Yes, please." Virginia's sweet potato pancakes were amazing.

"Me too," said Marple, nibbling on a slice of leftover cider cake, another of Virginia's specialties. Recently, Virginia had begun to honor the building's history as a bakery by turning out an irresistible array of muffins, breads, and desserts. The aroma of the pancakes mixed with the aroma of the thick-cut bacon from the oven.

Poe rubbed his head, trying to clear the ache and fog from his brain. A massive injection of protein and carbs was exactly what his weakened system needed. And, as usual, Virginia seemed to anticipate it.

"Virginia, you're spoiling us," said Marple.

"It's the farmer in me," said Virginia. "I like feeding people."

As Poe had learned, Virginia was raised in rural Pennsylvania, the only daughter of a Quaker dairy farmer. When she realized she was not cut out for country life, she moved to New York, bringing her farm recipes, her Quaker discipline, and her love of animals with her.

Virginia dropped a half slice of cooked bacon into Baskerville's huge maw and tossed a much smaller piece to Annabel, then slid a fresh platter of pancakes onto the table and lifted the lid off a small ceramic dish. "Honey butter," she said. "Made it yesterday."

Poe looked up from his plate. "Virginia, sit," he said. "Stop cooking and eat."

"Already did," said Virginia, wiping her hands on a dish towel. She was always the first one in the office, even though her apartment was several blocks away. "I'll just have coffee."

She sat down on a stool across from Poe and Marple and looked out over the first-floor office space. Then she let out a long sigh. "It's not the same without Mr. Holmes, is it?"

Poe's nerves were already frayed. By the kidnapping. By the momentous secret Helene had shared with him. But for some reason, this was the breaking point. He slapped his hand on the countertop and muttered through gritted teeth, "Will everybody please stop stating the obvious?!"

Virginia sat up straight, her eyes wide. "I'm sorry," she said, her voice quaking, "I just..."

Marple put her hand on Virginia's forearm. "Don't worry about it. Mr. Poe is simply frazzled by the case." Virginia already knew all about the hospital kidnapping. It had led the local news that morning.

"Six babies," said Virginia. "So horrible."

Poe put down his fork and looked over at Marple. "Everybody misses Holmes," he said. "You. Me. Virginia. The dog too, no doubt. I think it's time."

Marple cocked her head. "You mean...?"

"You know exactly what I mean."

Marple slid off her chair and looked across the table. She wiped the last bit of honey butter off her lips with a napkin. "Hold down the fort, Virginia," she said. "Mr. Poe and I are going on a road trip."

CHAPTER 9

"ARE WE ABSOLUTELY sure this is a good idea?" asked Marple. She was now having second thoughts about the mission, not least the toll a ten-hour return trip might take on her sleep-deprived driver.

"What? Surprising him?" asked Poe. "It's the best possible idea."

"What if we trigger him? Throw him back into his old patterns?"

"Are you saying *we* might be a bad influence on Brendan Holmes?"

"No," said Marple after a moment's thought. "Probably the other way around." Whether the trip was prudent or not, the truth was she couldn't wait to see him.

They were heading up Route 79 toward Ithaca, New York, in Poe's '66 Pontiac GTO—a better cruising machine than the Charger, he claimed. Marple couldn't really tell the difference. To her, all of Poe's flashy muscle cars were loud and uncomfortable. Fun to drive, maybe, but not great for the passenger. All jerky shifts and engine whines. Marple much preferred sedate high-end sedans from Uber Black, but Poe loved to drive, and she wasn't about to deny him that small pleasure. Not in the mood he was in.

They were west of the Catskills now, about halfway to Ithaca, two and a half hours northwest of the city. Along the way, they passed bare fields with isolated farmhouses and small towns that had seen better days—the kind of places where Marple loved to indulge two of her favorite hobbies: antiquing and bird-watching.

"How long has it been?" asked Poe. "Since he left."

"Two months, eleven days, six hours," said Marple. She'd been keeping count. She could have added the minutes.

Marple absolutely agreed with Virginia. The office was not the same without Holmes. Without him, the place lacked a certain drive and energy. Fortunately, the workload had been light since he'd been away—minor cases, easily disposed of, or ongoing investigations that could afford to simmer for a while. At least until last night.

Even on small cases, Marple missed her partner's deductive skills and technical savvy. As a detective, he was one of a kind. She missed their everyday camaraderie too. The banter. The discussions. Even the arguments. Holmes, Marple, and Poe. The magic of three. One on one, she sometimes found Poe's moodiness exhausting.

Marple looked over at him, his hands tight on the steering wheel. So far on the drive, Poe had been quiet for long stretches, seemingly lost in his own world. Except for the ten times he had tried to speed-dial Helene—without result.

"Is something on your mind, Auguste?"

"Nothing I want to talk about right now."

"All right, then…" Time for a distraction. Marple turned on the radio and pressed Scan. Reception was iffy until the receiver locked on to a classic rock station, which came in loud and clear.

When Marple recognized the bass line to "Every Breath You Take," she cranked up the volume and began singing along, adding a sweet high harmony to the lead vocal—the one about watching somebody's every step, every word, every move.

"This should be our company theme song," said Marple, humming along when she ran out of lyrics she knew. Poe stared ahead at the road. Something was eating at him, Marple could tell. She also knew enough not to pry. At least not at the moment. Patience. It was a lesson she had learned from countless interviews and interrogations over the years. Give the dam time to burst on its own.

Marple kept humming along with Sting as she pulled out her iPad and started zipping through international crime reports. As her fingers flew across the keys, she thought about how much the world had changed since she was a fledgling investigator. It didn't seem that long ago. Now even Interpol had a presence on social media.

She spent the next couple of hours digging down to a file of current investigations around the world—cybercrimes, government corruption, counterfeiting. A few firewalls and keywords later, she landed on a confidential report from London. Four infants had recently gone missing from a private, upscale hospital in Kensington. The authorities were keeping it quiet. Somehow they'd even managed to keep the parents out of the media.

"Aha!" she said. "Take a look at this!" She held the screen up so Poe could see it.

"Not now," said Poe. "We're here."

Marple looked up and put away her iPad. They were approaching a set of fieldstone pillars with a thick iron gate. No engraved plaque told visitors that this was Lake View, but as the gate immediately swung open upon their arrival, Poe eased through the entrance and onto a winding gravel road. A minute later, the rehab center rose into view. The brick building had an almost Norman design, with wood and natural stone around the entryway, some of its hues blending in with the surrounding woods. In the distance, Marple could see sunlight reflecting off Cayuga Lake.

As they pulled up to the entrance, she smiled when she spotted Holmes on the front porch, the only Black man in the row of residents sitting in huge Adirondack chairs. His shaved head gleamed, and his bare feet rested on a small stool. He wore a plush white robe over pajamas.

"Do you think he knew we were coming?" asked Poe.

"Well, he *is* Holmes after all."

Poe pulled the car to a stop in a visitor parking space. Marple opened her door and stepped out. She waved. Holmes waved back. He wiggled his bare feet.

"He looks content," said Poe. "Maybe he's planning to stay through the fall."

"No," said Marple. "He's ready to leave. I can feel it."

CHAPTER 10

AS MARPLE AND Poe ascended the wide porch steps, Holmes jumped up from the chair and held his arms out wide, like an actor owning a stage. Then came a pronouncement at the top of his voice. "'How small we feel with our petty ambitions and strivings in the presence of the great elemental forces of nature!'"

"I'm glad to see you've been catching up on your reading," said Marple. She moved in to give him a hug. He felt solid and looked healthy.

"The country atmosphere has changed me for good," said Holmes. He took a deep breath and let it out with a burst. "'How sweet the morning air is!'"

Poe looked irritated and impatient. "Are you just going to keep quoting from mystery novels," he asked, "or can we have a serious conversation?"

"You've come to drag me back to that great cesspool, haven't you?" said Holmes.

"How are you feeling, Brendan?" asked Marple. "How are things going with the program?"

"I'm clean, Margaret," said Holmes. "Renewed, restored, and reformed."

Marple had to admit that his eyes seemed clearer, and he was definitely full of pep.

"Brendan," she said, "if you're really better, and I truly hope you are, it's time to come back to work. We've got a huge case on our hands, and we need your—"

"Let's work *here*!" Holmes interrupted. "Join me! I'm sure we can find two vacant rooms." He started pacing across the porch in his bare feet, ignoring the other residents. "The woods are so stimulating!" he said. "Cool nights, wind through the leaves, the occasional scream of madness." He paused and leaned against a porch rail. "I can see why my mother liked this place."

Poe walked over and cleared his throat. "Brendan, I have something to tell you." He looked back at Marple. "I have something to tell *both* of you."

Marple stepped up and cocked her head. Was this what had made Poe nervous all day? Was there something he needed to get off his chest? She and Holmes followed him to an empty corner of the porch. Poe stared up at the treetops for a moment. Then it spilled out.

"Helene is pregnant. I'm the father."

Marple reached over and gave Poe's sleeve a hard tug. "Auguste! We've been driving together for five hours and you kept this to yourself?"

"I wanted to tell you both at the same time," said Poe. "Get your gut responses at once."

Marple's gut response was shock, but she didn't let it show. The timing seemed poor. Auguste and Helene had known each other barely four months. It was too early in the relationship. "Well, I think it's wonderful," she said after a moment. "You two make a terrific team." This part she meant. She liked Helene a lot. And maybe having a child would get Poe past his old sorrows and bring a little brightness into his life. God knew he'd had enough gloom.

Holmes turned toward them both, his back to the railing, his expression grim. "Personally, I *am* concerned," he said. "For poor Helene!" He grabbed Poe by the shoulders. "Does she have any notion what it will mean to be linked for eternity to the dark and unfathomable Auguste Poe?"

"Brendan! Stop it!" scolded Marple.

Suddenly, Holmes broke into a broad smile.

In a snap, Marple could tell that the old Brendan was back. She glanced at Poe. From his expression, she could tell that he saw it too. Holmes reached out and pulled them both into a tight embrace. "You didn't take me seriously, did you?" he said. "About staying here?"

"You sounded pretty convincing," said Marple.

Holmes stepped back. "Wait here," he said. "I'll just be a moment."

He pulled open the front door and bolted into the building. A few seconds later, he emerged with his duffel bag slung over his shoulder. He headed down the porch stairs toward the car, still in his robe, pajamas, and now slippers. He turned back as his partners stared.

"What's the problem?" he asked. "I showered this morning. Four times actually. I may be sober. But I'm still obsessive."

CHAPTER 11

THE DRIVE BACK to Brooklyn was strangely silent and awkward. After an initial burst of energy, Holmes seemed sullen. Marple tried to brief him on the hospital kidnapping, but he seemed oddly distracted—more focused on the passing scenery than on coming up with his usual theories and paths of investigation. Behind the wheel, Poe had turned brooding and uncommunicative again. He'd apparently given up on trying to reach Helene from the road.

After a few more stabs at conversation, Marple ended up spending most of the time on her iPad. First, she arranged to have Poe's '77 Trans Am, the car he'd lent Holmes months earlier for the drive to Ithaca, transported back to Brooklyn. She then set an alert for reports of other missing babies. So far, only New York and London. She'd asked Virginia to dig up a contact in Scotland Yard, London's Metropolitan Police. Maybe they'd be willing to compare notes. By the time Poe pulled the GTO up in front of the firm's Brooklyn headquarters a little before 7 p.m., she was a bit nauseated from staring at her screen.

As Marple climbed out of the car, she saw three figures emerge from the front door. Virginia. Baskerville. And Helene Grey.

The huge dog got to Holmes first, jumping on him with enough force to knock him backward. "Desist, you beast!" Holmes shouted in mock alarm before giving the dog an affectionate pat and a vigorous scratch between the ears.

"Baskerville! Down!" Virginia called out. The dog obediently dropped to his haunches and sat panting on the sidewalk. Virginia stepped past him to give Holmes a firm hug. "Welcome back, Mr. Holmes," she said, her forehead on his shoulder. "It hasn't been the same without you."

"I'll tell you one thing, Virginia," said Holmes. "The oatmeal cookies in rehab don't hold a candle to yours."

Grey stared for a few moments at Holmes's sleepwear and slippers. She waited patiently on the front step as he approached. "Glad to have you back," she said. "I'm sure you've heard that we really need your help."

"We'll see about that," said Holmes cryptically. He brushed past her and walked inside. Grey gave Marple a questioning look.

Marple shrugged. She watched as Poe pulled the GTO into the loading bay, then pushed a button to close its garage door after retrieving Holmes's duffel bag from the trunk. Then he walked over to the detective. "I've been trying to reach you," he said.

"I know," she replied. She turned and walked inside. Virginia stepped back into the doorway and pulled a leather leash from a hook. She looked at Marple. "Sorry to run, Miss Marple," she said. "I've got to take Baskerville for his walk. We'll be back in half an hour."

"Don't be silly," said Marple. "Go on home for the night."

"Really?" asked Virginia. "I'm happy to come back and help Mr. Holmes get settled."

"No," said Marple. "Leave that to me."

"Okay, then," said Virginia, clipping the leash to Baskerville's collar. "See you in the morning."

When Marple walked inside, she saw Holmes in the kitchen and Poe halfway up the staircase with Holmes's duffel bag over his shoulder. Grey was standing awkwardly in the entryway.

Marple felt the urge to say something. *Congratulations. When are you due? Boy or girl?* But she held back. Not the time. Not her place. Helene might not even know that Marple knew.

As soon as Poe got back down to the first floor, Grey cleared her throat and cocked her head toward the door. "Got time for a walk?" she asked. Poe nodded. They headed out through the front door together and then turned, walking past the row of windows.

Marple was a top-notch lip reader, but all she could pick out was Poe saying, "Let's go to the park." Grey's lips weren't moving at all.

Marple turned to Holmes as he walked over. "What do you think? Is Poe definitely the father?"

Holmes nodded and headed for the stairs. "As my namesake would say, 'the probability lies in that direction.'"

"In that case," said Marple, following right behind him, "'now is the dramatic moment of fate.'"

She knew her Conan Doyle as well as Holmes did.

Maybe better.

CHAPTER 12

POE WALKED SIDE by side with Helene as they entered Irving Square Park, the garden spot of Brooklyn's Bushwick neighborhood, with the old lampposts marking their route. The broad stone pathway led past happy couples and young families catching the last of the early autumn day. When Helene's hand brushed his, Poe took it gently and squeezed. His heart was pounding. Helene squeezed back, staring straight ahead. Two kids on scooters shot past them, wheels humming against the pavement.

"In case you were worried," said Helene, "the baby is yours. Couldn't be anybody else's."

Poe felt a flash of anger. He jerked his hand away. "Why would you say that? Do you think I suspected you of sleeping around? Is that why you wouldn't return my calls?"

"I needed a little time," Helene said as she kept on walking. "Maybe I wanted to leave you a shred of doubt—in case you didn't want any part of this. Anyway, it wasn't intentional. I must have skipped a pill by mistake."

Poe immediately felt guilty. He blurted out, "Ethinyl estradiol is only 99.7 percent effective," he said. "So there's a 0.3 percent chance that it would have happened anyway."

Helene stopped and gave him a look. "That sounds like something Holmes would say." She put a hand on his shoulder. "I don't care about chemical formulas right now, Auguste. I want to know what you're *feeling*. About this. About *us*. I want to know what's really going on in your mind."

Poe wrestled with what to say next. It was the same thing he'd been wrestling with for the past fifteen hours. He loved Helene. He was sure of that. She was the best thing that had happened to him in a long time. But at the moment, that was about the *only* thing he was sure of.

"To tell you the truth," he said, "what's really going on in my mind is: I'm not sure I'm cut out to be a parent."

Helene nodded. She let her hand slide off his arm. She looked up and stared into the distance across the park. "Right," she said. "That makes two of us."

CHAPTER 13

SHIRTS. SOCKS. SLACKS. Briefs.

Marple sat on the silk sofa in Holmes's bedroom and watched as he carefully unpacked his duffel bag, item by item. In typical Holmes fashion, everything was immaculately pressed and impeccably folded.

"You have no idea what it took to get an ironing board in that place," he said.

Marple ran her hand over the sofa cushion. "I missed you, Brendan," she said. "More than I thought I would."

Holmes gave her a slightly embarrassed smile. "I was a handful before I went away," he said. "I know that."

A handful? That was an understatement. Marple flashed back to all the times Holmes's drug habit had put their PI licenses—and their lives—in jeopardy. But through everything, she and Holmes had kept a strong bond. Comrades to the end.

The duffel was almost empty now. The last item Holmes pulled out was a small prescription bottle. "Buprenorphine," he said, rattling the pills inside. "My new best friend."

"Not methadone?" asked Marple.

"Methadone is Schedule II," said Holmes. "Buprenorphine is Schedule III. On paper, lower potential for abuse."

"On paper," Marple repeated.

"Correct," said Holmes. "Says so in all the literature."

As he put the small white bottle on the bedside table, Marple saw a slight tremor in his hand. She leaned forward. "Brendan, are you all right?"

Holmes clenched and unclenched his hands. "I'll let you know in a second," he said. He sat down on the end of his bed, facing Marple. "I have a confession to make," he said.

Marple felt a flutter inside. She tried to deflect it with humor. "Look, Brendan. We already know you stole the bathrobe."

"Margaret, I'm serious. I realized something up there at the funny farm." Holmes clasped his hands tightly in his lap, as if to keep them from twitching. "My instincts are shot. I'm through as an investigator. I'll never work a case again." He lowered his head. "This is the end of Holmes."

What? This was not the colleague and friend she knew. Brendan had many flaws, but lack of confidence had never been one of them. "Don't be ridiculous," she said. "You just got back. You need time. Auguste and I can take up the slack until you—"

"There's something else," said Holmes, cutting her off. "Something that might shock you even more."

Marple's mind started spinning. But before another word could pass, the sound of glass shattering violently came from downstairs.

CHAPTER 14

MARPLE JUMPED TO her feet and rushed out onto the interior balcony that overlooked the first floor, Holmes right behind her. Looking down, she saw Poe flailing around in the kitchen, slamming cupboards and kicking the baseboard violently. There was a broken cocktail glass at his feet, surrounded by a small, shiny puddle. He was already pouring himself a replacement for the drink he'd dropped—or thrown.

Marple headed for the staircase. Holmes followed. "Auguste!" she called out. "What happened? Where's Helene?"

All three were in the kitchen now, crowded around the center island. Poe took a deep sip from his new glass. "Duty called," he said grimly. He slammed the glass down hard enough to splash the contents onto his sleeve. He looked at Holmes, then at Marple. "Well, I was right. It's true," he said. "The baby's mine." Poe picked up the glass again and downed the rest of his drink in one gulp. "God, I pity this child!" he moaned.

Holmes leaned in close to his partner. "So you'd rather it was somebody else's?"

Poe shook his head. "No. Of course not."

"Then what are you so upset about?" asked Marple.

Poe held up his empty glass. "*This,* for one thing. It's in the genes, you know."

"The baby has twenty-three chromosomes from each of you," said Holmes. "With any luck, Helene's genome will be dominant."

"Brendan," said Marple. "Not helpful."

"I didn't exactly act the part of the overjoyed papa," said Poe. "I may have chased her away."

"It was a shock," said Marple. "You're still adjusting. Let things breathe."

Holmes squared his shoulders and cleared his throat. "This may not be the best time, Auguste, but I'm afraid I have some news too." He glanced at Marple. "I'm quitting the firm."

Then, without another word, Holmes turned and walked out the front door.

Poe faced Marple, clearly agitated. "Did you know about this?"

"He told me he was shaky," Marple replied. "I didn't think he would actually quit."

"Should we go after him?"

Marple shook her head. "Not now."

Poe grabbed another glass from a tray and poured Marple a drink from his bottle. He stopped mid-pour. "Sorry," he said. "I forgot you don't drink bourbon."

Marple grabbed the glass and knocked back the booze in one gulp.

"I do now," she said.

CHAPTER 15

THE BOURBON DID not agree with her. Marple was still awake at midnight when she heard Holmes return to his apartment next door. At least he hadn't fled the city. Or the country.

Better not to press him tonight, she decided. Maybe his outlook would change in the morning. Poe had turned in hours earlier, his melancholy over Helene's pregnancy apparently doubled by Holmes's announcement. Marple noticed a flicker of movement in a corner, near the base of a reading table. Her heartbeat quickened, then settled. It was her mouse-hunting cat, Annabel, a gift from Poe, who understood Marple's intense aversion to rodents. The feline had done an excellent job keeping them at bay since she'd moved in.

Marple slipped out of her apartment with her laptop and tiptoed down the hall to the firm's private library. She always relished the peace and quiet after everybody else was asleep. She pressed the code on the security pad and heard the subtle click of the lock release. Inside, the surroundings were as warm and comforting as an English parlor. No wonder: Marple had designed the room herself.

She settled into a cozy armchair, surrounded by bookshelves that held the greatest mystery stories of all time—the collected works of Sir Arthur Conan Doyle, Edgar Allan Poe, and Agatha Christie—and opened her laptop. The internet connection on the Ithaca trip had been patchy and slow. But concealed in the shelves of the library were modems and signal boosters that rivaled the Pentagon's. Thanks to tweaks by Holmes, speeds here were absolutely blazing. If Marple was in the mood to download a movie, she could do so in seconds. But she was here for business, not pleasure—in fact, about as far from pleasure as she could imagine.

The first thing she did was cover her laptop camera. Considering where she was headed, she wanted to be sure that her exploration was one-way only. She clicked on the Tor browser and started her descent into the dark web.

In seconds, she was surfing through a morass of sites hosted on private overseas servers—anonymous, untraceable, nearly impossible to shut down. It was like gliding through a bazaar of sleaze and decadence. Marple could practically hear the greedy merchants shouting out their offers of stolen credit cards, elephant ivory, homemade explosives, false identities. It was all there for the taking—for a price, of course, and from some very malevolent purveyors.

Marple's search was specific and depressing. With a few more clicks, she easily accessed a trove of black-market adoption sites. There was a seller's market for healthy babies, no questions asked, as long as your money was good and your ethics were flexible. Babies to order. Hair, skin, and eye color of your choice. Vaccinated or not, according to your personal medical convictions.

Marple uploaded photos the parents had given her of the six missing St. Michael's babies to compare with online images, but she realized that the infants had been mere minutes old when their proud parents had snapped those pictures. It was the longest of long shots, so remote that she doubted the FBI had even tried it. Even with the latest biometric software, facial recognition was notoriously sketchy for infants.

Marple set her laptop to auto-scan, watching thumbnail images of babies zip by like tiles on a game board, until they melded into a single blur. A distinct tone and a freeze-frame would indicate a match. But after thirty minutes, there was nothing. The search was merely wallpaper. The babies of St. Michael's had simply disappeared off the face of the earth.

Marple had no clue where they were, but she had a theory about why they'd been taken. And it cut right to her heart.

CHAPTER 16

THE NEXT MORNING, Brendan Holmes woke up in his own bed for the first time in months. It felt like waking up in a prison cell. Instead of windows open to the lake breeze and the sound of chirping robins, the sole window over his bed was clamped shut against the honks and hums of Brooklyn traffic.

And the odors! Holmes was a hyperosmiac—a super-smeller. It was a blessing and a curse. A blessing when it helped him quite literally sniff out a buried body or hidden explosives. A curse when he gagged on the stench of uncollected garbage on the street below. This morning, even the aroma of fresh coffee from the first-floor kitchen hit him wrong. There was no other way to put it: his apartment didn't feel like home anymore. He was miserable. When he'd walked out the day before, he'd seriously considered catching a cab to JFK and just getting on a plane, any plane, to anywhere. Then he'd realized that he didn't have his wallet. Or his passport. Or his pills. Poor preparation. Not like him.

Holmes stood up, reached for his prescription bottle, and

took his daily dose of withdrawal medicine, sticking the little orange pill under his tongue. He had studied every detail of the chemistry, of course — the sublingual absorption, the low intrinsic activity at the opioid receptor, the reinforcing subjective effect — all properties that were supposed to make him feel something close to normal. Instead, they just made him feel dizzy. As soon as the pill started dissolving, he felt like throwing up. But he didn't. *Stick with the program,* he told himself. *All twelve steps. One day at a time. One pill at a time.*

When he opened the front door of his apartment — still in his pajamas — he could feel the buzz of activity downstairs. He looked over the balcony. Virginia was busy at her desk, her eyes locked on her computer screen, headphones on, fingers flying across her keyboard. Baskerville sat like a sentry by her workstation.

As Holmes walked down the staircase, he picked up a thread of conversation from the kitchen. His partners were talking about the kidnapping case.

Correction. His *ex*-partners.

Marple looked over as he walked up to the counter. "Put some clothes on, Brendan. We've got a meeting with the task force in an hour."

Interesting ploy, thought Holmes. Marple had obviously chosen to deal with his resignation by pretending that it simply hadn't happened. Treating him like he was still part of the team. Appealing to his sense of responsibility.

Nice try.

"Maybe *you* do," said Holmes. He walked to the far end of the counter and plucked a pumpkin muffin from a plate. He saw Marple glance at Poe, who slid off his stool and picked up the pursuit, with a slightly different tack.

"Brendan. Please. We need you on this. This could be the biggest case the firm ever had. The most important case. They're *babies*, for God's sake! If you had been in that maternity unit with me and Margaret, you'd have been on board in a heartbeat."

"Emotion clouds efficiency," said Holmes. He tore a piece from the muffin and popped it into his mouth.

"That's exactly why we need you," said Marple. "Your logic. Your objectivity. Auguste and I stared into those poor parents' eyes."

"We promised them help," said Poe. "We promised them *you!*"

"You had no right to speak for me," said Holmes. "You knew where I was."

"We did," said Poe, his tone sharper now. "But we didn't realize you'd given up."

That cut a bit. Holmes tossed the rest of the muffin into the trash and headed back toward the staircase. "I need rest," he said. "My medication makes me drowsy." His foot was on the first step when Poe called out.

"Do it for Helene!"

Holmes stopped. He turned around.

"That's right," said Poe. "You have no idea what she's going through. Captain Duff, the new head of the Major Case Squad, is a nightmare. He's trying to cut her off at the knees. She's operating on zero sleep. Her own maternal hormones are probably not helping..."

Poe was laying it on a bit thick, but Holmes liked Detective Lieutenant Grey. She was a tireless investigator, and she'd brought the firm in on a couple of career-changing cases. Holmes straightened his shoulders and walked back into the kitchen.

"All right. I'll do it. This one meeting. For Helene."

"Bravo," said Marple.

"It's the least I can do," said Holmes. He stared straight at Poe. "The poor woman deserves one level-headed male in her life."

CHAPTER 17

BY THE TIME Marple and her partners walked into the St. Michael's task force war room at One Police Plaza, it had already been humming for over twenty-four hours. The place reeked of body odor and burnt coffee. Marple saw Holmes wince, and worried that his sensitive olfactory bulbs would be overwhelmed. She grabbed his arm. "Steady, Brendan."

Most of the clearly sleep-deprived occupants were NYPD detectives or techs. A few wore blue windbreakers with FBI stenciled on the back. On one wall, scans of six newborns were lined up like yearbook photos, captioned only with a gender and the parents' surname. "Girl Pickard," "Boy Bronson," and so forth. Otherwise, they looked pretty much interchangeable. Across the room, Captain Graham Duff looked up in annoyance.

"*Again?*" he called out. "Who the hell invited you people?"

He slammed a folder down and started across the room. Helene Grey stepped up from a table nearby and blocked his way. "I did, Captain. Maybe they can help. Fresh eyes."

"Fresh brains," added Holmes. "From what I can see, everybody in this room is mentally depleted—including you, Captain. No offense."

Duff stared for a second, then narrowed his eyes. "So this is the mighty Holmes. The missing link." He leaned in with a faux-confidential whisper. "Where have they been hiding you?"

"I was taking a self-improvement course," said Holmes. "I highly recommend it."

"What are we looking at here?" asked Marple, diverting everybody's attention to a huge monitor at the front of the room. The image on the screen was segmented into six rotating scenes of beautiful city apartments and luxury houses. It looked like the home page for a high-end realtor's website.

"We've tapped into the parents' laptops and phone lines," said Grey.

"You mean the people who hired us?" said Poe. "Isn't that an invasion of privacy?" Marple noticed that Poe and Helene were barely looking at each other.

"We have their permission," said Duff. "On the basis of security and efficiency. Spared us the need for warrants. In my mind, they're all persons of interest."

"Agreed," said Holmes. "It wouldn't be the first time I've seen a client in cuffs."

The observation sounded cold, but to Marple, it showed that her partner's analytical mind was at least partly engaged, which was a good thing. She took a step closer to the screen. The captions at the bottom of the images matched the surnames of the babies. As the visuals rotated, she recognized a few of the parents pacing through the frames. The scenes confirmed something else they all had in common:

Money.

Even seen through laptop lenses, the rooms were dazzling. One was a high-ceilinged loft filled with Craft Revival antiques.

Another was surrounded by glass, with a stunning river view. A third sat near the top of a Manhattan high-rise, looking out over Central Park. The audio on the feeds was muted, but the faces that occasionally loomed into view all looked severe and drawn.

"The world's most depressing Zoom meeting," muttered Poe.

"The parents are sitting at home, waiting for ransom calls," said Duff. "If we get a hit, we'll trace it from here."

Holmes turned away from the screen and swept his gaze across the busy room, his expression grim. "There won't be any ransom calls, Captain." He waved his hand toward the screen. "This is all a waste of time and money."

Marple was encouraged to hear that Holmes's intuition matched hers — even if their conclusions were equally bleak.

"Mr. Holmes is right," said Marple. "These babies aren't hostages. They're merchandise."

CHAPTER 18

JUST THREE MINUTES later, after a few more tense exchanges with Duff, Holmes had had all of the cramped war room he could tolerate. The smell in the crowded room was getting to him. Plus the apparent futility of the operation.

He turned to Marple. "This is worse than useless," he said. "If you want my help, I need a firsthand look at the crime scene."

"I agree," said Poe. "Let's start earning our fee." Holmes could tell that his partner was eager to leave for reasons of his own. Grey had returned to her station near the front of the room. She was tapping on a keyboard, her nose close to her laptop screen. Holmes looked back when he reached the door with Marple and Poe. Grey didn't even look up.

Poe's blue '73 Plymouth Road Runner was waiting across the street. It was a short drive from NYPD headquarters to St. Michael's. Poe pulled into the small employee parking lot.

Marple pointed at a metal sign in front of the parking space. "Doctors only, Auguste," she said. "You'll get towed."

Poe reached under his seat and pulled out a stack of printed placards, each about the size of a magazine cover. He picked one that read, DOCTOR ON MEDICAL CALL. Beneath the lettering was an official-looking stamp and a caduceus symbol. He tossed it onto the dashboard, face up. "Cheaper than med school," he said.

As they walked across the street toward the entrance, Holmes noticed a local TV crew, camera ready, obviously sensing a scoop.

Holmes realized this was exactly what he'd once craved. Bigger cases. More visibility. National buzz. Except now he didn't want any of it. He wanted to go back to bed. But he didn't want to break a promise, especially to Margaret.

Focus, he told himself as they headed for the entrance. *This is your last case.*

Holmes led the way through the revolving door and headed for the elevator bank. A podium emblazoned with a large NYPD shield stood in the way, bordered by ropes and brass stanchions. A sturdy cop stood behind the barrier. "Hospital ID," he said, holding out his hand.

Holmes looked at Poe, wondering if he might have some fake medical credentials to go along with his fake parking pass. But Poe clearly hadn't anticipated the obstacle. It was Marple who stepped up to the podium and pulled out her PI identification card. "Holmes, Marple, and Poe, private investigators," she said firmly.

The cop didn't even glance at the card. "Hospital ID only," he said. "Sorry."

"You're not sorry," said Holmes. "You're just obstinate. Why don't you put in a call to Captain Duff. Graham Duff. He's in charge of this investigation."

"Captain Duff was here this morning," said the cop. "He specifically told me to watch out for you three — and to not let you past this point."

Holmes turned to Poe. "Maybe you should call Helene?"

Poe looked down. Clearly, that was the last thing he wanted to do.

"Never mind," he said. "We're going up." Poe started to elbow his way past the podium toward the elevator, and Holmes followed suit. Suddenly, three more cops emerged from behind a marble partition. Within seconds, Holmes found himself in a hammerlock, being shoved back toward the entrance. He twisted around to see Marple and Poe right behind him. They were being manhandled by two other cops. Then a woman's voice cut through the lobby.

"Hey! Officers! Knock it off!"

The cop holding Holmes stopped an inch from the revolving door and loosened his grip. By the time they all turned around, a tall fifty-something woman in a white coat was waving a laminated ID card in the cop's face.

"Dr. Revell Schulte," she said. "Head of maternity. I know these people. I'll vouch for them." She clipped her ID back onto her coat. "And stop using gestapo tactics in my hospital."

All three cops let go and shuffled back to their stations across the lobby.

"Dr. Schulte," said Marple. "We saw you in the unit the night of the kidnapping."

"You did," said Schulte. "I saw you too."

"This is our partner, Brendan Holmes."

"Late to the party, I'm afraid," said Holmes.

"This is no party," said Schulte.

She led them into an elevator and up to her office in a corner of the maternity unit. Rather than a wood-paneled refuge filled with medical texts and possibly an articulated human skeleton, the room was spare and functional, no more impressive than a real estate office—except for the framed diplomas on the wall. MS from Columbia. MBA from Stanford. MD from Harvard.

Schulte slipped behind her desk and sat at the edge of her high-backed chair. She gestured toward the waiting-room-style chairs facing her desk. Holmes took a seat. Marple and Poe did the same.

"Thanks for the rescue downstairs," said Marple.

"I've been tossed out of bars," said Poe, "but never a hospital."

Schulte showed no reaction to the quip. She sat quietly, looking from Holmes to Marple to Poe. For a few long moments, she said nothing. Then: "Thirty years ago, I was walking home from the library one night when two men grabbed me from behind. They punched me in the side, tried to pull me into a car. I screamed and kicked my way loose. Then I ran to the nearest police station. I told them what happened, showed them the scratches on my arms, the bruises on my ribs. They took a report. Sent me home. And did nothing."

"They never caught anybody?" asked Marple.

"It was a Saturday night in the city," said Schulte. "I'm not sure how hard they looked." She leaned forward over her desk. "Look. I'm not a big fan of the police. But I've read everything about you three. I saw you on TV and in the papers all summer."

Holmes allowed himself a tight smile. He had wanted their firm to have a significant profile in the city, and now it did. He looked up to see Dr. Revell Schulte staring at him as if she knew what he was thinking.

"I don't care how famous you are," she said. "I care how *good* you are. I need you to find my babies."

She stood up behind her desk and headed for the door. "Come with me."

CHAPTER 19

MOVING THROUGH THE halls with Dr. Revell Schulte was like following a rock star backstage. She walked tall and straight, her grey-flecked ponytail bobbing against her collar. Poe noticed that junior staff avoided eye contact as she passed, while senior staff gave her deferential nods. But when she pushed through the door into the main security station a minute later, it was a different story.

In the dimly lit room, several techs sat in front of monitors and control panels. Unlike the medical staff in the halls, the techs didn't seem to have any particular regard for Dr. Schulte. They didn't even look up from their stations. A squat man in a business suit wheeled his chair back from a large console but didn't even bother to stand up as the doctor led the way in. Poe picked up a distinctly condescending vibe.

"Delivery rooms are in the other wing, Doc," the guy said, jerking his thumb.

Poe could tell that he was joking. But also *not* joking. This man did not welcome their unexpected company. Schulte made the introductions brief. "This is Clint Baxter, head of security for the hospital. Clint, meet Holmes, Marple, and Poe." She pointed at the three PIs in succession, like ticking items off a supply list.

"Holmes...Marple...Poe," Baxter repeated slowly. "Like the old mystery books."

"Right," said Holmes. "Except we're flesh and blood. Here in person. Doing your job."

Baxter flashed a fake smile, the kind that told Poe he was nervous, insecure, or both. "Yeah. I've heard of you," said Baxter. "Why are you here?"

"They're working the kidnapping case," said Schulte. "The parents have hired them privately, and they're working with the NYPD. I want them to have total access."

Baxter's fake smile faded. "Sorry, Doc. That's not your call."

Marple stepped forward, clearly impatient with the preliminaries. "Tell me, Mr. Baxter, have you figured out how the intruders cut the feed for the two-minute gap? How they knew exactly which tapes fed which cameras? Or why they missed the old Panasonic unit near the loading dock? Have you established the chain of custody for the maternity unit security bands?"

Baxter narrowed his eyes and cleared his throat. "That's all part of our internal investigation, Miss Marple." He gave her an unsubtle once-over. "Or is it Missus?"

"Miss. Ms. Ma'am. Margaret. Your Excellency. Your choice." She reached into her pocket and held out a thumb drive. "Plug this in for me, will you?"

"Hold on," said Baxter. "You're not turning my department into your private office. If you want to—"

"Clint," Schulte interrupted, "would you like to know what the board is saying about your department right now?"

Baxter's face turned even more sour. He snatched the flash drive from Marple and stuck it into a port. "What's this?" he asked gruffly.

Marple stepped right up beside his chair. "These are files I pulled from the phones of parents on the maternity floor on the night in question. While your cameras were down, people were busy snapping away. And they entrusted me with the images. Maybe you or Dr. Schulte can ID some of the people in the shots."

Schulte moved forward and rested her hands on the headrest of Baxter's chair. Poe admired the power move. Baxter sat in his chair with his arms folded, feet planted on the floor, trying to maintain an illusion of authority.

The first image showed a smiling but exhausted mother posing with two nurses in a delivery room. "That's Alvarez and Huggard," said Schulte. "RNs. Been here forever."

Marple tapped the keyboard. In the next picture, a new mom, shiny with sweat, gave a weary thumbs-up to the camera while a medical team huddled in the background, slightly out of focus. Poe recognized the mother as the wife of alpha-male dad Sterling Cade.

Schulte pointed to a woman in light-blue scrubs. "That's Phoebe Platt. Just started her pediatrics rotation." Behind the young doctor stood a woman in burgundy scrubs, her face obscured by a monitor. "Can't tell who that is," said Schulte. "A nurse, for sure."

"It's Ellie Tellman," said Marple. She recognized the body shape and the cornrows.

"You know her?" asked Schulte.

"We met yesterday," said Marple. She flicked through the rest of the pictures one at a time as Schulte picked out an assortment of residents, attendings, and aides, some of them repeating from one shot to another. Every once in a while, Baxter chimed in with a name. At the end, the sequence rotated back to the first image.

"Wait," said Poe. "Go back one."

Marple pressed the reverse key, returning to a photo of a mom cradling her tiny baby in the recovery room. At the edge of the frame, a slender woman in pale pink scrubs was frozen in mid-step, halfway out the door, her face in profile.

"Who's that?" asked Poe.

"That's Keelin Dale," said Schulte. "She's an LPN. Also our lactation consultant. She helps the new moms get started with breastfeeding, offers assistance if they need it."

"Does she handle all the babies?" asked Marple.

"Typically, sure," said Schulte. "She often brings them back and forth from the nursery to the moms for feedings."

"Can we talk to her?" asked Marple.

"I'll call her station," said Schulte. As the doctor pulled out her iPhone and tapped the screen, Poe glanced at Holmes, who was leaning back against a console. His eyes were down. He looked sullen, disengaged, off his game.

"Who's this? Katy? Hey. It's Dr. Schulte. Keelin's on today, right?"

Poe couldn't hear the other side of the conversation, but he saw Schulte's expression shift from impatience to irritation.

"Okay, thanks," she said, ending the call. She looked at Marple. "Keelin didn't show up for her shift."

"Is that unusual?" Marple asked.

"It's a first," said Schulte. She turned to Baxter. "Clint, can you pull up Keelin's profile?"

Baxter turned his chair to a side table that held a Dell computer. He flicked his fingers over the keypad and brought up a profile image of an attractive young woman with auburn hair and a sprinkling of freckles across her cheeks, then clicked to the personal info page.

Poe squinted at the screen. He pulled out his cell and took a photo of Keelin's phone number and Jersey address.

"She's new," said Schulte. "Here two months. Terrific references. I'll try her home phone..."

"No, don't," said Marple. "You might make her nervous. Better to let us go find her."

Poe followed as Marple speed-walked out of the security station and down the hall to the elevators. When he looked over his shoulder, he saw Holmes hanging back.

"Brendan! Let's go!" he called out.

Holmes stopped short and shook his head. "I told you I was good for one meeting today. Not three. I need you to believe me when I say I'm done." He folded his arms and leaned back against the wall. "I want my name off the front door."

The elevator door opened. "This is not the time for debate, Brendan," said Marple. "We'll talk later." As the elevator door closed, Marple lowered her voice and said to Poe, "I can't worry about him right now."

Poe nodded but said nothing. Marple seemed itchy and out of sorts. Maybe she was off her game too.

CHAPTER 20

AS USUAL, POE'S sleek blue Road Runner turned heads as he sliced through crosstown traffic. The powerful Plymouth was the latest addition to his impressive muscle car collection, and it was a real attention-getter.

Marple was not impressed at all. She ignored the gawkers as she tapped her fingers on the passenger-side armrest. When they reached the Holland Tunnel under the Hudson River, traffic appeared to be backed up for the entire length of the tube.

"We would have been better off on a moped," said Marple.

"How far is Keelin Dale's place?" asked Poe, straining against his seat belt as traffic inched forward.

"About half an hour," said Marple, "if you can ever get us out of this wormhole." She could tell that Poe was resisting the urge to hit the car's horn, with its ridiculous cartoon *beep-beep*. When they finally broke into daylight on the Jersey side of the tunnel, they passed a pair of parked police cars at the exit, lights flashing.

"Maybe we should ask for an escort," said Marple.

"I doubt they could keep up," muttered Poe. Marple realized that he felt the need to reassert his vehicle's dominance. He revved the Plymouth's hefty V8 and roared around the southbound curve of Route 78. Marple held on tight as Poe did his best to blast past every vehicle in his path.

Less than ten minutes later, they entered the downscale Greenville neighborhood, a mix of prewar apartment buildings and single-family homes. Poe pulled into a space across from a renovated two-unit frame house with matching front doors.

"Keelin's place is on the left," said Marple, sliding out of her seat.

They walked up the steps and looked around. Traffic on the side street was light, and the only pedestrian in sight was an Amazon driver stepping back into his truck a few houses up. Marple knocked on the door while Poe pressed his face against the front window.

"Anything?" asked Marple.

Poe shook his head. He waited for a few seconds, then pulled a thin metal tool from his pocket.

The lock was nothing special. A stainless-steel Defiant, probably twenty-five bucks from Home Depot. Poe had it open in ten seconds. He put his hand on his Glock in its holster. Marple looked for an alarm pad or a trip wire. Listened for a dog. Scanned for cameras. Nothing. The place was quiet, and all the lights were off.

Marple stepped in beside Poe as he closed the door.

"Keelin?" she called out. "Miss Dale? Anybody home?"

No response.

They moved slowly through the living room toward the back of the unit. The apartment was small but tidy, furnished in contemporary young-adult style. Lots of medium-grade furniture, a good-sized TV, and a few discount-store shelf units.

As Marple walked through the archway into the small kitchen, she saw Poe's head whip around, as if he'd heard something.

Then she heard it too.

A baby crying.

CHAPTER 21

MARPLE RAN BACK through the living room to the entryway. Poe rushed up next to her. She peeked outside through the glass panel beside the front door. On the stoop next door, a Hispanic woman was unfolding a stroller with one hand, like some kind of magic trick. In the crook of her other arm, she held a red-faced baby with dark curly hair.

The crying had stopped. Now the baby looked irritated. And it was no newborn.

"Eight months at least," whispered Marple as the woman fastened the baby into the stroller. "Probably fifteen pounds. And wrong profile."

"Not wealthy enough?" said Poe.

"And not white enough, I suspect," said Marple. "The two newborns who *weren't* taken from the nursery were infants of color. One Black, one Asian. Their parents' assets are equal to all the others. But those babies weren't touched. I suspect we'll find that the selection wasn't coincidental."

Marple turned back toward the staircase leading to the second floor. She and Poe both kept their backs against the wall as they climbed the steps. Poe unholstered his gun.

Marple held her small handbag close to her side. It contained her keys, her ID, and a small canister of pepper spray. Though she sometimes carried a little .22, as a rule, Marple preferred to let her partners handle the firearms.

The landing at the top was dark, but they could see a sliver of light from a partly open door on the left.

They took the rest of the stairs quickly and flattened themselves on either side of the door. Poe listened for footsteps or running water or the sound of snoring. But all he could hear was the hum of traffic from the busy street at the back of the building.

Marple peeked through the opening. She nodded at Poe. He nudged the door open and stepped into the bedroom, arms extended, pistol pointed. Marple hung tight behind him as he swept the room. Empty, except for a stripped double bed and a small dresser. Marple put her hand on another doorknob. *Bathroom,* she mouthed.

Poe nodded. Marple pushed the door open. Poe stepped through first. "Clear," he said.

The Plexiglas shower stall still showed condensation, and a damp towel hung from a hook behind the door. The air smelled of lemon. Marple put her fingers on the wooden knob of the medicine cabinet door and gently tugged it open. A dozen black marbles rolled out and clattered into the sink and onto the floor tile.

"What the hell is this?" asked Poe, dodging the tiny glass balls with his feet.

Marple smiled. "It's what a young lady does when she wants to hear if an overnight guest is going through her things."

"That's diabolical," said Poe.

"My mother always set the same trap before dinner parties," said Marple.

She leaned toward the cabinet and rustled through the narrow shelves. Nothing unusual. Deodorant. Toothpaste. Cotton balls. Aspirin. On the top shelf was an amber-colored prescription bottle with no label. Marple took it down and untwisted the lid. She shook a couple of small oval blue tablets onto her palm.

"Halcion," she said.

"How can you tell?" asked Poe.

Marple held one of the blue pills up to his face. The word "Halcion" was imprinted on it.

"Remind me," said Poe. "Insomnia?"

"Insomnia, anxiety, panic disorders," said Marple. "It's a benzodiazepine. Highly addictive."

"Okay," said Poe. "Maybe she's nervous. Maybe she has a hard time nodding off." He shoved around the contents of the cabinet. It was an old-fashioned unit set into the wall, probably original to the apartment, the kind that still had a narrow slit in the back for disposing of used razor blades. Poe slid a bottle of hydrogen peroxide over to one side.

"Hold on," he said. "Look."

Marple peeked into the cabinet. With the weight of the bottle to one side, the bottom shelf tilted up slightly at the opposite end. Poe stuck his pistol back into its holster. He grabbed a pair of tweezers from the top shelf and slid the tiny tongs between the bottom shelf and the cabinet frame. The shelf was loose along its entire length.

Marple plucked all the toiletries out and dumped them one by one into the sink.

Poe pried the thin wood up all the way. Marple grabbed a

small hand mirror and reflected the light from the ceiling fixture into the gap.

"Hello, there!" said Poe.

Marple looked in. Set between the studs underneath the cabinet was another shelf, about six inches down. Resting on the shelf were four clear plastic bags, secured with twist ties. Marple reached in and pulled out one of the bags. It was filled with Halcion tablets, *hundreds* of them.

"Guess what," said Marple, dangling the bag from her fingers. "Our lactation consultant is a benzo junkie."

"Or a dealer," said Poe.

"Freeze! Both of you!"

Marple looked up to see a rifle barrel in her face.

CHAPTER 22

"SHOW ME YOUR hands!"

The man was tall, in his fifties or sixties, wearing a dark toupee that contrasted sharply with his greying stubble. His muscle had gone to fat, but Marple could tell he knew how to handle a weapon. Maybe ex-military. Or ex-cop. The rifle pointing at them was an M27 automatic.

"We're private investigators," she said. "We're looking for Keelin Dale. Five six. Slender. Reddish hair. Freckle-faced."

"She's a nurse at St. Michael's in the city," said Poe.

"I know who she is," said the man with the gun. "I'm her damn landlord." He jerked the gun toward Marple. "What's that?" He nodded at the bag of pills in her hand.

"We think your tenant may have a drug problem," she said.

"Or a drug business," said Poe.

"I don't know anything about that," said the landlord. "Come out here." He backed into the bedroom and gestured with the barrel of the gun. "Slowly."

Marple dropped the bag of pills into the sink with the other cabinet contents. Poe stepped into the bedroom, his hands raised to chest level. "Can I show you my ID?" he asked, sliding one hand under his jacket.

"No," said the landlord curtly. "But since you're heading that direction, you can show me your gun."

Poe slid his Glock out slowly, keeping his fingers away from the trigger. He bent his knees and placed the gun on the floor. Marple stepped beside him.

"I'm Margaret Marple," she said. "This is my partner Auguste Poe. Holmes, Marple, and Poe Investigations. As I said, we're PIs on a case."

"Holy shit!" the landlord muttered. "You're *them!*" He lowered his gun and broke into a grin. He had stunningly white dentures. "I saw you guys on TV this summer. Channel 5."

Poe let out a breath and dropped his hands. "Correct. That was us." Local stations couldn't get enough of them this past summer. *Our fifteen minutes of fame,* Holmes called it.

"Isaac Wright," said the landlord, letting his gun hang loose in one hand. "I live across the street. Saw you break in. Very smooth."

"You need to spend more on your locks," said Poe.

"Any clue where your tenant is?" asked Marple.

"Left an hour ago," said Wright. "By taxi. With a couple of suitcases."

Marple turned to the left and pulled open a pair of accordion closet doors. The main rack was empty. So was the shoe organizer and both overhead shelves. Dozens of empty hangers rattled together on one side.

Wright stepped over and looked in. "I don't get it," he said. "She only moved in a few months ago. Why the hell would she bug out without telling me?"

"Well," said Marple, "looks like the lady emptied her closet. That's way too many clothes for a vacation."

CHAPTER 23

THE LOGICAL DEDUCTION was that Keelin Dale must've gone to Newark International. Marple agreed. Why would she opt for JFK or LaGuardia when there was a perfectly good airport just half an hour away?

As they headed west on Route 78, across Newark Bay, Poe reached under his seat and pulled out his stack of placards. He handed them to Marple. "Find something appropriate," he said, swerving around a dump truck.

By the time he screeched to a stop in front of international departures, Marple had jammed a NJ TRANSIT — OFFICIAL BUSINESS placard against the inside of the windshield. The wording was bolstered by a pair of New Jersey state logos and an excellent facsimile of the governor's signature.

"Nice choice," said Poe.

The blue Road Runner got a couple of curious looks from the baggage handlers as Poe and Marple sprinted across the sidewalk. Inside the terminal, Poe paused at a monitor and scanned the departures list. He was looking for destinations without extradition treaties. A hunch, but one that had paid off in the past.

"There's a 2:15 to Rabat!" he called out. Morocco was a non-extradition country.

Marple was way ahead of him. He caught up with her at the TSA checkpoint, where a Plexiglas barrier separated the entry concourse from the departure gates. Behind the barrier, passengers shuffled through their preflight choreography. Belts off. Shoes off. Arms up. Poe worked his way down the side of the barrier to get another angle on the queue.

There! Skinny black jeans. Maroon blouse. Auburn hair pulled into a bun.

Freckles in abundance.

Poe caught Marple's eye and pointed. She nodded. Positive ID.

Poe watched as Dale dropped her purse, phone, and laptop into a bin and pushed it toward the scanning machine. She slipped out of her heels and placed them on top of her carry-ons. From what Poe could see, she was traveling solo. Marple slid over to his side.

"What now?" he asked. He knew their PI licenses wouldn't get them past the TSA screener. And they had no powers of arrest anyway. "I could fake a heart attack," he offered. "She *is* a nurse."

"Do you really think a lactation specialist would be your first responder?" asked Marple. She was fishing through her purse. Poe looked back at the TSA line. Dale was already standing in the body scanner, arms over her head. *Dammit!*

"Got it!" Marple pulled out her passport and started tapping away on her iPhone.

"What are you doing?" asked Poe.

"What do you think?" said Marple. "I'm buying a ticket to Morocco."

CHAPTER 24

EVEN WITHOUT A change of clothes, Margaret Marple was fully prepared to take an eight-hour flight to North Africa. But she hoped it wouldn't come to that. As she approached the gate B45 departure area, she spotted Keelin Dale sitting by herself in the row of seats closest to the wall, legs crossed, reading a *People* magazine.

Marple held her phone at hip level, snapped a quick photo, then sent it to Poe. She knew her partner must be fuming back in the main terminal. This should teach him to never leave home without his documents.

Marple strolled slowly past the gate a few times, watching to see if Dale made contact with anybody else in the waiting area. She didn't. Just kept flipping through her magazine. After a third pass, Marple walked casually up to the desk, asked the gate agent for the latest departure update, then took a seat with a clear view of her prey. She held her phone in her lap and tapped out a text.

YOU'RE BEING FOLLOWED

She sent the message to the cell number that she'd seen listed on Dale's profile page. Marple's perfect visual memory came in handy in moments like these.

She waited a few seconds for the vibration to hum inside Dale's handbag. The nurse pulled out her phone and looked at the screen. Her whole face tightened. She abruptly unfolded her legs and slid up to the edge of her seat. She looked furtively around the waiting area and smoothed her hair nervously.

Interesting, thought Marple. *A trained operative wouldn't have reacted at all.* Whatever she was up to, Dale was an amateur, not a pro.

Even with her subject plainly in her sights, Marple knew that her options were limited. She couldn't make a citizen's arrest without actually witnessing a crime. She couldn't restrain Dale or sedate her without risking a charge of assault or false imprisonment. Sometimes Marple wished she'd taken the academy route and worked her way up to detective. It would make situations like this so much easier. On the other hand, there was something to be said for creativity.

She sent another text.

LADIES ROOM. NOW. HIDE THERE.

Keelin almost dropped her phone when the text arrived. She stood up and walked from the carpeted waiting area onto the concourse. The lavatories were only about fifteen yards ahead, past a Cinnabon stand. Marple followed close behind. But not too close.

As Dale walked through the curved entry to the women's side, Marple hung back long enough to pull a yellow mop bucket out of a utility alcove and stretch a mop handle across it to partly block the entrance. It was as close to an out-of-order sign as she could manage on the spot.

When she stepped into the lavatory, a woman with a large backpack was washing her hands at one of the sinks. Of the five stalls along the wall, only one was occupied. The woman held her hands under the air dryer for a few seconds, then finished the job by wiping her hands on her Giants sweatshirt as she walked out.

Marple leaned against the sink directly opposite the closed stall. She pulled out the unmarked prescription bottle from Keelin's apartment and shook out the contents. She could hear shallow breathing from inside. The tips of a pair of stylish shoes were just visible under the door.

Marple sent another text.

COME OUT. BE CAREFUL.

She heard a muffled, "Oh, Jesus." Then a flush. The door latch turned. Keelin Dale stepped out of the stall, eyes wide, arms tight to her sides, clearly terrified.

Marple extended her hand and opened her palm. It was filled with oval blue pills.

"Nurse Dale," she said. "Any more where these came from?"

CHAPTER 25

POE KNEW THEY had to work quickly and carefully to stay on the right side of the law. Technically, this was a conversation, not an interrogation. The trick was to keep Keelin Dale from recognizing the difference.

Marple had extracted the frazzled nurse from behind the security barrier with a vague threat of exposing her as a drug thief. Now the three of them were sitting in a cluster of public seating in front of a wall of glass near the main airport entrance.

"Who are you?" asked Dale. "Are you the police?"

Poe could see how nervous and flustered the nurse was. He glided right past her legitimate question. "Let's not talk about us," said Poe. "Let's talk about you."

"The pills," said Marple, following up quickly. "We've traced them to you."

"How?" asked Dale. Her hands were clasped so tightly her fingertips looked scarlet.

"Never mind how," said Poe. "Did you take them from St. Michael's?"

"God, no!" said Dale. "Do you know how hard it is to get drugs from a hospital these days?" She shook her head. "It's like Fort Knox in there."

Marple held off for a few seconds, then tipped the next domino. "Easier to steal babies, right?"

Dale bit her lower lip. Her pale skin blanched, making her freckles stand out even more. "Omigod, omigod..." she mumbled. She tried to avoid eye contact, but Poe leaned over to stare right at her, pressing the advantage.

"You're an addict, Keelin. We're very familiar with the type. Poor judgment is one of the symptoms. So is risk-taking behavior."

"Somebody found your weakness," said Marple. "Promised you a lifetime supply of Halcion. Enough to deal, if you wanted, and make a tidy profit. No more fake scrips. All you needed to do was provide some simple information about the maternity unit."

Dale was in tears now. "They said nobody would get hurt. They promised the babies would be ransomed in no time. They only picked babies with rich parents."

"Rich *white* parents," said Marple.

"That wasn't my idea!"

"Whose idea *was* it, Keelin?" asked Poe. "Who are we talking about? Who's behind this?"

"Who's your contact?" asked Marple. "Do you have a name?"

She and Poe were playing off each other, ping-ponging their questions before Dale could catch a breath.

"I don't know!" she finally shouted. A passing businessman looked over. Dale lowered her voice. "I talked to somebody on the phone. A woman. I used burner phones, like she told me. I threw them into the compacter after each call. I wasn't on call the night it happened. That was part of the deal. They told me to fly to Rabat and wait until everything got worked out. They said nobody could touch me there." She took a deep shuddering breath. "The babies," she said, almost in a whisper. "Did they get the babies back yet?"

Suddenly, a riot of red and blue lights blasted through the window. Dale jumped up. "Oh, Christ! You *are* cops!"

"No, Keelin," said Poe. "I promise we're not."

Marple looked outside. "But we know a few."

A New Jersey State Police SUV screeched to a stop outside, followed by an NYPD patrol car. An unmarked sedan with flashing dashboard lights pulled in front and parked at a hard angle near the entryway. Helene Grey stepped out. Poe rapped on the glass until she spotted him.

In a few seconds, the police were through the main doors, hands on their guns. The two New Jersey troopers approached first. "Keelin Dale?" one of them asked. Two NYPD uniforms were right behind.

Dale turned to Marple. "Are they arresting me?"

Grey stepped between the troopers and held up her badge. "Keelin, I'm Detective Helene Grey, NYPD. Right now we just want to talk. That's all."

"I'd go if I were you," said Marple. "Believe me, you're a lot safer with them than you'd be with whoever is waiting for you in Rabat."

Dale turned to Marple with a pleading look. "Will you come with me?"

Poe realized that, for Keelin Dale, Marple had become the least of three evils, right below the cops and the kidnappers. The panicked nurse desperately needed a friend.

"Of course I will," said Marple. She glanced at the troopers and held Keelin's forearm. "No cuffs here. We're walking out together."

Poe watched as Marple and Dale exited, sandwiched between two cops, and slid into the back of the NYPD patrol car.

Grey sat down next to him. "Auguste, are you insane?"

"I called you, didn't I?" he replied.

"Right. After you chased down a prime suspect on your own."

"A prime suspect *we* identified. I trusted Margaret to bring her in."

"Sometimes I think you guys trust each other a little too much," Grey muttered.

"Anyway," said Poe, "I don't think Dale can identify anybody. They were smart enough to keep her at a distance. She was just a cog in the machine."

"We'll see," said Grey. "I'll have New Jersey get a warrant for a legit search of her apartment. We can press her on the pills and see if her memory improves on the kidnapping." She stood up, pulled a business card from her pocket, and handed it to Poe.

"I've got a doctor's appointment tomorrow morning," she said. "If you want to be there, fine. If you don't, I'll understand." Before Poe could respond, Grey turned and walked out the sliding doors. Poe watched her thank the New Jersey troopers before she climbed into her sedan and led the small motorcade toward the airport exit.

He glanced down at the business card.

Exactly what he'd been afraid of.

CHAPTER 26

HOLMES SAT AT the far end of the communal table in their first-floor office space, with Poe and Marple on either side at the other end. They were all staring down at their laptops.

"I don't understand," said Virginia, in the seat at the opposite end of the table. "How are they keeping such a tight lid on this over there?" At Marple's direction, Virginia had gathered everything she could find about the London hospital kidnappings. There wasn't much.

"We Brits can be quite tight-lipped," said Marple. "As long as somebody doesn't leak it to Fleet Street, they might be able to contain it for a little longer."

Baskerville lay under Virginia's chair, panting loudly. From where Holmes sat, he could smell what the hound had for breakfast. He glanced absently at Virginia's report, organized in a meticulous Google Docs template. But his mind was else-where—or nowhere. The buprenorphine had that effect, making him groggy and detached. Logically, he understood how critical this case was. But mentally, he was having a hard time mustering his mojo.

"All wealthy white families," said Poe. "Same as here."

"One of the mothers is the niece of an MP," said Marple. "That may be how they're controlling it. Claiming national security."

"What do you think, Mr. Holmes?" asked Virginia.

"About what?" Holmes replied numbly.

"Do you have any theories? Anything else I should be searching for?"

Holmes stared at Virginia for a second, then looked at both of his partners. Apparently, they had not broken the news about his departure to their eager assistant. They had decided to leave it to him.

Fine. No time like the present. He closed the lid of his laptop.

"I guess you haven't heard, Virginia," he said. "I'm finished."

"Finished?" Virginia wrinkled her brow and stared at him. "What do you mean, *finished*?"

"I mean I'm finished with investigation, Virginia. Finished with the firm. I'm quitting."

"We're in discussions," said Marple, clearly trying to soften the blow.

"There is no discussion," said Holmes coldly.

Virginia pushed back from the table. "No! Mr. Holmes! You *can't!*" Tears started to glisten in her eyes. "You've only just come back! You *can't* leave again, not for good!"

"Yes, I can," said Holmes. "Sorry."

Virginia stared at him for a few seconds, shaking her head. Then she stood up and walked through the office toward the front door, wiping away tears with the back of her hand. Baskerville jumped to his feet and followed her.

"Virginia, wait!" Marple called out.

Too late. The door slammed.

Poe stared at Holmes. "Now look what you've done!"

"She'll be fine," said Holmes. "You all will. In fact, you'll be far better off."

Marple shifted to a chair closer to Holmes. She leaned her arms on the table and looked at him. "Brendan. Look. I know the stress you're under—"

"You have no *idea* the stress I'm under!" Holmes shouted, pounding the table with his fist. "Tell me something, Margaret—have you ever been addicted to anything stronger than *tea*?"

Marple rocked back. "I'm sorry. You're right. Maybe I don't understand."

Poe leaned in. "Here's what I understand, Brendan. We've got six missing babies—ten if you count the ones in London—and no real leads."

"You've got the nurse," said Holmes.

"Who most likely knows nothing," said Poe. "They can hold her for drug possession, but they'll have a hard time proving conspiracy to commit kidnapping unless they know who she conspired with. She's a small fish."

"A fingerling," said Marple.

Holmes stared at the table. His muscles ached. He hadn't slept well since leaving Lake View. His mouth felt dry. In his opinion, his withdrawal drug had all the negatives of an illegal drug habit with none of the positives. He no longer felt like himself.

Marple rested her hand gently on his wrist. "Brendan, please."

Holmes jerked his hand away. He wasn't about to fall for her soft touch. Or her tough love. Not this time.

"Help us crack this case," said Poe. "Then you can leave. I'll drive you to the airport myself. Muscle car of your choice."

"For God's sake, Brendan," said Marple. "They're *babies*!"

Holmes could feel his stomach churning. His skin itched under his suit. More than anything, he wanted this conversation to be over. But he knew his partners well enough to understand that they weren't about to give up. They were as tenacious as he was. At least, as tenacious as he *used* to be. He looked at Marple, then at Poe.

"Just this case," he muttered. "This *one* case. I work it my way. And then I'm gone."

Silence all around.

Holmes could tell that his partners didn't like the deal. But it was the only one on the table.

CHAPTER 27

LATE THAT NIGHT, Holmes started keeping his end of the bargain. At least that's how he saw it. His partners had succeeded in chasing down a person of interest, even if she seemed to be a dead end. And Marple in particular seemed to have a solid grasp of the workings of the hospital.

Now it was his turn.

Holmes craved human intelligence, and he needed to test his own faculties. Were his powers of deduction and intuition as dimmed as he assumed them to be, or might he still have a flicker of his old genius left? Only one way to find out.

When he walked into the Cops & Docs bar at midnight, he had to suppress his olfactory reaction. It wasn't just the smells of beer, perfume, and body odor. Those were right on the surface, and not entirely unpleasant. More potent was the background blend of urine and bleach from the restrooms, the scent of disinfecting wipes from the supply closet, the sting of ammonia from last night's floor mopping. He had to let it all wash over him and then press it back while he engaged his frontal lobe and visual cortex.

The place was packed with the expected clientele, mostly off-duty cops and hospital workers, some still wearing scrubs or vests marked ER or EMT. The atmosphere was humming at what Holmes estimated to be about 85 decibels, which included the music from the ceiling speakers. Loud but tolerable. At least for a short stretch.

As he shouldered his way through the crowd from the door to the bar, Holmes repeated, "Pardon me," and offered polite nods. He had a charming smile and he knew how to deploy it. But tonight it seemed to be having a negative effect. Everybody he glanced at — male or female — either ignored him or flat-out turned away.

When he finally reached the bar, Holmes slid onto a stool and tried to catch the attention of the bartender, a well-muscled guy with a thick moustache. It took some effort. When the man finally walked over, wiping his hands on a towel, he appeared to lack the traditional barkeep bonhomie.

"Is it me," asked Holmes, "or is this place a little clannish?"

"No," said the bartender. "It's you."

"Why? Am I overdressed?" Maybe a custom-tailored suit had been the wrong choice. Force of habit.

"You're a pariah." The bartender pointed behind the bar. Holmes leaned over to look. He saw photos of himself and his two partners lined up like mug shots, their names labeled underneath. "Some top cop told the police and hospital people not to talk to you. *Any* of you."

"Top cop?"

"Tall, skinny guy."

"Captain Duff?" asked Holmes.

"Sounds right." The bartender placed a coaster in front of Holmes. "Look. Makes no difference to me. I'm here to sell drinks. What can I get you?"

"Club soda," said Holmes. The clean-cut guy at the stool next to him got up and walked away. Holmes noticed the bold NYPD on the back of his windbreaker as he left.

A second later, his place was taken by a young woman with a halo of blond curls and heavily shadowed blue eyes. Late twenties. Black leggings, leather jacket, Wet Leg band T-shirt. She smelled of citrus and cinnamon.

Holmes smiled at her. She smiled back. It was a start.

"Undercover?" he asked.

"In a way," she replied.

She caught the bartender's eye with no effort at all. "Hey, Lou!" she called out. "Shot of Jameson!" She gave Holmes an appraising look. "You don't belong here," she said.

"I could say the same about you," Holmes replied. His soda and her shot arrived at the same time. He raised his drink. "*Salut.*"

She tapped her glass against his and knocked back the whiskey.

Suddenly, Holmes felt clammy all over. He could feel himself sweating under his suit. His head started pounding. Was it the young woman's fragrance? Or was he simply no longer capable of talking intelligently to strangers?

He stared down the bar and saw the glow from a hundred backlit bottles. His hands started to tremble around his glass, shaking the ice cubes inside. He realized that he was about to violate one of the cardinal rules from his time in the woods. An *unbreakable* rule. But he couldn't help it. He needed to tamp down his nerves and build up some confidence.

He raised his hand. The bartender looked over.

"Vodka, neat," Holmes called out.

"Well, now," the woman said. "One of us just got a little more interesting."

CHAPTER 28

HOLMES CLEARED HIS throat. The vodka molecules had started to pass through his blood-brain barrier and he was feeling the effects. The woman had ordered a beer chaser to follow her shot.

"Can I tell you something?" said Holmes.

"Why not?" said the young woman. "That's what bars are for."

"I'm here on an investigation," he said. "I'm a private investigator."

"Can't be all that private," the woman replied. "You just told me."

"I'm Brendan Holmes."

"I know," said the woman. "From your picture." She nodded at the printout behind the bar. "I'm Callie Brett." She held out her hand. Holmes shook it gently. Her skin was cool and damp from the beer bottle.

"Listen. I need to talk to somebody from the hospital," he said. He was starting to feel the full impact of the alcohol now. "But everybody's avoiding me." He realized his sentences were starting to spill out in a loose order. "It's very important. Very important investigation. Urgent."

"You can talk to me," said Callie. "I don't work there anymore."

A hospital worker? Not a cop? Holmes would not have deduced that about her. Had he missed something obvious? He tried to cover his surprise with a rudimentary question. "And when did you leave?"

"Twenty-four hours ago."

"You quit?"

"I did."

"What did you do there?"

"Pediatrics resident."

"You're a doctor?" Holmes blinked. His normally sharp instincts were way off.

"You look surprised," said Callie. She took a long sip of her beer. "I knew I should have worn my stethoscope." Then she smiled again.

Holmes found himself making a quick mental adjustment. So much for his powers of perception. They were obviously wrecked. But now he had to capitalize on the opportunity. Make up for the deficit. Difficult. His brain was swimming. His head was heavy. But he did his best to spin out a line of questioning.

"Did you by any chance notice any strangers in the maternity unit recently?" he asked.

"You mean besides the dozen new patients a day and their families?"

"Anybody unusual," said Holmes. "Anybody who stood out. Anybody who didn't belong."

Callie tilted her head and squinted toward the ceiling for a few seconds. She looked back at Holmes. "Some people came in last week from HavenCare. Corporate types. Two women."

"HavenCare?"

"Yep. That's the reason I quit. HavenCare is the conglomerate that's planning to suck up St. Michael's. Along with everything else."

"St. Michael's is going corporate?"

"Within six months."

"You didn't like that idea?"

"Joining the evil empire?" said Callie. "No, I didn't. St. Michael's is—was—one of the few independent hospitals left." She rolled her beer bottle between her palms. "Look. I get the efficiencies of scale, the records sharing, the administrative streamlining. I sat through all the presentations. I really liked the idea of nobody looking over our shoulder, watching our every move. You know what I mean?"

"I do. Absolutely," said Holmes. He felt the same way about needless supervision, had always preferred to work independently. "So, where are you going?" The word "going" had sounded odd as he spoke it. More like "gong."

"Denver," said Callie. "Small clinic. Privately owned. Obviously."

"How were they dressed?" Holmes was aware of his own non sequitur, and the fact that his head was hanging lower. It felt like a lead weight. He saw Callie lean over, her head tilted sideways.

"Hey," she said. "Are you okay?"

"Can you describe them?" Holmes could feel his words oozing out. Not crisp. Not authoritative. Not good.

Callie slid off her stool and leaned into his face. "What's up?" She called to the bartender. "Lou! How many has he had?" Lou held up one finger. She turned back to Holmes. "Are you *on* something?" She shook him by the shoulders. "What are you taking, Brendan?"

The subject has become the inquisitor, thought Holmes. His guard was now totally down. "Buprenorphine," he mumbled. "Sixteen milligrams." He badly messed up the next word: "Sublingually."

Callie grabbed his arm. "Buprenorphine? Are you kidding me?" She pulled his chin up and squeezed his cheeks. "You know that booze on top of bupe can be fatal, right? *Do you know that?*"

"I don't really care," said Holmes. At the moment, that was the absolute truth.

It was his last thought before his head hit the bar.

CHAPTER 29

MARGARET MARPLE'S APARTMENT cupboard was fresh out of tea, which was why she was prowling the first-floor kitchen at 1 a.m. Virginia always stocked a supply of Margaret's favorite chamomile in a tin by the microwave.

As she reached for the tin, the front-door bell rang. She turned and looked at the wall clock. It was late for visitors but not unheard of around here. She walked through the empty office to the entryway and looked at the security monitor.

It was Holmes. With an attractive young woman.

Margaret pressed the lock release and opened the door. The woman's blond curls were damp from the mist outside. Holmes looked logy, not himself. His herringbone jacket was rumpled, and his tie was askew. There was a small lump on his forehead. A sedan with an Uber placard was idling at the curb behind them.

"Margaret?" the woman asked.

"Margaret Marple, yes."

"You know this guy?"

"I do," said Marple. "He's my business partner. Who are you? What happened?"

The woman had a solid grip on Holmes, her hand on his upper arm. "I'm Dr. Brett. Callie Brett. Brendan had a little incident tonight."

Marple's heart started pounding. *"Incident?"*

"He's fine. Just mixed two substances that should never be mixed. I stayed with him until he stabilized."

Holmes twisted free and stepped through the doorway. "Like she says, I'm fine."

Dr. Brett took a step back toward the sidewalk. "Okay, Margaret. He's all yours now. But do me a favor. Watch him tonight—and do not let him anywhere near the liquor cabinet."

"Of course," said Marple. "How do you two...?"

"We just met," said Brett, holding up her hands as if to plead innocence. "Bar buddies, that's all."

"Thank you for bringing him home, Doctor," said Marple.

"No problem," said Brett. "Good luck with your investigation." She pressed her palms together in prayer formation. "Please find those babies." Callie Brett turned away, and waved good-bye as she slid into the back seat of the Uber.

"Dr. Brett gave me an interesting lead," said Holmes. He lurched toward a desk with a computer. "I need to follow up..."

Marple pulled him back. "The only thing you're doing right now is walking upstairs and going to sleep. What in God's name did you get into tonight?"

Holmes looked morose. "I'm sorry," he said, eyes down. "I've told you—I can't be trusted anymore. I've lost the gift."

Marple helped him up the stairs. "Not the gift for damaging yourself, obviously."

Holmes seemed to gather strength as they walked toward his apartment. He planted his palm on the security pad outside his door. The lock clicked open. He made an awkward bow. "Thank you, Margaret. I'll see you in the morning."

"You'll see me before that," she said. "I'm sleeping on your sofa."

She gave him a nudge and stepped into the apartment foyer with him. "Go put yourself to bed," she said. Then she grabbed him by the arms. "And starting tomorrow, we'll have no more of this. As long as you're a partner here, *you are still Holmes!*"

"Wait," said Holmes. "I need to tell you something."

"Now what?" said Marple. She was tired, and her irritation was showing. She realized that Holmes was staring at her intently.

"Margaret," he said softly, "I'm in love with you."

Marple walked to the linen closet and yanked out a blanket and pillow. "No, Brendan. You're in an altered state."

CHAPTER 30

POE COULD NOT remember ever feeling this uncomfortable, or this out of place.

At 8 a.m., at a small private clinic, Detective Helene Grey lay on an examination table with her midsection exposed. Her blouse was unbuttoned to the bottom of her bra, and her slacks were pulled down to her lower abdomen. The room was dim, except for the glow from a small monitor at the head of the table. A petite Asian woman in a lab coat applied a shiny coat of gel to Grey's belly.

"I'm Andrea," the tech said with a smile. "I warmed it up for you."

"Thanks for that," said Grey, her voice low.

"So let's take a peek," said Andrea. She pulled an ultrasound wand from its cradle and placed it a few inches below Grey's navel.

Auguste Poe stood off to the side, arms folded across his chest, his heart pounding so hard he thought the device might pick it up. He wondered if it had been a mistake to come along. To Poe, it seemed like Helene was a lot more comfortable with the technician than she was with him.

Poe kept his eyes on Grey's face until the monitor lit up with an image—black and white, fanned out and wider at the bottom. It looked like shifting sand or storm clouds, grainy and rippling. As the tech moved the wand, a small black void appeared near the center, an irregular oval.

"There's the gestational sac," Andrea said softly. "And here..." She pointed to a tiny, indistinct shape near the margin. "That's your baby."

Poe felt adrenaline rush to his gut. Grey craned her neck for a better view. The tech tapped some keys and a cluster of digits appeared on the right side of the screen. "Let's see what we can hear," she said. She pressed another key. A spiky graph pulsed across the bottom of the screen. A tiny speaker blasted what sounded to Poe like somebody bending a sheet of aluminum back and forth. *Warp, warp...warp, warp...warp, warp...*

"That's the heart?" he asked.

"It is," said Andrea. "A hundred and fifty beats a minute."

"Is that good?" asked Grey. "It sounds fast."

"Perfectly normal," said the tech. She shifted the wand a few inches and leaned forward toward the screen. "Hold on."

"What's wrong?" asked Grey. Poe saw her jaw clench. He felt a quiver in his knees. His mouth went dry.

"Give me one second..." said the tech, angling the wand again. The black opening disappeared, then reappeared on the other side. Or did it? Another wiggle of the wand. The first opening appeared again. Then *two* openings together, side by side, like mirror images.

"Whoa," said Andrea. She pressed a key. The sound came again, a little slower this time.

"What's that?" asked Poe.

"It's another heartbeat," she replied. "Another baby." She looked at Grey, then at Poe. "Congratulations, guys, you're having twins."

"Dear God," said Grey softly.

Poe felt the sound from the machine like it was throbbing inside his own head.

He reached over and patted Helene's hand gently as it rested on the exam table.

Then, without a word, he turned and walked out of the room. He didn't stop until he reached a bench near the sidewalk—where he almost passed out.

CHAPTER 31

POE WAS STILL reeling an hour later when he walked in the front door of the building in Brooklyn. Virginia was in the kitchen with Baskerville at her hip.

"You were up and away early this morning, Mr. Poe," Virginia called out.

"Correct" was all he could say. He'd been equally terse with Helene. She had mumbled something like "We'll talk." He had nodded. Then they'd each gone their separate ways.

Poe looked up to the balcony level and saw Marple emerge from Holmes's apartment. Her skirt and blouse were rumpled, and her hair was uncharacteristically untamed. Holmes followed close behind in a robe and silk pajamas.

Virginia's eyes widened at the sight of Holmes and Marple descending the staircase together. Poe stared at Holmes as the pair approached the table.

"So," he said. "You and Margaret are roommates now?"

Holmes gave him a dismissive wave. "Margaret was my sofa sentry last night. For some reason she thought I needed monitoring."

"Monitoring for what?" asked Poe.

"Nothing," said Holmes. "Abundance of caution."

"How is everybody this morning?" chirped Marple as she took her seat. Even in her rumpled state, she seemed cheerful. "I hope we all remember what we're up to this morning."

Poe slid his mug across the table. Virginia filled it with coffee. "Don't tell me it's another goddamn task force meeting," he mumbled.

"I'm not setting foot in that place again," said Holmes. "Nothing but a den of underachievers." Virginia pushed a cup of coffee in front of him and then turned to fetch the hot kettle from the stove.

"This is totally different," said Marple. "You've probably forgotten. We're scheduled to be on a panel at the crime-writers' convention at the Marriott Marquis."

Poe leaned across the table. He narrowed his eyes and cocked his head. Had he heard correctly? "What? A *writers'* convention?"

"Yes," said Marple. "We committed to it back in . . ."

"July," Virginia finished, pouring steaming water over the tea strainer in Marple's favorite mug.

"That's correct," said Marple. "And we keep our commitments."

"Well, I wasn't part of that, Margaret," said Holmes. "Besides, why in God's name would we waste time at a crime-writers' convention when there are actual crimes to solve? Missing babies, remember? Distraught parents? The case you both talked me into working?"

Virginia lit up as she handed Marple her steaming mug. "Mr. Holmes! You're staying?!"

"A temporary reprieve," said Holmes.

Poe took another sip of his coffee. "Margaret," he said. "Brendan's got a point. You must be kidding."

"I know we're busy," said Marple. "Think of this as a refreshing respite. And there's a lot we can learn from crime writers. We all know that."

Poe rubbed his eyes. He felt emotionally exhausted, and his nerves were raw.

With everything on his mind, this was the last thing he needed, today of all days. "Waste of valuable time," he said firmly. "I'm not going."

"You certainly are," said Marple. "I made a promise."

Poe was working hard to keep his temper in check. "Margaret. You can't go making promises for all of us."

"And yet I did," she replied evenly. "You were spending a weekend with Helene when I made the arrangements. And Brendan was incommunicado in Ithaca. But like us all, I'm authorized to speak for the business. As an equal partner."

"Then *you* go by yourself," said Holmes. "As the representative of the firm."

Poe saw Marple's features relax while her shoulders tightened slightly. It was the same demeanor he'd seen her adopt with balky suspects. Sweetness, underpinned with steel.

"The contract specifies Holmes, Marple, and Poe," she said, "and that's who they're getting." She turned to Holmes. "This is perfect for you, Brendan. Now that you're about to retire, you'll have time to write a crime novel of your own."

She patted his wrist lightly as she sipped her tea. "Maybe you can pick up some tips."

CHAPTER 32

THE STRETCH LIMO arrived at the office exactly at ten, as specified in the contract. Marple slid in first, followed by her partners.

"So *bourgeois*," said Holmes, settling awkwardly against the plush leather.

"An underpowered coffin," muttered Poe.

"Oh, will you two stop whining?" said Marple. She was excited about this event and not about to let these spoilsports dampen her spirits. The limo pulled away from the curb and headed for Manhattan.

Holmes stared out the tinted side window. "Let's hope nobody else gets kidnapped while we're on this lark."

"By the way," said Marple, "I have a call in to Scotland Yard about their kidnappings. Maybe we can compare notes with their team." After a long search, Virginia had finally located a promising contact, a young London constable named Ben Dodgett who seemed willing to assist them. Marple hoped to help him unlock the London investigation, which in turn might unlock their own one.

"How long did you say this event will be?" asked Poe, drumming his fingers on an armrest.

"There's a panel discussion, then lunch," said Marple brightly. "Maybe a little mix and mingle too."

"I trust we're being compensated," said Holmes.

"Yes, and quite nicely," said Marple. "I've already donated it to the Friends of Firefighters."

"Margaret. *Really?*" said Holmes. "A little consultation would be nice."

"Well, it never hurts to be on the good side of the fire department."

The limo soon eased through Times Square and pulled up in front of the hotel. Marple saw a skinny young man with an iPad and a headset pacing anxiously on the sidewalk. The instant the limo rolled to a stop, he hurried over and pulled open the rear door.

"Hey, guys. Glad you're here," he said. He was talking very fast, and his forehead was shiny with perspiration. "I'm Adam, from the events office. Sorry to rush you, but we had to move your panel up. You're on in"—he glanced at his watch—"five minutes."

"What happened to the schedule?" asked Holmes.

"You won't believe it," said Adam. "John Grisham cancelled at the last minute. Totally out of character. He's usually so reliable."

Poe frowned. "So it takes three of us to make up for one of him?"

"Be quiet," said Marple, pushing him out of the car. "Just go."

Adam led the way through the main entrance and then through a back hallway to a service elevator, muttering anxiously into his headset the whole time. After a short, smooth ride, the doors opened onto a backstage space filled with folded banquet tables and extra PA equipment.

Marple peered through a gap in the curtains isolating the backstage area and saw a brightly lit dais facing a huge ballroom. It looked like every seat in the audience was filled, and the place was buzzing.

When they approached the few steps leading up to the stage, Adam stopped and adjusted his headset. "Hold here," he said, lifting his hand. "They're introducing you right now."

Marple heard the amplified clatter of fingers on a microphone. She saw a slender woman in a maroon business suit leaning over the podium. "Ladies and gentlemen, welcome!" As the woman waited for the audience to settle, she glanced quickly toward the wings. Adam gave her a thumbs-up. The woman turned back toward the ballroom and leaned into her introduction.

"As crime writers, we all know the names of our next panelists. I suspect that most of us grew up worshipping these names. But while many of you now solve crimes in make-believe, this team solves them in real life. I'm pleased to introduce three of New York's most celebrated private investigators: Brendan Holmes, Margaret Marple, and Auguste Poe!"

The ballroom erupted in applause. Adam swept his arm toward the stage. Marple turned to her partners. "Remember," she said, "this is supposed to be fun. And we could actually get some business out of it."

At the last second, she reached up to fix Holmes's necktie. "And you, my friend, might get a book deal."

CHAPTER *33*

POE WAS PARTIALLY blinded by the stage lights as he walked across the dais with his partners. When he sat down at the table, with a microphone aimed at each of them, the glare was less piercing, and the audience came into view—maybe a thousand people or more.

The ballroom was set up with rows of chairs fanning toward the back in four neat sections. In the center of each aisle, volunteers in matching outfits stood facing the stage, cradling wireless mics.

Poe recognized the woman who had introduced them. She was now seated in the moderator's chair. It was Anna Spahr, a New York crime reporter from the local NBC affiliate. Her perfect teeth gleamed as she leaned forward in her chair and looked across the stage at them.

"Welcome, Holmes, Marple, and Poe!" she said, drawing another quick burst of applause. "If the audience will indulge me, I'll ask the first question." She glanced at her note cards, then looked up again. "Please tell us what first drew you to the world of crime investigation."

Poe tried hard not to roll his eyes. In his peripheral vision, he saw Holmes lean toward the table mic in front of him. "Truth, justice, and the American way," he said somberly. Then he slumped back.

There were a few snorts and titters from the audience. Then Poe heard Marple's voice crackle through the room.

"Crimes are like puzzles, aren't they?" she said. She'd dialed up her accent, sounding chipper enough to bounce off the walls, instantly lifting the mood. "I think we all like solving puzzles. And when we solve a crime, whether it's in a story or in the real world, it's incredibly satisfying. Am I right?"

This drew positive murmurs and a solid ripple of claps.

Poe sighed and settled into his chair. *How long will this take again?* But the next fifteen minutes or so moved relatively quickly, with Marple doing the bulk of the work keeping the audience charmed.

"Impostors!" A loud voice from the audience.

Spahr whipped around and placed her hand above her eyes to peer past the lights and into the crowd. "Please!" she said. "If you have a question, one of the ushers will bring you a microphone."

Poe sat up straight in his chair as one of the volunteers approached a very tall bald man with glasses. He took the mic. "Just kidding," he said, breaking into a grin. "You're among friends here. But let's face facts. Clever as it is, Holmes, Marple, and Poe is a publicity stunt, right?"

Poe squinted. He recognized the man from his book jacket photos. It was Harlan Coben, a bestselling crime author and winner of the Edgar Award, named after...who else? Edgar Allan Poe.

"I'd like to hear your *real* origin story," Coben said. "If you dare." He handed the mic back and sat down to hearty chuckles and pats on the back.

Poe leaned forward and cleared his throat. "Mr. Coben is right," he said. "We're frauds." Awkward silence. Poe lowered his head, and his voice. "We actually met in a mystery book club as under-grads at—"

"*No!* He's lying!" Holmes interrupted. "He's very good at that. It was at a murder mystery dinner party in Secaucus fifteen years ago. At one point in the evening, the three of us found ourselves locked in the library—"

"With Professor Plum and Colonel Mustard," added Marple brightly.

A big laugh from the crowd.

"Hold on!" A female voice from the other side of the room.

Poe looked over. He spotted a slightly built woman with bright red hair. In her first two words, he had picked up a slight Irish lilt.

"What is it with these false identities?" she asked. "How do you expect us to believe this claptrap?"

"Do you mind giving us your name?" asked Spahr, trying to reassert control.

"I'm Tana French," said the woman.

Christ! thought Poe. Another highly successful crime author. And another damned Edgar Award winner. They were beset by the best.

Marple spoke up again. "I have something to say, and I've never said this before. Don't let it leave this room, but my actual name is not Marple." She paused for a beat. "It's Christie." Some genuine gasps from the crowd.

"Oh, *please!*" Another female voice, this time from the front row. Poe looked down as an usher walked over with a mic. The speaker had thick brown hair and a round, open face. "Hello. My name is Lisa Gardner."

Dear God, make it stop, thought Poe. Another great crime writer, with a famously analytical mind.

"If you can't be honest about who you really are, why should we believe a word you say?" Gardner asked.

Poe looked over at Holmes, who seemed played out. But not Marple. She was obviously loving this. She leaned forward, her arms resting on the table. "Why *not?* Don't we accept the over-the-top tales you tell? Willing suspension of disbelief, right? And speaking of playing with names, Ms. Gardner, would you care to identify Alicia Scott?"

A burst of chuckles from the crowd. Gardner tightened her grip on the mic and glanced around before replying, "Everybody here knows that Alicia Scott is a pseudonym I used when writing romantic suspense. It's a pen name. A simple literary device."

"Is it?" asked Marple. "How can we be sure which name is the real you? If you like, we'd be happy to investigate."

Poe leaned toward his mic. "No charge."

Amid the guffaws that followed, Anna Spahr walked briskly to the podium and made a broad show of looking at her wristwatch. "Well, ladies and gentlemen, as you know, our schedule has been thrown a little out of whack. So let's thank our panelists and head out through the rear exits for a little reception and more conversation."

Poe was the first one off the stage, as light applause echoed in his ears.

Marple was next. "Wasn't that delightful?" she said. She turned to Holmes. "Be honest, Brendan. Won't you miss the spotlight?"

Holmes scowled. "Not for one second."

CHAPTER 34

WHAT A NIGHTMARE.

For Holmes, the lobby reception was worse than being onstage. Out here, there was no insulation from the clingy crowd. And the panel session had apparently only boosted curiosity from the attendees. The small talk was excruciating. Holmes realized that the same people who spent their days crafting snappy dialogue often had no flair whatsoever for normal conversation. As he sipped the club soda Marple had handed him, he started to fantasize about an escape. Maybe through the hotel kitchen . . .

"Brendan Holmes? Incredible! I've been waiting all morning to meet you!"

Christ, please. Not another one.

Holmes looked down. The man's head barely came up to his chest. The voice was scratchy. Not from cigarettes. With his superior olfactory sense, Holmes would've detected even the faintest scent of nicotine. Maybe a vocal polyp.

"I'm Oliver Paul," the man said, thrusting his hand forward in a way that gave Holmes no choice but to shake it. The palm was soft, fingers uncalloused. Not a tradesman or blue-collar worker. Maybe an office worker or technician. God forbid another writer.

"My pleasure," said Holmes. It was by far the biggest lie he had told that day.

"Do you mind?" asked Paul, pointing to a corner a few yards away. "I hate crowds as much as you do."

Holmes followed him over. He noticed that the man's left eye did not fully focus. It didn't wander, exactly, just pointed a few degrees off axis. Unsettling.

"I'm sure you hear this all the time," said Paul, leaning in, "but I'm a bit of a detective myself."

Paul was correct. Holmes had heard it more times than he could count. From cab drivers, waiters, deliverymen, doctors, drug dealers...

"And what are you investigating, exactly?" asked Holmes. He flicked his gaze over Paul's shoulder, searching for Poe and Marple, hoping for rescue. He spotted them locked in a spirited debate with Harlan Coben, who loomed over both.

"To tell you the truth," said Paul, "I've got enough material for a great crime novel. Better than anything Sir Arthur Conan Doyle ever came up with."

"Is that so?" Holmes had heard that before too. It always made him slightly queasy.

"But to tell you the truth," said Paul, "I could really use your help."

"To tell *you* the truth," said Holmes, "I've decided to step back from the business. In fact, I'm thinking this might be my last public appearance."

"That would be such a loss," said Paul. "Please. Let me tell you what I've uncovered. It will only take—"

A chime rang out from the ceiling speakers, then an announcement. A pleasantly insistent female voice. *"May I have your attention please. At this time, will our panelists and invited guests please proceed to the dining room for the Masters Luncheon. Thank you."*

"I think that's me," said Holmes, draining his soda glass. "Nice to meet you." He brushed past Paul as fast as basic human courtesy would allow.

"Wait!" came the scratchy plea from behind him. Holmes didn't look back, pretending not to hear. He caught up to Poe and Marple as they walked through the door into the intimate function room.

"Saved by rubber chicken," muttered Holmes.

CHAPTER 35

"WE'RE OVER THERE," said Poe, pointing to a table across the room. The luncheon setup had no more than fifteen tables, set close enough to allow easy chatting. Holmes had been hoping for a little more isolation. A soundproof booth would have been nice.

The tables were set for four, with white damask tablecloths and tasteful floral centerpieces. Waitstaff in dark slacks and crisp white shirts hovered on the periphery. The aromas of grilled beef, broiled swordfish, and—yes—baked chicken emerged from behind cushioned doors.

"Is this absolutely necessary?" asked Poe under his breath. "We have more important things to attend to!"

"The hard part is over," said Marple. "Enjoy your lunch."

Holmes pulled out Marple's chair for her and helped her settle before taking his seat to her right. Poe sat down on her left. The other tables filled with VIP guests. At a table nearby, Tana French was telling a bawdy story, her Irish accent seemingly deepened for the tale.

"Looks pricey," said Poe, glancing around the elegant room.

Holmes stared at the empty chair at their table and wondered who the no-show was. Probably Grisham. And then...

"Now. Where were we?"

Oliver Paul pulled out the chair and sat down. Holmes almost jumped out of his seat.

"No need to call security," said Paul, holding up his hands. "I assure you I paid for the all-access experience. I'd hate to tell you what this seat cost!" He looked across the table, from Holmes to Marple to Poe. "But what an honor to be sitting with the three of you!"

Holmes let out a brief sigh, then put on a thin sheen of civility. "Margaret. Auguste. This is Oliver Paul. He and I were just talking in the lobby."

"Charmed," said Marple.

"Same here," said Poe.

"Has Brendan told you?" asked Paul in his scratchy voice.

Marple laid the napkin in her lap. "Told us what?"

"Maybe he wants to keep it to himself," said Paul, "solve it on his own."

"Solve what, exactly?" asked Poe.

"My case!" said Paul. "I've been working on it for years. Haunting. Impossible. I call it 'The Mother Murders.'" He spoke quietly, as if he were afraid other guests would overhear. "Great title, right?"

A waiter appeared and began to pour wine into the goblets at each setting. Marple casually floated her palm to cover Holmes's glass. "I'm sorry, Mr. Paul," she said. "Are we talking about an actual crime or a crime story?"

"Maybe both!" Paul replied with an awkward wink. "It could be the next *In Cold Blood*!"

"That's a high bar," Holmes said. Though Oliver Paul did remind him a bit of Truman Capote, at least in the height department.

"This is one of the greatest mysteries *ever*," said Paul. He looked around the room. "Way better than anything these hacks could dream up."

Holmes felt the blood rising in his neck. In a flash, his decorum completely dissolved. "Oh, for God's sake, Mr. Paul, spit it out!"

"There," said Paul calmly. "See how good I am? I've got you hooked already."

Amid the buzz of room conversation, Holmes heard the hum of a cell phone. It was coming from Poe's jacket pocket. He watched Poe pull out the phone, glance at the screen, and jerk back in his chair. Poe turned the screen so that Holmes and Marple could see it. **SCHOOL BUS MISSING**, the text read. **PUTNAM COUNTY / DRIVER + 5 KIDS**.

Poe and Marple stood up quickly, almost in unison. "I'm sorry, Mr. Paul," said Marple. "We have to go."

Holmes didn't stir.

"Brendan!" said Poe, shaking the back of his partner's chair. "Come on!"

"No," said Holmes. As much as he wanted to escape this particular room, he felt it necessary to make a stand. "You two need to learn to work without me."

"Brendan," said Marple. "We managed without you all summer. But this looks like more missing children. And you agreed to help."

"Not today," he said. "You go. This is the future. *Your* future."

"We'll talk about this," said Marple curtly. "You promised." She nudged Poe on the shoulder and followed him out of the room.

"Endive salad," the waitress announced as she set down an elegantly arranged plate of greens at each place, ignoring the two empty chairs. Holmes picked up his fork.

Oliver Paul leaned across the table. "I know what's going on with you, Mr. Holmes," he said. His tone was gentle and soothing, in spite of the rasp. "I know you've been in a...facility. You're afraid you've lost your touch—that old Holmes magic."

Holmes set his fork down on the table. *Enough! Who does this obnoxious little groupie think he is? And where did he get his information?*

"Incorrect!" Holmes said brusquely. "And as for the old Holmes magic"—he stared directly into Paul's good eye—"I'm afraid I never had it." He pushed back his chair and tossed his napkin onto the table. He pointed a finger at Paul. "Do *not* follow me," he said.

Then he turned and headed for the door.

"Hey, Holmes! Where are you going?" It was Harlan Coben, calling out from two tables over. "Off to search for your true self?"

CHAPTER 36

"CAN YOU *PLEASE* let me drive?" begged Poe.

"That's not happening," said the driver.

"Well, then, at least *push* it! This is an emergency!"

Poe and Marple sat in the back of the courtesy limo as it made its way north from the city. The chauffeur had been expecting a simple return trip to Brooklyn. Instead, they'd commandeered him and his vehicle for a mission to rural Putnam County, more than an hour out of his way.

"Don't worry," said Marple. "We'll pay the extra charges."

Poe heard the driver mutter under his breath. "Damn right."

As the enormous Lincoln got up to speed, Marple plumbed her iPad for any information on the incident. Police feeds. Social media. FBI threads. "Nothing," she said. "How did your source find out about this?"

"Margaret," said Poe, "you know I can't give away *all* my secrets." He looked out the window as the scenic Hudson Valley rolled by. Poe considered Marple and Holmes his closest friends in the world. He trusted them with his life. But there were still select pockets of information he kept to himself. Bank accounts. Safe houses. And contacts who could be trusted to feed him information about crimes minutes after they were committed.

In some ways, he rationalized, his secrecy was for their protection. It gave them plausible deniability in case he ever needed to go rogue. Besides, there might come a time when he'd need to disappear altogether, and for that he would need his own private network. People only he knew.

The car turned off the main road onto a narrow two-lane. "Up there!" Poe called out to the driver.

The GPS coordinates had led them to the middle of nowhere. Brown farm fields ran off in every direction, interrupted here and there by a patch of green or a thin stand of trees.

Poe knew from his on-the-road research that the nearest town was Tompkins Corners, population 9,000—about the same as the number of people who lived in a single Manhattan block. He'd been told to look for law enforcement in this spot, and his intelligence was correct. There was a lone police car blocking the road straight ahead, and two young officers standing in the road.

When the massive stretch pulled to a stop near the Putnam County Sheriff's Office unit, the two officers bent down to peer through the tinted windows.

The driver craned his neck around. "What's going on? What are we doing here?"

"Relax," said Marple, patting the back of his seat. "Enjoy the scenery."

Poe turned to Marple. "Welcome to the country," he said. "I think the last time these guys saw a limo was on prom night."

"Be nice," said Marple. "If you treat them like rubes, we'll get nowhere."

As Poe and Marple exited the car, another local police unit

pulled up, lights flashing. A female officer and her male partner climbed out. The woman gave Poe and Marple a quick once-over. Then the limo.

"Kardashians in town?" she asked.

Marple held out her private investigator's ID. Poe did the same. He decided to let Marple do the talking.

"I'm Margaret Marple. This is my partner Auguste Poe. We're private investigators from New York, working a kidnapping case. Six babies went missing from a Manhattan hospital almost three nights ago."

One of the cops from the first car spoke up. "Well, what we're missing here is a school bus. Not babies. Third graders."

"How many kids?" asked Poe.

"Five," said the female cop. "Plus the bus driver. They were near the end of the run." She stood with her legs apart, hands on her hips. Power stance. She jutted her chin out as she spoke. "How'd you two find out about this so fast, all the way down in the city?"

Suddenly, the country air filled with the sound of sirens. Everybody looked to the south. A pair of state trooper SUVs appeared over a crest, bracketing an unmarked blue sedan. They pulled to a stop on the other side of the road. The sedan door whipped open.

Poe groaned. "You've got to be kidding..."

Captain Graham Duff crossed the road in three long strides and stopped in front of the two PIs. "How in the name of hell did you two get here first?" he asked.

Marple smiled. "In case you haven't heard, Captain, we're very good at what we do."

Poe looked across the road to see if Helene Grey was in any of the vehicles. She wasn't. He felt partly guilty, partly ashamed, and partly relieved. He wasn't quite ready to face her yet.

Duff turned to the quartet of local cops. "Graham Duff, NYPD," he said. "Whatever information you have to share about this case, you share it with me." He jerked his thumb over his shoulder at Marple and Poe. "And whatever you do, keep them away from the parents." Poe wasn't surprised at Duff's final dig. "Folks up here can't afford them anyway."

CHAPTER 37

TWENTY MINUTES AFTER leaving Oliver Paul at the luncheon, Holmes was still wandering Times Square. The shooting galleries and garish porn shops it had been known for were purged decades ago. Theater lights and massive LED displays instead blinded him as he walked.

After a while, Holmes headed east along 45th Street. He was a creature of the city. As he walked, he navigated without thinking. He turned north, walked a few blocks, then east, then north again, dodging cabs and delivery bikes by instinct.

He was in a dark mood. As he walked under yet another skeleton of scaffolding, he angled his body to let a couple with a stroller ease by. He thought about the missing babies, and about the message Poe had received, but felt totally useless and out of touch. In his mind, his career was over. He could accept that his partners were furious with him, but he hated that they were disappointed in him. He felt he'd let them down in every possible way.

When he looked up, he found he was on Park Avenue, approaching 59th Street. At the corner, he looked right. In spite of his depression, he felt a small lift in his chest when he noticed he was by one of his favorite places on the planet.

Holmes crossed the street and opened the front door of the Argosy Book Store. Unlike Times Square, it hadn't changed much at all since his first visit as a child. Same patterned ceiling. Same cozy clutter of desks, shelves, and bins—all crammed and overflowing with books. Same posters and framed artwork leaning against desks.

Even the scents were the same, only more intense. Worn leather, wood polish, binding adhesive, aging paper. Absolutely intoxicating.

Holmes wound his way past the tourists and aficionados until he found himself in a small alcove behind a worn maple table. He ran his hands across the densely packed shelves, tapping the rounded spines as he went. Melville. Austen. Dickens. Tolstoy. Joyce.

At one point his hand simply stopped, like a divining rod over hidden water. When he glanced up at the shelf, the book was staring him right in the face. His heart jolted. He hadn't even been looking for it. But there it was.

Holmes pulled the volume off the shelf. The cover was blue buckram, finely textured, with an inset illustration of a downcast figure in formal clothes, holding his hat loosely behind his back. He had the expression of a man visiting a sick friend, or attending a funeral.

Below the illustration, in thin lettering, sat the title: *Adventure XXIV. The Final Problem. By Sir Arthur Conan Doyle.* Holmes looked down to the bottom of the inset. His eyes widened. "From *The Strand Magazine.* Vol. VI: December 1893." A collector's edition!

Holmes tucked the volume under his arm and carried it to the checkout desk in front. The clerk was a young man with stringy blond hair and a pale complexion.

"How much?" asked Holmes.

The clerk took the book and entered some digits into the computer.

"One hundred," he said.

One hundred? Holmes was almost hurt. "It's worth more than that," he said.

"You're probably right," said the clerk, tucking a strand of hair behind his ear. "I won't tell if you don't."

Holmes reached into his wallet and pulled out his Amex card. He handed it to the clerk, forgetting that it was an unnecessary step. Force of habit. The clerk glanced at the card before reaching over and sticking it into the device on the counter.

"Interesting name," he said. "Coincidence?"

"Not quite," said Holmes.

As the clerk slid the book and receipt into a bag, he leaned over. "You know Sherlock gets killed off in this one, right?"

Holmes nodded and took the package. "Maybe Sir Arthur had the right idea."

CHAPTER 38

EIGHT THE NEXT morning.

Holmes felt warm sun pouring through his bedroom window, but his mood was still gloomy. He had gone to bed early, before his partners came home. He realized they hadn't called him once the whole day about their trip to the country.

Maybe they were finally getting the message.

He showered once, shaved his face and scalp, then showered again. He reached into the bathroom cabinet and took his daily dose of medication. When he stepped back into the bedroom, an aroma coming from the kitchen downstairs hit him like a wallop. He dressed quickly and stepped out onto the balcony.

"Good morning, Mr. Holmes!" Virginia waved to him from in front of the stove. She wore a blue-and-white chef's apron and held a mixing bowl in the crook of her arm.

Holmes walked to the end of the hallway and down the staircase to the first floor. His olfactory bulbs became more aroused with every step.

"Miss Marple and Mr. Poe are out already," said Virginia.

"You're probably hungry." As usual, she had anticipated his first question and his immediate need.

"What in heaven's name are you making?" asked Holmes.

Virginia smiled. "Waffles with toasted pecans." She held up a small cruet. "With warm maple syrup, of course." She gestured toward the table. "Sit, Mr. Holmes. I'll bring your coffee."

Holmes closed his eyes and drew a deep breath, taking in the essence of sizzling batter and butter from the griddle, with hints of vanilla and roasted nuts. The aroma took a direct line to his limbic system, stirring memories he hadn't felt since childhood. Holmes knew this recipe very well. It was his mother's.

But he had never mentioned it.

Then the plate was in front of him, with a mug of fresh coffee alongside. The waffles were thick and golden brown, flecked with the crushed pecans and dripping with rivulets of syrup. He picked up his knife and fork and took his first taste. Incredible. Almost overwhelming. He savored the warmth, the texture, the flavors.

He looked over at Virginia. "Where did you learn to make this?" he asked. She was already rinsing the mixing bowl in the sink. "Not sure," she said with a shrug. "Things just come to me."

Holmes nodded. The girl had a sixth sense. Poe had been the first to notice it, and Holmes had seen it in operation many times. Their young assistant was always one step ahead of the game and, at times, seemed to know things that reason said she simply should not.

Holmes wolfed down the waffles and wiped his mouth with a napkin. If comfort food was Virginia's way of making him feel at home, it had worked. At least for the moment. Holmes scraped the last morsels from his plate and licked his fork. "I need your help," he said.

Virginia finished drying the bowl and set it on the counter.

She brushed back a streaked lock of hair—green today. "Sure," she said. "Anything."

"Background check," said Holmes. He gave her what details he knew about Oliver Paul.

"Got it," said Virginia with a quick nod. She dried her hands and walked over to her desk at the far end of the floor. A half minute later, she was back, balancing a MacBook on one palm, tapping keys as she walked. She sat down across from Holmes and put the laptop on the counter. She peered at the screen, moving her lips slightly as she absorbed the data.

"Let's see . . . Oliver James Paul? Tell me if this is the one you're interested in. Age thirty-six. Last known residence Queens. No criminal record. No military service. No current vehicle registrations." Virginia's fingers flicked around the keypad, then hovered. "Interesting," she said.

"What is?" asked Holmes.

"No obvious social media activity. He's totally dark. Except for all these publications. Dozens of them."

"About crime?" Holmes asked.

"No," said Virginia, clicking on one of the files. "About . . . chronometer mechanisms." She tapped a few more keys, then looked up. "Oliver Paul is a watchmaker. He has a shop in the East Village."

Holmes pulled out his cell phone. "Text me the address."

Virginia's whole face brightened. "New case?" she asked.

"Not likely," said Holmes. But something in him was stirring. He couldn't deny it.

Couldn't hurt to pay the little creep a visit.

Unofficially, of course.

CHAPTER 39

BY NOON, HOLMES was standing in the shadow of a pizza parlor awning and staring across Avenue B toward the address Virginia had sent him. The sign over the entrance said SMALLTIME, and the pun was totally apt. The entire clock shop was only about three times as wide as the front door, squeezed between a vape store and a pharmacy. The sign on the door said OPEN, but Holmes had yet to see a single customer enter or exit.

The powerful aromas of garlic and oregano from the pizza kitchen assaulted his nostrils. Time to move. He walked across the street, peeked through the front window, then opened the door and stepped inside.

The ceiling was low and the air was pungent. A dehumidifier near the entrance ended its cycle with a metallic rattle. Holmes cocked his head. The air was now filled with the sound of ticking from every direction, creating a disconcerting white noise.

The walls of the shop were lined with timepieces of every kind—alarm clocks, calendar clocks, cuckoo clocks—from polished antiques to neon-hued 1970s cubes to contemporary atomic models. Hanging at the top of one wall was a classic Standard Electric schoolroom clock. An imposing grand-father model was set into one corner, its brass pendulum visible through a glass-paneled front.

"*Yes!* I knew you'd come!" An excited voice from the back of the shop. Holmes recognized the rasp immediately. Oliver Paul emerged from a curtained-off back room and leaned over a glass counter.

"Good morning, Mr. Paul," said Holmes. "You said you were an amateur sleuth. You didn't tell me you were a watchmaker."

"Because I knew you'd find out. And please, call me Oliver." Paul reached across the counter for a handshake. Holmes could feel Paul trembling with excitement. A double-eyed jeweler's loupe rested on his forehead, giving him the look of an eager insect. "I guess you couldn't resist my story," he said.

"You haven't told me a story yet," said Holmes. "All you gave me was a somewhat provocative title. 'The Mother Murders,' correct?"

"Exactly," said Paul. "I have everything right here." He ducked below the counter. Holmes could see Paul's back hunch over as he tugged at something underneath. After a few seconds, he resurfaced with a tattered file box, straining slightly under the weight of it. He slid the box onto the glass countertop. "My notes on the case," Paul pronounced.

He started to lift the lid off the box, but Holmes reached over and pressed it firmly back down. "No notes," he said. "I only want to know what's in your head. Otherwise, I won't help you."

"No problem," said Paul, tapping his temple. "I have it all col-lected and collated."

He pushed the box to one side, then slipped out from behind the counter and walked to the front of the shop. He flipped the door sign so that CLOSED faced out. On his way back, Paul rubbed his hands together in glee. He returned to his spot behind the counter and settled onto a metal stool.

"You said *murders*, Oliver. Plural. How many are we talking about?"

"Twenty-three," said Paul. He paused for a moment. "Soon to be twenty-four."

Suddenly, the grandfather clock began to chime. In the next second, the shop was filled with a dissonant chorus of pings, gongs, chirps, and trills.

Holmes blinked as Paul called out over the cacophony. "Do I have your attention now?"

CHAPTER 40

HOLMES COVERED HIS ears and waited for the din to subside. When the clocks returned to their insistent ticking, he rested his arms on the countertop and focused intently on the diminutive watchmaker.

"All right," said Holmes, "tell me everything."

In spite of his initial distrust of Oliver Paul—or maybe because of it—Holmes could feel himself coming alive in the moment. He was alert to Paul's posture, his gestures, his expressions. As always, he was especially attuned to the olfactory blend of bacteria and perspiration from the apocrine glands—a clear indicator of stress. For a super-smeller like Holmes, it was more telling than a lie detector. But as Paul spoke, his body exuded only confidence. Which meant that he was either delusional or telling the truth.

"I've been investigating these murders since they began," said Paul. "They go back more than two decades."

"Two decades is a long time," said Holmes. "Why haven't the police solved any of these crimes over all these years?"

"For one thing, police are lazy and unobservant," said Paul. His voice took on an extra rasp as he shifted to a lower register, more intimate and confidential. "You know I'm right."

Holmes maintained his poker face, giving away nothing. He wasn't about to endorse Paul's subjective opinions about law enforcement, even if they matched his own. He was determined to follow the advice of his namesake and concentrate himself on the details. Facts. Data. Proof. That's what mattered.

"These homicides," said Holmes. "Where did they occur?"

"All over the country, in small jurisdictions," said Paul. "But here's the thing: they weren't classified as homicides. They were all ruled to be accidents."

"*Fatal* accidents," confirmed Holmes.

"Correct," said Paul. "Deadly mishaps around the home or office. All conveniently unwitnessed." Paul leaned forward. "Did you know, Mr. Holmes, that more than four hundred fifty people die from accidents every single day in this country?"

"Is that all?" asked Holmes. The number seemed low. In his experience, Americans were stunningly careless with cars, guns, drugs, and liquor.

"Tell me about the victims," he said.

"All female," said Paul. "All married women, all mothers. Hence, 'The Mother Murders.' Do you want to hear something even stranger?"

"Always," said Holmes. He had to admit that the watchmaker knew how to build suspense.

Paul lowered his voice again. "It's about the timing. Every one of the murders happened on the same day of the year."

"What day?" asked Holmes.

"September 30th."

Holmes glanced at the calendar clock over Paul's shoulder.

Today was September 25th. He felt a prickle on the back of his neck as Paul delivered the kicker. "That's right, Sherlock. Only five more days until another mom dies."

Holmes controlled his breathing and kept his tone even, doing his best to appear dispassionate and rational. "Why are you on this case, Oliver?" he asked. "What makes you so obsessed with it?"

"Very simple," said Paul. "The first victim was my mother."

CHAPTER 41

FIFTY MILES NORTH, Margaret Marple stood at the edge of a Putnam County cornfield as Auguste Poe stepped into the tattered rows.

"This is where the school bus was abandoned?" Marple asked.

Poe pointed ahead to a patch of trees near a drainage gulley at the edge of the field. "Parked down there," he said. "Covered in camo netting. Hidden from the road and practically invisible from the air."

Marple nodded. The bus had already been towed to the municipal garage. But in terms of evidence, it had turned out to be an empty shell. No prints. No traces of blood or other bodily fluids. No clothing. No weapons or shell casings. The five children, all eight years old, had disappeared without a trace, leaving their backpacks on their seats. Marple scanned the photos of the bags on her iPad as she walked. The kids had scrawled names across the backs in thick marker or glitter pen. *Olivia. Ava. Lucas. Grace. Logan.*

No trace of the driver. Bill Barnes. Sixty years old. Ex-Army. Former security guard. Marple flicked to his photo. Massive guy with a woodsman's beard. New to the job but, by all accounts, a gentle giant. The kids apparently called him Hagrid.

She and Poe had made the trip back up here from Brooklyn in Poe's '77 Trans Am, which was a lot speedier than the limo—though, as Marple had pointed out, a lot less comfortable. She'd considered asking Holmes to join them but decided against locating him and goading him to come along. She knew the pressure of the writers' convention yesterday had put him in a sour mood, and figured the trip out here in a cramped sedan would only make things worse.

"Do you think he's serious about leaving for good?" Poe called out from a few furrows away.

"I haven't given up on him," said Marple. "But we can't let the work suffer in the meantime." She exchanged her shoes for calf-high Wellingtons, which she pulled up to cover the legs of her tweed trousers. She stepped into the field and followed Poe along a set of deep, wide vehicle tracks.

A few sections of crime-scene tape had come loose from stakes at the border of the field. They wafted in the breeze like tattered yellow ribbons.

Poe's boots crunched through the remnants of the season's corn stalks, now brown and dry. Marple stopped next to him. There was no obvious connection between the missing third graders and the missing St. Michael's babies. Marple had been immersed in studying the black market for newborns. But older kids? The possibilities made her shiver.

"Chowchilla," Poe muttered under his breath.

"Pardon?" said Marple.

"Chowchilla, California—between Fresno and Modesto. Back in 1976, some kidnappers hijacked a school bus and hid the kids underground in a quarry. Perfect crime, until the bus driver and the kids dug their way out."

Marple scanned the empty field. "Nothing underground here, I assume."

Poe shook his head. "The FBI did a good job. Heat-seeking drones, body-sniffing dogs, ground-penetrating sonar. Not a single hit. The kids aren't buried. At least not anywhere in this field."

Marple and Poe walked carefully between the corn furrows. Poe pointed at a set of heavy-duty tread marks leading away from the bus. "Tractor marks," he said. "More than two weeks old. No new vehicle tracks. And not a single footprint leading away from the bus."

Marple looked up, scanning the clear blue sky. "Perplexing," she said. "It's like they were all spirited away by a spaceship."

When she glanced back in Poe's direction, he was standing still in a corn row, his eyebrows slightly raised.

"Margaret," he said, "you are a never-ending source of inspiration."

CHAPTER 42

HOLMES HAD DELIBERATELY left Oliver Paul hanging, without committing to help with the so-called Mother Murders. "Not sure I can take it on," Holmes had said, "in light of my other obligations." But that was pure misdirection. In his mind, he was already working the case. Maybe, he thought, this was an investigation he felt he could own and control. Alone.

He'd mulled over the facts, choosing to believe for the moment that Paul was relating them accurately. The consistent victim profile suggested a serial killer, except that the time span was too broad and the geography too scattered. Wandering murderers like Ted Bundy were rare. Holmes knew that most serial killers picked a hunting ground and stuck to it, like Jack the Ripper's preference for Whitechapel or Dahmer's attachment to Milwaukee. And few had the patience or incentive to make a killing look like an accident. In fact, many psychopaths enjoyed taking credit for their work.

Before leaving the shop, he'd also managed to inveigle Paul into giving him a steep discount on an antique pocket watch—a 1911 Audemars Piguet. The exquisite timepiece was resting in his jacket right now, along with a trusty notebook, pencil, penknife, and small set of folding opera glasses.

Now, on the third floor of the main branch of the New York Public Library on Fifth Avenue, Holmes was digging into the facts of twenty-three seemingly unrelated, seemingly accidental deaths.

The century-old Rose Reading Room was filled with massive tables running in parallel rows. Brass lights illuminated the polished wood, and bookshelves lined the walls. It was as close to heaven as a bibliophile could get, even if most pages were now being read on computer screens. Holmes was busy at a terminal himself, accessing the library's database of eleven thousand newspapers.

His search centered on accident reports from editions across the country, filtered by date. The work was tedious and time-consuming. File after file. Page after page. He assumed that some of the same details might be crammed into Oliver Paul's file box, but no matter. Holmes took pride in doing his own research. And he didn't want it tainted by an amateur's methodology.

Most of the stories Holmes located took up no more than an inch or two of column space, sometimes complemented by a separate follow-up obit. The victims were not famous or wealthy or otherwise notable. They were just dead—in a pattern of banal, but tragic, mishaps. An electrocution in Whitefish, Montana. A fall in Sedona, Arizona. An asphyxiation in Doylestown, Pennsylvania. A propane explosion in Round Top, Texas. And so on...

Hour by hour, one by one, the incidents fell into place on his list. Fatal one-woman accidents in homes, businesses, or campsites, all in towns with small police departments. There was very little to link the accidents except the September 30th date and the fact that each of the victims was a married mother.

The only exception to the pattern was one of geography. The first article was from the *New York Post,* almost exactly twenty-three years earlier. An accidental bathtub drowning in a Harlem town house on September 30th. Victim: Abigail Agnes Paul. Age thirty-eight. Pronounced dead at the scene.

As he mined for details, Holmes realized he was getting the familiar tingle. His detective instincts were fully aroused. The thought flickered in his mind that maybe this was the case that could save him—the one that would let him strike out on his own again, where he could do things his way, without interference from anybody.

But in the next second, doubts started flooding his mind, the computer screen swimming in front of his eyes. His pulse was racing. He felt his lips go numb. It wasn't a panic attack. He'd felt those before and survived them. This was different. And worse.

As he looked around the reading room, he started to perspire. He felt like everybody in the room was looking at him, judging him, threatening him. It was as if all the same worries and insecurities that had sent him to rehab were buzzing and scratching again in his brain. He felt helpless. Hopeless. He felt like screaming. The urge was too overwhelming. Couldn't be stopped.

And so he let it out. At the top of his lungs.

Right in the middle of the library.

CHAPTER 43

TWO BURLY SECURITY guards arrived in seconds. They grabbed Holmes under the arms and lifted him bodily from his seat. He struggled against their grip, but it was no use. His muscles felt slack. No strength or coordination.

"I demand to talk to the library director!" Holmes protested as the guards pulled him out through the reading room foyer.

"We'll get you on her schedule," said one of the guards.

"You don't understand," said Holmes. "I'm a patron! A *generous* patron."

"We appreciate it," said the second guard. "You're also a disturbance."

The guards walked Holmes briskly downstairs to the Fifth Avenue exit and pushed him through one of the ornate front doors and onto the front steps. He felt like a seed that had been spit out.

Holmes straightened his jacket and took a few moments to collect himself. Slowly, he settled back to normal—or at least functional. He no longer felt like screaming. But his brain was still buzzing. He needed to get back to work. He pulled out his new watch and checked the time against his cell phone. Dead accurate. It was 5 p.m. on the nose.

Holmes slipped the watch back into his pocket and pulled up the Uber app on his phone. He punched in a destination and was assigned a car two minutes away. He walked down the broad library steps and leaned against the base of one of the massive marble lions guarding the entrance.

When his Uber, a dark-green SUV, pulled up, Holmes hopped into the back seat.

"Headed for Harlem?" the driver asked.

"That's right," said Holmes. "Marcus Garvey Park. Corner of Madison and 124th."

"You got it," said the driver. He made a left on East 40th and headed across town toward FDR Drive.

Riding north along the East River, Holmes felt the same twinge he always got when he approached a murder scene, no matter how old it was. It was a blend of anticipation and voyeuristic excitement. Places of death had always held a special fascination for him. They made him feel alive.

Holmes hadn't bothered to check who currently resided at the Harlem address where Oliver Paul's mother had died. Whoever it was, Holmes figured he could charm his way in. If not, as Marple had taught him, the PI card often worked wonders.

The Uber driver made great time uptown, beating almost every light. It wasn't long before they were pulling up alongside the black wrought-iron fencing that bordered Marcus Garvey Park. Holmes climbed out and paused to get his bearings. Then he walked slowly along the street, checking numbers, until he reached the address named in the *Post* article.

The building was a classic four-story brownstone with granite steps leading up to a set of polished wood doors. For a location this close to the park, Holmes estimated the building's value would be at three million plus. Gentrification in action.

He walked up the steps and rang the bell. A woman's voice crackled through the speaker near the door. "Yes?"

"Hello. My name is Holmes. Brendan Holmes. I'm a private investigator working on a cold case in the neighborhood. I'm wondering if I could take a quick look at your apartment."

There were a few moments of silence. Then, without another word, the buzzer sounded. Easier than he'd expected. Holmes turned the knob and pushed the door open. As soon as he stepped into the entryway, he heard footsteps on the other side of the interior door. Another set of locks clicked open, this time by hand.

The door opened into a dark interior hallway. At first it was hard to see the figure inside.

"Sherlock! You found me!"

The familiar rasp.

It was Oliver Paul.

CHAPTER 44

"WELCOME!" SAID PAUL with a broad grin. "Come in!"

Holmes did his best to hide his surprise. "I thought you lived in Queens," he said.

Paul turned to lead the way up the elaborate wood staircase to his apartment.

"We did," he said. "But when this place came back on the market, we couldn't resist."

"We?"

As Holmes walked into the apartment, a woman emerged from the kitchen. Young. Attractive. Her brunette pixie cut complemented her delicate features. She was accompanied by two little girls, one in her arms, the other clinging to the leg of her jeans.

Oliver slid behind the woman and rested his hands on her shoulders. She was about an inch taller than he was. "This is my wife, Irene. Irene, this is Mr. Holmes. I call him Sherlock, for short."

Holmes suppressed the urge to roll his eyes.

"I've heard all about you," said Irene, jostling the little girl in her arms. "Sorry, my hands are full." Her accent was British. The two girls were silent and shy, turning their heads away as Irene introduced them.

"This is Lily," she said, nodding toward the girl she was holding. She reached down to tousle the hair of the girl grabbing her leg. "And this little Klingon is Brenda." Both the girls were dressed in T-shirts and animal-patterned shorts. Their toenails were painted bright pink.

"Lovely children," said Holmes. "How old?"

"One. And not yet two," said Paul.

"Irish twins," added Irene with a little smile. She glanced at Paul. "Well, we'll leave you to it." She and the two tiny girls moved as a unit up the narrow staircase to the top floor.

"Come in," said Paul, waving Holmes into the living room. The décor was a tasteful mix of classic and contemporary. Holmes glanced along the bookshelves. They were lined with tome after tome on watchmaking and repair. He wasn't surprised to see a gorgeous Georgian-style clock resting on the mantel.

"I see you bring your work home," said Holmes, rubbing his hands over the polished walnut.

"Restored it with my own two hands," said Paul. "Wrote an article on it." He took a step toward a shelf and pulled out a thin magazine. "Would you like to read it?"

"Maybe later," said Holmes. He was ready to get down to business.

"Please," said Paul, gesturing toward the sofa. "Sit."

Holmes eased himself down onto the plush cushions. Paul took a seat in an armchair.

"It doesn't make you uncomfortable?" asked Holmes.

"What?" asked Paul.

"Living here," said Holmes. "In the place where your mother died."

Paul smiled and shrugged. "That's why I bought it," he said. "To feel close to her." He leaned forward in his chair. "Would you like to see where it happened? I know that's why you're here."

Holmes looked up. "If it wouldn't trouble you..."

"Not at all," said Paul. "Follow me."

He led the way up the narrow set of stairs to the bathroom on the top floor. When they reached the landing, Paul stopped. Holmes could hear splashing water and the sound of a woman singing in a high-pitched voice. He could smell lavender and lemon in the air.

"Dammit!" said Paul. "I think Irene is giving the girls a bath."

"In that case, a peek would be inappropriate," said Holmes. "Another time."

They walked back downstairs to the living room. Holmes took his place on the sofa again. Paul leaned against the bookshelves.

"Where were you that night?" asked Holmes.

Paul stared at the floor for a moment, then looked up again. "At a friend's house down the street. I was thirteen."

"And your father...?"

"Gone," said Paul. "Years before. Left us some money but not much else."

"So your mother was alone in the house?"

Paul nodded. "She loved her baths," he said. "Took one every night before bed to help her sleep. The coroner thought she'd had a little too much wine that evening. Accidental drowning, he ruled it, with alcohol as a contributing factor."

"But you think it was murder."

"I'm sure of it," said Paul. "The first of many."

"How did you and your mother get along?" asked Holmes.

Paul smiled. "I can see where you're headed, Sherlock. And I don't blame you for thinking it. After all, you're a great detective. But I was just a kid. And she was my mother. We all love our mothers, don't we?"

CHAPTER 45

THE LATE BRUNCH at the office the next morning featured Virginia's latest baking experiment: maple blueberry scones. Poe took his first bite. Incredible.

"These are amazing, Virginia!" he called out.

"Enjoy!" came Virginia's cheery reply from her desk, with her massive dog guarding her workspace.

Poe looked across the table at Holmes. "Virginia said you made a visit to the Lower East Side yesterday." Holmes brushed a few scone crumbs from his chin.

"St. Michael's?" asked Marple from the other side of the table.

"No," said Holmes. "Just buying a watch." He pulled the expensive antique out of his pocket and laid it on the table. "See?"

Poe leaned forward to examine the timepiece. "Perfect," he said. "You'll make a great railroad conductor." His cell phone buzzed in his pocket. He grabbed for it and checked the screen.

Finally! It was Helene.

She hadn't responded to his phone calls or texts for forty-eight hours—not since they'd parted at the clinic.

The message was terse. **BATTERY PK ESPLANADE. 30 MINS.**

"It's Helene," said Poe. "I have to go."

Holmes turned in his seat. "Is it about the baby case?"

"No, it's personal," said Poe. "Wish me luck."

"Of course," said Marple.

"Not me," said Holmes. "I'm saving my good wishes for Helene."

Poe hadn't said a word to his partners about his trip to the clinic, or the fact that he was now an expectant father times two. The only person he wanted to talk to was Helene. Even if he wasn't exactly sure what to say.

His GTO was parked in the spot that was once the building's loading bay. He pushed a button to open the garage door, then started the car up and pulled away, heading in the direction of Manhattan. He didn't know what to expect, or what he wanted. He'd spent the last two days—and nights—thinking about those two tiny heartbeats, and how much they'd terrified him. Could he get over it? Maybe he could. For Helene.

Poe found street parking near the north end of The Battery, where he could see across the Hudson River to New Jersey. He took out his phone as he walked down the broad, tree-lined path and tapped a quick text. I'M HERE.

Two seconds later, he heard Helene's voice. "So am I."

Poe whipped around to see her standing three feet behind him. "You're tailing me?" he asked.

"Don't be so suspicious," she said. "I saw you pull up."

Poe reached out to hug her. Her arms felt stiff, not welcoming. He couldn't blame her. He couldn't blame her if she punched him in the face.

They started walking side by side in the direction of the harbor. "Look, Helene. I'm sorry," said Poe. "About the other day. I didn't know what I was in for. I didn't know what to say. I was overwhelmed—couldn't handle it."

"I noticed."

"Over the years," Poe continued, "I've been shot at, knifed, beaten up, thrown down stairs. But nothing prepares you for a shock like that."

Grey gave him a tight smile. "It wasn't a felony, Auguste. It was a sonogram."

"You're right. I know. Listen. I'm not sure how we're going to do this. But I'm willing to try. I just need—"

"Auguste, wait." Grey stopped in the middle of the pathway and turned to face him. "I came here to tell you something. I've made a decision."

Poe reflexively glanced at Helene's belly, then reached for her arm. "Are you okay? Is everything...?"

Grey stepped back. "I'm fine," she said. Her eyes flicked down at the ground, then up again, looking straight at him. "Auguste, I quit the force."

Poe wrinkled his brow. "The task force?"

"No," said Grey. "The police department. The whole thing. I turned in my gun and badge. I'm finished."

Poe found himself stammering. "Wh-why? Why would you—?"

"I'm leaving to have these babies, Auguste. Somewhere far away from here." She placed one hand on her belly. "I'm thirty-eight. I can't be on the job and do *this* job too."

"Wait!" said Poe. "You can't just...Hold on! I need more notice than this!"

"No, you don't," said Grey. "Because you're not coming with me." She stepped forward and put her hands on Poe's shoulders. "You said it yourself, Auguste—and you showed it at the clinic. You're not ready for this. I don't know what happened in your past, but whatever it is, it's making it hard for you to handle the future. Even a good future. Work on that. Then maybe we can talk."

Poe could feel his face flushing with anger. "Dammit, Helene! They're my kids too!"

"Yes, they are," said Grey. "But for now, they're living inside my body, and this is the way it has to be—for all four of us."

"I can't let you..."

Grey held up her hand. "Stop, Auguste. Don't fight it. This is the right thing. The babies and I need you, but first you need to solve the St. Michael's case. You, Margaret, and Brendan. *Those* babies need you. Those parents need you. The task force needs you. Even Duff needs you. He just doesn't know it."

Poe lowered his head. He suddenly felt exhausted. Drained. Defeated. Even his voice was weak. "When do you leave?" he asked. "Can we at least take a few days to—"

"No," said Grey. "I'm leaving today." Poe felt his knees crumple. He backed up to a park bench and sat down, head in his hands. Then he looked up again, his eyes red and brimming.

"I love you, Helene."

"I know that. I love you too, Auguste."

He waited a few moments, then started to stand up. "I'll walk you to your car."

"No, don't," said Grey, pushing him down gently. "It'll only make it harder for me. Please. Stay here." She gave him a small pat on the head. "Besides, this way I know you won't stick a tracker under my fender."

Poe managed a small smile at the joke. Even though his face felt numb. "Will you let me know what's going on," he asked, "with the pregnancy and everything?"

"I'm not leaving the planet Earth, Auguste," said Grey. "And I'm not doing this to punish you. I just know it's for the best.

And so do you." She leaned forward and planted a soft kiss on his forehead. "We will see each other again. I promise."

Poe nodded. He felt like there was a rock sitting in the back of his throat. He stared at the pavement as Helene walked away. When he heard the sound of her car starting, he stood up and watched her drive off.

Across the street, beyond the now-empty parking space, Poe spotted a corner bar with a neon bottle in the window.

He headed straight for it.

CHAPTER 46

HOLMES WAS WAITING impatiently with Marple in the lobby of an apartment building on Central Park West when Poe slid out of a cab, late for a 5 p.m. appointment the three had promised to keep. Holmes was peeved at Poe's tardiness but even more curious about his meeting with Helene. He knew Marple felt the same.

"How did it go?" he asked as Poe walked in. From the slack expression on Poe's face and the scent on his breath, Holmes knew the answer.

"Not the time," Poe replied tersely.

"Very well," said Marple briskly. "Let's focus on the moment. The people upstairs are counting on us. And they've already paid an upfront fee."

Thanks to Poe, the team was overdue for a meeting with the parents of the six missing St. Michael's babies. Holmes had resisted the gathering, but Marple had insisted on it. "These people are victims," she reminded her partners. "But some *could* be co-conspirators. Pay attention to eyes and body language."

"Yes, Margaret," said Poe numbly. "We know the drill."

Marple opened her purse and handed Poe a pack of breath mints. Then she turned to the building's Nordic-looking concierge. "We're all here now."

The concierge picked up a handset and mumbled a few sentences sotto voce, then nodded toward the elevator. "Penthouse level."

Holmes stood aside and let his partners enter first. They made the ride up in silence. A half minute later, the doors opened onto the foyer of a stunning split-level unit. Through the windows on the far side, Holmes could see the autumn foliage in Central Park, muted by early evening shadows. Twelve adults were gathered in the huge living room, huddled in tense conversation.

When Holmes and his partners walked in, every head turned and the whole room went silent. A man who seemed to be in charge walked straight over. "Where the hell have you been?" he demanded. He looked angry enough to throttle someone.

Holmes recognized the man right away: Sterling Cade, the alpha-dad Marple had told him about. The penthouse belonged to Cade and his wife, Christine.

"Our apologies," said Marple in her most soothing tone. "Personal matter."

Cade did not seem mollified. "We're paying you to concentrate on our case," he said. "We expect your full attention."

"You have it," said Holmes crisply. "We're here."

"And you'll notice," added Poe, "that the police are not."

Cade's wife stepped up beside her husband. "He's right," she said. "The police don't do anything but tap our phones and laptops and tell us to be patient." Christine Cade's eyes were red, and she looked worn and haggard.

Marple gestured toward the living room. "Shall we?"

Holmes was happy to let his partner do most of the talking, especially with a hostile audience. Empathy was Margaret

Marple's superpower, and in situations like this, he had seen it work wonders.

Behind Sterling Cade and his wife, the other parents clustered together. Holmes and Poe held back as Marple spoke with each couple in turn, working the room like a master psychologist. Holmes saw that a catered buffet had been set up at the far end of the room, but the food looked mostly untouched. Nobody was here for canapés.

Marple addressed the group. "You've all met me and my partner Auguste Poe the other night at the hospital." She nodded to her right. "This is our third partner, Brendan Holmes. I'm glad to say that he's now fully engaged in the investigation. And we are lucky to have him. We've spent—"

"It's been four days!" shouted one of the dads, interrupting her. "What the hell have you found out?"

Holmes recognized the irate father from Marple's file and the task force video feed. Aston Norris, corporate attorney, Lincoln Center board member, St. Michael's benefactor. His wife, Penny, held tightly to his arm.

Norris went on, his tone increasingly bitter. "We hired you guys because you're supposed to be sharper than the police. Smarter. More resourceful." His upper lip curled into a bitter sneer. "Maybe we were wrong." Nods and murmurs from the rest of the crowd.

Marple took a small step toward the parents, letting them almost engulf her. She looked patiently from face to face and waited for complete silence before speaking again. Holmes admired her restraint. He probably would have shouted right back.

"We have no suspects yet," said Marple softly. "But we have a theory about the crime. As Mr. Norris says, it's been four days—four days without a single contact or demand." Marple paused to let this sink in. "The police haven't told you this, but I will. Ransom is not the motive here. Your children were not taken because they were born to wealthy parents. That's a distraction. My belief is that they were taken because they have a specific set of genes. A certain pedigree."

Another dad stepped forward. "Christ, somebody might as well say it."

This time it was Garrett Dean, a money manager for a group of even wealthier families. "You mean it's because they're *white,* right?"

Dean's comment unsettled the room even more. Several of the parents looked horrified. Others lowered their eyes.

"You're saying we're dealing with racist kidnappers?" asked Sterling Cade.

There was a new flurry of shouts and protests. Holmes watched Marple stand firm in the face of the storm, letting it roll over her.

The parents are right to be furious, Holmes thought — especially with him. He felt like a total fraud. He shouldn't have come in the first place. But he couldn't afford another screaming fit. Not with this crowd. Not in front of Poe and Marple.

As the parents closed in on Marple, Holmes turned away and slipped past a gleaming grand piano. He opened a sliding door to a narrow patio facing the park. He stepped out onto the porcelain tile. From the room behind him, he could hear Marple's gentle accent rising against the babel.

Holmes leaned on the metal railing and looked down to the busy street below. His mind buzzed with calculations. Ten stories. Not high enough to achieve terminal velocity but at least seventy or eighty feet per second. With a headfirst orientation, it would be a quick and merciful ending. Two blinks, one stunning shock, then eternal peace.

"Believe me, I've thought about it too." Poe's voice. Right behind him. "More than once."

Holmes didn't turn around. He just continued to stare out over the park. From the corner of his eye, he saw Poe step up to the railing beside him. "So what holds you back?" Holmes asked.

"Simple," said Poe. "I've still got too much to make up for on this side of life. You do too."

Holmes spun around and glared at his partner. He said nothing. He was in no mood for commiseration—or a sermon. He turned and walked back through the apartment toward the elevator, passing Marple, who was still preoccupied with the anguished crowd.

A couple of the parents looked up as he walked by, but for Holmes, they barely registered.

He was now on a mission of his own.

CHAPTER 47

STOMACH ROILING, HOLMES walked to Columbus Circle and hopped on a subway line heading downtown. He stared out a clouded-over window and tapped his feet impatiently as the subway car rattled under midtown on its way to lower Manhattan.

The fifteen-minute journey felt like hours. Holmes exited at Canal Street and walked as quickly as possible up the filthy staircase to the street, holding his nose against the stench of greasy fast-food wrappers and stale urine.

He moved at a brisk pace, trying not to think about where he was headed. His rational brain knew it was the last place on Earth he should be going. But his rational brain was no longer in charge. His reward circuit was running the show, and it was desperately seeking stimulation.

He was close now, and the pull was strong.

A light rain started to fall, misty and chilly. Tourists pulled out umbrellas or ducked under awnings. Dusk was falling, and colored store lights reflected off the newly slick pavement. Holmes made a turn down Baxter Street and then hooked into an alley between a bar and a bail bond shop. At the far end, set deep into the building wall, was an entrance he hadn't visited in months. Two months and sixteen days, to be precise.

As Holmes reached the shadowy alcove, he bent his head against the rain. His heart was racing. He could almost see his dealer's twisted lip, feel the small packet of heroin in his hand, the sensation in his nostrils, and the gentle flood of euphoria through his body. He looked up and stopped. His dealer's door was boarded up. A bright pink notice was taped at eye level.

CONDEMNED BY THE CITY OF NEW YORK.

Holmes slumped back against the wall as rain dripped down his face. He was itching for a hit—*aching* for a hit. But he didn't have the energy to track down his old source or ferret out a new one, not when the risk of getting dosed with fentanyl would be dangerously high.

His head was spinning. He'd already taken his buprenorphine for the day. Should he stick another tablet under his tongue? He mentally called up the list of questions from his discharge instructions. *Feeling anxious?* Affirmative. *Sweating?* Yes, even in the rain. *Eyes watering?* Ditto. His mind skipped down to the last question on the list, the one that determined definitively if extra medication was indicated.

Do you feel like using right now?

More than anything!

Holmes pulled out the pill case that held his travel supply—two extra pills of bupe. He turned the case over in his hand. He placed his thumb on the plastic clasp. The morphinan alkaloid molecules were supposedly arranged in a way that would quell his craving for heroin and keep him on an even keel. Instead, he was convinced the pills were messing with his mind.

Holmes needed a fully functioning brain. He'd made a commitment to his partners and he couldn't let them down, especially Margaret. And to prevent that, he needed his head to be clear. Unclouded. Back to its natural state. Whatever the hell that was.

Holmes flicked the pill case open, then walked to a storm drain and dropped the pills one by one through the grate. He turned up his collar and headed for the train to Brooklyn.

Brendan Holmes, licensed private investigator and chronic substance abuser, was officially off his meds.

CHAPTER 48

NINE THE NEXT morning.

Marple shielded her eyes against the glare as she walked up the curved suburban pathway toward HavenCare headquarters, the conglomerate in the process of acquiring St. Michael's. The sunlight reflected sharply off the sleek facade of Building A, one of seven on the beautifully groomed campus just north of Bedford, New York.

"Norman Foster," said Holmes, walking beside her.

"Who?" asked Marple, not even looking at him. She was still annoyed at Holmes for walking out on yesterday's meeting, but gratified that he'd agreed to come along this morning. After all, it was his fortuitous meeting with Callie Brett that had provided the lead.

"The architect who designed Apple Park's main building in Cupertino," said Holmes. "He did all this too."

"Makes a statement," said Poe. He was one step behind, looking around at the expanse of tempered glass and steel latticework.

"Thirty billion in profits last year," said Marple. "That's an even *bigger* statement."

"Can't blame St. Michael's for wanting to join the club," said Holmes. "It's like linking up with the mothership."

Holmes seemed antsy this morning—more antsy than usual these days—but Marple could sense him trying to focus. She hoped he would be on his best behavior. Poe too. Between her partners' various afflictions and addictions, Marple was feeling more like a babysitter than a colleague of late. It was exhausting, always having to be the adult in the room.

Marple had prepped her partners for this meeting on their way up. Dr. Frank Stone, HavenCare's head of community relations, was the man in charge of avoiding embarrassment for one of the largest healthcare conglomerates in the country. According to published interviews, he had graduated at the top of his med-school class at NYU but had hung up his white coat a decade ago. Now, like Poe, he was said to be partial to Brioni suits. Marple guessed he'd realized that managing hospitals was far more lucrative than actually working in one.

The three of them entered the building through a thick revolving door. They checked in with a receptionist, who handed them plastic clip-on badges, then waved them through security and pointed them toward the executive elevator on the other side of the vaulted lobby.

A short while later, they were escorted into a large conference room overlooking a patch of Westchester woods. An enormous marble conference table hung suspended from the ceiling by two thick cables. Despite a lack of other visible support, the table felt solid and immovable. Marple saw Holmes bending sideways in his chair, running his hand underneath the slab as if he were trying to decode a magic trick. She yanked on his sleeve as the conference room door opened.

"Everybody does that" came a voice from the doorway. "I can't quite figure it out myself."

Marple recognized their host from his viral TED Talk "Health-care on Mars," and from Virginia's detailed research. She was impressed that Stone arrived with no entourage, no assistant, and no lawyers. Of course, there was no telling who was watching via the tiny cameras in the ceiling. In rooms like this, Marple always assumed she was being watched.

"Dr. Stone," said Marple. "Thank you for meeting with us. We're—"

"Holmes, Marple, and Poe," said Stone brightly. "I know your work." He glanced back toward the door. "Are we waiting for anybody else? FBI? NYPD? Anybody from St. Michael's?"

"We're here on our own," said Poe.

"Representing the parents of the missing children," Holmes added.

"I can't imagine what those poor people are going through," said Stone, shaking his head. "How can I help?"

Stone exuded sympathy. Of course, Marple realized. That was one of his professional tools. Maybe the vestigial remains of his old bedside manner. She pulled out her iPad, tapped a key, and slid the screen across the table.

"This is surveillance footage from the maternity floor of St. Michael's a few days before the kidnapping," said Marple. She watched Stone's face as he peered at the footage of two young women in business suits casually walking the hospital corridor. They appeared to be on their own, with no official escort.

One of the women held her iPhone in front of her for part of the time, apparently recording as she walked. Patients and hospital personnel passed by without paying them any attention. At one point, the two women stopped a doctor, apparently asking her for directions. She'd turned and pointed them toward the nursery.

Marple froze the frame and indicated the woman in the white coat.

"That's Dr. Callie Brett," she said. "These women told her they were from HavenCare, doing a facility evaluation. Do you recognize them?"

Stone looked closely at the image, then shook his head. "Sorry, I don't. But that doesn't mean anything." He looked up at Marple. "We've got more than a thousand employees on this campus alone, a thousand more spread out across the country. Nothing from facial recognition?"

"No matches," said Marple. This was true, but it wasn't the *whole* truth. Holmes, Marple, and Poe had obtained the footage from their inside source, Dr. Revell Schulte, but they had yet to share it with the authorities. Marple knew they were walking a fine line by withholding evidence this important, but she felt their first obligation was to the parents and their babies, not to the NYPD. And certainly not to Captain Duff.

"What reason did Dr. Brett say these women gave for being there?" asked Stone.

"Checking the facilities," said Marple. "Equipment. Floor space."

"September 20th," said Stone, squinting at the date beside the time code. "I can help with that." He pulled out his iPhone and started tapping away as he talked. "We have a team devoted to onboarding at St. Michael's. I'll check their schedule." He opened a program, tapped a few more keys, scrolled for a few seconds, then looked up. "Sorry. Nobody from our team was at the hospital that day. And my guess is that it would have been a larger contingent anyway. This hospital is a very important acquisition for us." He clicked out of the program and slid the iPhone back into his pocket.

"So I was right," said Poe. "These ladies were casing the place."

"Does that mean we're looking at the kidnappers, posing as HavenCare representatives?" asked Stone.

"Not likely," said Holmes. "Different skill sets."

"We have a nurse who's confessed to tipping off an outside contact," said Marple. "But she doesn't seem to know anything else about the kidnapping."

"Keelin Dale," said Stone. "The drug addict. I heard about her arrest. She's no longer a hospital employee, of course."

Marple reached down and opened her purse. "There is one more thing..." She pulled out a small green ankle band and dangled it from her finger.

"That's a NovaGen," said Stone. "Standard in all our maternity units. I believe St. Michael's has started using them on our recommendation."

Marple handed him the band. "Actually," she said, "that's a counterfeit."

"We tested it," Holmes said, "and found that it's been programmed to register a signal at rest, but *not* when near an alarm trigger."

"The label on the inside says, 'Manufactured in Great Britain,'" said Poe. "Is that where the real ones are made?"

"It is," said Stone, turning the device over in his fingers and looking closer. "Could've fooled me. Medical devices are big business over there. It's very lucrative."

Marple reached to take back the band. Her mind flashed to the four infants missing in London.

"Interesting," she said. "Sort of like the business of selling babies."

CHAPTER 49

NINE HOURS AFTER the meeting with Dr. Stone at HavenCare, Holmes was feeling exhausted and frustrated. The meeting in Bedford had been a waste of time, totally unproductive. To his great disappointment, he hadn't detected any signs of evasiveness in Dr. Frank Stone. No wavering eyeline. No incongruent gestures. No scent of stress sweat. The doctor was either a sincere communicator or a practiced liar. Or both.

Holmes was also feeling guilty. Over an hour ago he'd left his partners at home, telling them he wanted to inspect the St. Michael's escape route one more time in the dark, to see if the forensics team had missed anything. Instead, he'd made an escape of his own—to Harlem. At this very moment, he was walking up the front steps of Oliver Paul's elegant brownstone.

Holmes pulled out his handkerchief and dabbed the sweat from his forehead. His body ached. He felt clammy and nauseated. He had predicted that the first seventy-two hours without his medication would be the worst, but he was determined to fight through it. Despite the challenge of going cold turkey, he stubbornly held to the belief that it was better this way.

Suddenly, his gut lurched. He bent over the metal railing, fully prepared to vomit into the bushes. Nothing came up. After a few seconds, the worst of the feeling passed. He stood up and pressed the door buzzer.

"Yes? Who's there?" Irene's voice.

"Irene, it's Brendan. Brendan Holmes."

"I'll buzz you in," said Irene.

At the sound of the buzz, Holmes pushed through into the vestibule. As he stepped inside, the interior door lock clicked open. He walked slowly up the staircase to Paul's apartment. He felt a bit like a kid playing hooky. He still hadn't told Marple or Poe anything about his little side project.

He rationalized his secrecy by telling himself that he didn't want to distract them from the kidnappings, but it was really the independence that excited him. He didn't want them to either discourage him or try to horn in on the case. For the first day or two, he'd thought of "The Mother Murders" case as a hobby. But it was quickly becoming a private obsession.

When Holmes looked up, Irene was waiting for him on the landing, one of her little girls in her arms. "Welcome back, Mr. Holmes."

"Call me Brendan," said Holmes, mounting the last few stairs. "Or Sherlock." He had initially resented Oliver's nickname for him, deeming it sarcastic and overly familiar. But he'd quickly realized that Paul wasn't using it in a disrespectful manner. He was using it very seriously, as if he were conferring a royal title. Holmes was getting used to it. In fact, he found himself getting oddly comfortable with the little watchmaker and his family. In some ways, they seemed almost normal.

He glanced at the child. Which one was it? What was her name? Linda? Glenda? *Brenda!*

He leaned forward. "How are you tonight, Brenda?" No reply.

Was the girl shy? Mute? What age did children start speaking, anyway? Holmes realized he had no idea. The girl lifted her head slightly off Irene's shoulder and gave Holmes a tentative smile.

As Irene led the way into the living room, Holmes spotted Oliver Paul sitting in an easy chair, cradling the other girl in his lap. Holmes racked his brain again. Lila? Lola? *Lily!*

The watchmaker looked up. He seemed surprised but pleased. "Sherlock! What a treat." He nodded to the sleeping child in his lap. "Excuse me if I don't get up."

"I hope I'm not intruding," said Holmes. Actually, he hoped that he was. He liked to catch people unawares. It was one of his favorite techniques. Spontaneous reactions could be very revealing. He scanned Paul's face for any hint of defensiveness, sniffed the air for any scent of anxiety. Nothing.

A cell phone jingled in the kitchen. "That's mine," said Irene. She set Brenda down and smoothed the girl's Disney-print shirt. "I'll be right back, sweetheart," she whispered.

"Please, sit," said Paul, pointing to the sofa.

As Holmes walked across the room, he could feel the little girl following him, toddling along in his shadow. As soon as he sat down on the sofa, Brenda pulled herself onto his lap by climbing the folds of his trousers. Holmes wasn't sure how to react. He'd never held a child in his life. Puppies, yes. And occasionally Margaret's cat, Annabel. But children, never. They were not in his social set.

Holmes felt the girl settle into position with her hip on his thigh and her head nestled against his torso. Her body radiated warmth, along with the essence of applesauce and soap.

"Looks like we have a new babysitter," said Paul.

Holmes shifted awkwardly, trying to be a good sport. "I'm afraid my hourly rate would be exorbitant," he said. He looked down at the toddler. Her thumb was tucked into her mouth and her eyes were closed. Holmes rested one hand on the armrest and the other on the little girl's shoulder—very lightly—as if she were an egg that might crack. He turned his head hopefully in the direction of the kitchen, but Irene had apparently taken the phone into a back room.

"Don't worry," said Oliver. "She'll be back soon. To what do we owe the pleasure?"

"All right, then," said Holmes softly. "If you don't mind, let's talk a little bit more about your mother."

"Of course," said Paul. "Moms are my favorite topic." He cocked his head to one side and gave Holmes that odd look, the look where only one eye focused. "How long since you've seen yours?"

Holmes felt a squeeze in his gut. The question threw him. Strange. Irrelevant. Inappropriate. "My mother?" he replied evenly. "My mother died a long time ago. I'm not here to talk about her."

Paul sighed gently. He tucked a small blanket over Lily's bare feet. "Passed away," he said. "That's what they told you. And I can understand why you'd want to believe it. Easier that way, I expect, considering her circumstances."

Heat prickled the back of Holmes's neck. He leaned forward, then eased back, trying not to disturb the sleeping child in his lap. Memories flashed in his brain. Painful memories. He shook them off and stared hard at the watchmaker. "What the hell are you talking about?"

"Don't look so surprised, Sherlock," said Paul. "I'm an expert on mothers. Yours was an insecure, narcissistic, self-destructive drug addict. But trust me, she is very much alive."

CHAPTER 50

MARGARET MARPLE PLUCKED a sweater from her chair, folded it neatly, and placed it on her closet shelf. She was straightening her apartment while mentally reviewing the facts of their case and puzzling over the mysterious two women in the maternity ward when she heard five sharp raps on her front door — two in a row, a pause, then three more.

Brendan.

She heard his voice in the hallway as she headed through her living room. "Margaret! It's me! I need to talk to you!"

Marple opened the door. Holmes pushed right past her, jittering with energy and wringing his hands.

"Hello," said Marple, still holding the doorknob. "Would you like to come in?"

"Sorry," said Holmes. He was pacing nervously. He looked confused and disturbed. His gaze was flitting all around the room.

"Brendan, what's wrong? Did you find something at the hospital?"

Holmes sat down heavily on Marple's love seat, eyes aimed at the floor. "I have a confession to make," he said.

Marple felt a quiver in her chest. *Not again.*

"Brendan, we've been through this. Whatever feelings you have are probably just..."

Holmes looked up. "I'm working on another case," he said. "I've been keeping it from you and Auguste."

Marple's shoulders stiffened slightly. She sat down on the edge of a chair. "I see."

"Remember Oliver Paul, the little pest from the writers' convention?"

"The one with the amazing story we never got around to hearing?"

"Yes. That's him. 'The Mother Murders.'"

Marple leaned forward. "You mean it's a real case? I thought it was just some wannabe detective fantasy."

"It's no fantasy," said Holmes. "I've done the research. Twenty-three women died over the past twenty-three years. A faulty electrical ground in a swimming pool. A leaky oven gas line. A mis-wired space heater. One a year, always on the same day: September 30th. All mothers. All deemed accidental. No suspects. No arrests."

"My God," said Marple, adding, "Odd pattern. Anything else?"

"Yes," said Holmes. "I think Oliver Paul has been investigating *me*."

"Why would you think that?"

Holmes took a deep breath. "Margaret, he knows things. He knew all about my little vacation in Ithaca. He seems to know what's going on in my mind. And tonight, he started talking about my mother."

"Brendan, you're rambling. Start at the beginning."

Marple could sense that Holmes was doing his best to center himself but was having a difficult time. She had tried to get him to open up about his past, though it always seemed like a door he wanted to keep sealed. She could have looked into it anyway, of course, but out of respect for Holmes, she'd never pushed. But now, for some reason, a significant piece of that history appeared to be spilling out in a flood.

"Growing up," said Holmes, "I knew my mother had problems. Mental issues. Drugs. For as long as I can remember, my father was always sending her away to one recovery program or another. She even spent time at Lake View. That's why I chose it."

"Your father was a doctor, correct?" said Marple. "I assume he had connections in the rehab world."

Holmes nodded. "One night, about twenty-five years ago, he sat me down in the living room and told me that my mother had died. He didn't tell me where or how. He said that he knew it would be difficult, but it was time to move on in life without her. And that was it."

"Was there a funeral?" asked Marple. "A memorial service?"

Holmes shook his head. "My father said that my mother never wanted anything like that. I hadn't seen her in years by that time. It was as if...one day she was off somewhere getting help. The next day she was gone forever."

"And what does Oliver Paul have to do with this?"

Holmes looked up. He cleared his throat. Marple could tell he was having a hard time getting the words out.

"Oliver Paul says that my mother is alive."

Marple blinked. "What?" *How cruel.*

"I think he could be making it up, but he's been right about a lot of other things. I need to see for myself." Holmes grabbed for Marple's arm. "And I need you to come with me. To be sure I'm not going crazy."

Marple felt a wave of compassion and a pinch of guilt. The timing could not be worse.

"Brendan, I'm sorry. I'm on my way to London. Virginia called while you were out. Scotland Yard is willing to cooperate with us on the baby case, and it can't wait. I'm taking the red-eye from JFK tonight." Her phone buzzed. She glanced at the screen and stood up. "Sorry. That's my Uber. Maybe Auguste can—"

"No, Margaret. I need it to be you."

She put her hands on his shoulders. "Then wait for me. We'll figure it out when I get back. I won't be gone long."

Holmes nodded, then stood up also and seemed to suddenly notice her small carry-on bag waiting by the door, with her laptop tucked into a zippered front pocket. He grabbed it for her, then they walked downstairs to the waiting car. "Good hunting, Margaret," he said, opening the rear door.

Marple could feel his confusion and disappointment. She hated to abandon him in this state. He handed over her bag, which she set, with her purse, on the floor mat, then she ducked back out.

"Listen to me, Brendan," she said. "For the sake of your mental health, don't go running off chasing ghosts until I get back. Work the baby case with Auguste. Stay put. Promise?"

Holmes nodded.

Marple climbed into the car. Holmes closed the door after her. Marple saw him standing with his hands in his pockets as the driver pulled away.

Marple was usually good at compartmentalizing. As the car crossed Jamaica Avenue and headed south, she did her best to focus on the long flight and daunting tasks ahead of her. But she also fretted about Holmes.

She worried that her partner had made yet another promise he couldn't keep.

CHAPTER 51

BY THE TIME Holmes got back to his apartment upstairs, he was sweaty and queasy again. It seemed to come in waves. He sat on the edge of his bed and stared at the drawer where he had kept his main supply of withdrawal meds. No more. The night he'd returned from Canal Street, he'd tossed out every remaining pill.

He picked up his phone and scrolled through a long list of messages from his rehab counselor—the one he was supposed to have been contacting every twenty-four hours since he left Ithaca. The phone number was right there. Maybe he should call. Check in. Find somebody to refill his prescription. *No, dammit! Weakness! A step backward!* He tossed his phone onto his side table.

He stood up and grabbed the back of a chair, suddenly unsteady on his feet. He crossed the room and opened the door to his closet. He knelt on the carpet and ducked his head under the row of impeccably organized shirts and suits. His fingers found the keypad of the safe embedded in his back closet wall. He pressed the code by feel and heard the whir of the small motor that released the lock. The door popped open with a satisfying click.

Holmes leaned over and peered into the tiny sanctum, the solid steel box where he had always kept his heroin stash. But of course that was gone too.

Now he reached into the safe and lifted the thin felt liner that covered the floor. Underneath was a single yellowed envelope with one edge ripped open. He pulled it out and sat back against the closet door, his heart pounding.

From the envelope, he carefully extracted a one-page letter, written in elegant script. Holmes held it up under the closet light and read it slowly, absorbing every line. The words were very familiar. He'd probably read this same letter a hundred times before. In many ways, he'd built his life around it.

It was the last thing his mother ever gave him.

CHAPTER 52

SEVEN THE NEXT morning.

Auguste Poe was on his second cup of coffee when he saw Holmes slumping his way down the staircase to the first floor. The air was filled with the scent of cinnamon. Virginia's apple-spice muffins. New recipe. A basket of the treats sat on the table, still warm from the oven. Poe took one onto his plate and broke it in half, drooling over the warm apple filling and sugar-crumb topping.

As he reached the first floor, Holmes inhaled deeply, then called out, "Virginia, stop! You are overwhelming my senses!"

Virginia's head turned away from her computer screen, her hair streaked with a striking new tint. Purple today.

"You're welcome!" she called back.

Holmes walked past Poe to pour himself a cup of coffee. "Margaret's flown off," he muttered.

"I know," said Poe. "London. She told me yesterday." He stared down into his coffee mug for a few moments. "I should probably tell you: Helene's gone too."

Holmes sat down at the table, his hands wrapped around his

steaming coffee mug. "What do you mean, gone? Gone where?" He reached over for a muffin.

"Apparently," said Poe, "she decided that she and the babies would be better off without me."

"Babies?" said Holmes, his eyebrows shooting up. "Plural?"

Across the office, Virginia rolled toward them in her desk chair, nearly running over her dog. *"Babies?"*

Poe let out a long sigh, then jerked his head to invite her over. No sense in going through this twice. Virginia hurried over to the table, eyes wide and alert.

"What's going on here?" she asked.

"To bring you up to speed," said Poe, "Helene is pregnant. I'm the father. And we just found out she's having twins."

"Twins? When were you planning to tell us?" asked Holmes.

"I knew it," said Virginia softly, almost to herself.

"What do you mean?" asked Poe.

"I could feel it," said Virginia. "The day Mr. Holmes came home from Ithaca. Helene was here waiting for you. I could tell there was something different about her. It was a very confusing vibe, so I didn't want to say anything. Now it makes total sense. She was pregnant. Pregnant with twins."

"So she's taking a leave from work?" said Holmes.

"Not a leave," said Poe. "She left. She quit her job."

Holmes looked incredulous. "Quit? For God's sake. To go where?"

"No idea," said Poe. "She didn't want me to know. She just got in her car and drove off."

Poe could feel Virginia's energy building, ready to burst. "I'm not pushing," she said, "but I could track her social, find her relatives, friends, reach out to her FBI contacts, check her OB-GYN's office..."

Poe shook his head. Nothing there he hadn't already thought

of. "No," he said. "If Helene wants to disappear, she knows how to do it. For all I know, she could have a whole new identity by now. She could be running a coconut stand in Belize. The fact is, she wanted some space, and I'm giving it to her. She didn't really give me a choice."

Holmes set his coffee mug down and stared across the table at his partner. "So there we have it, Auguste. The women in our lives have totally abandoned us."

Virginia looked from Poe to Holmes and waved her hand in front of their faces. "Hello. Not *every* woman."

CHAPTER 53

MARGARET MARPLE'S PLANE had touched down on Heathrow's rain-drenched northern runway at half past nine in the morning, London time. Marple hated red-eye flights, especially in this direction. She'd been fitfully awake for almost the entire journey across the Atlantic. Now she was exhausted and ready for a nap—just when she knew she needed to be at her most alert.

It didn't help that she'd been thinking about Brendan Holmes the whole way. But now it was time to focus. She needed to compartmentalize. Missing children—that was what she needed to concentrate on.

As she walked through the Jetway into the terminal, Marple hoped the passport control queue wouldn't be too long. As soon as her shoes touched the carpet of the arrival gate, she heard her name called.

"Miss Marple!"

She looked up. Standing right outside the area of disembarkation was an attractive young police constable. He wore the familiar trim, multipocketed uniform jacket and matching trousers of the Metropolitan Police, with a tie knotted neatly beneath a crisply starched white collar. He held his helmet with its royal insignia under one arm, and his beaming smile showed off his perfect white teeth. *If somebody were hiring a model for a British bobby,* thought Marple, *this fellow would be a good choice. He looks like a bloody recruitment poster.*

Well done, Virginia, she thought.

Marple stepped out of the flow of exiting passengers and walked up to the officer. "I'm Margaret Marple," she said. "And you must be..."

"PC Ben Dodgett, ma'am. Welcome to London."

"Please. It's Margaret."

Dodgett gestured toward a narrow corridor marked NO ENTRANCE—OFFICIAL USE in several languages. "Shall we, Margaret?" The entrance was guarded by a solider in camo fatigues.

Margaret fumbled with her passport. "What about customs?"

Dodgett was already moving past the soldier and toward an alarmed exit door. "Already sorted," he said, looking back. "Need help with the rest of your gear?"

Marple straightened the straps of her bag across her shoulder and slid her passport back into her purse. "No, I'm fine, thank you very much." She already felt her accent thickening, as it always did when she touched English soil.

The door was guarded by two more soldiers, these two in black tactical gear.

Dodgett pulled out a thin plastic card. One of the soldiers took it and placed it against a scanner. Marple heard the door release. The other soldier pressed his back against it, his rifle slung across his chest. The door swung open to a caged metal stairway, which led outside, where the damp English air was filled with the smell of jet fuel and the rumble of taxiing planes. On the edge of the airfield tarmac, an unmarked sedan was idling. A driver in a dark suit stood by the open rear door. Marple immediately spotted the thick armor plating and ballistic glass. This was no Uber.

"Here we are," said Dodgett.

The interior of the car smelled of polished leather and a faint, pleasant hint of tobacco, and it seemed to be soundproofed.

"I'm definitely traveling with you from now on," said Marple, sliding her bag and purse onto the seat beside her.

Dodgett leaned forward and tapped the driver on the shoulder. The car pulled away and turned down a road behind the terminal. Within a minute, they were on the M4, heading east toward London.

Marple settled back on the plush leather, with Dodgett beside her.

"Is this seat heated?" she asked, sensing warmth under her thighs.

"Too much?" asked Dodgett, reaching for a control.

"Not at all," said Marple. "It's lovely."

From the way they were shooting past other vehicles on the motorway, Marple estimated they were moving at least 80 miles an hour. But the only sound was a light hum from the tires. Dodgett was staring out the window at the passing blur, his helmet resting lightly on his knee.

"I don't suppose you realize the significance of your name," said Marple.

"I certainly do," he replied. "Same as the constable in *They Do It with Mirrors*. Happy coincidence."

"You know Agatha Christie's work?"

"Know it?" he said. "I'm a devotee. Big fan of Miss Marple—the original." He lifted his dark eyebrows. "No offense."

"None taken," said Marple. "I'm in the same camp. So which is your favorite Christie mystery?"

Dodgett's brow furrowed slightly. "Well, I usually say it's *They*

Do It with Mirrors, since that's the one in which my namesake is featured."

"Featured?" Marple teased. "Hardly. A minor character—let's be honest."

"True enough," said Dodgett with a grin. "Actually, my real favorite would have to be *A Pocket Full of Rye.*"

"Of course. Because Miss Marple turns to a Scotland Yard inspector for help."

"No. Because she is close to one of the victims."

"Right!" said Marple, running the plot in her head. "Gladys the maid. Poor girl. Strangled in the garden and left with a clothespin on her nose."

"Sometimes I do find Miss Marple a little detached," admitted Dodgett. "I guess I prefer it when things get more personal." After a beat, he added, "Can I tell you a secret?"

"Please," said Marple.

"Those books were what first got me interested in police work. The puzzles. The red herrings. The misdirection. The reveal. If only real life could be that tidy."

"I think I may have found a kindred spirit," said Marple. She turned to more fully face him. "Not to darken the mood, but what more can you tell me about the hospital kidnappings here?"

"Not much, I'm afraid," said Dodgett. "So far, all we have is a doula."

"A doula? Was she on duty the night of the kidnapping?"

Dodgett nodded. "She worked to support a couple of the mothers. Private, not on staff. Brought her in this morning. We suspect she knows more than she's saying."

"You have her in custody?"

Dodgett glanced at his wristwatch. "We can hold her for twenty-four hours. Plus another twelve if we think we can charge her for something serious. But it doesn't seem likely at the moment."

"I need to talk to her," said Marple firmly.

Dodgett looked over. "You understand that would be totally against protocol."

"I do."

Dodgett's sober expression lightened, and his blue eyes twinkled. "Well, for Miss Marple, perhaps we can arrange a professional courtesy."

CHAPTER 54

AFTER BREAKFAST, POE and Holmes headed to One Police Plaza in Poe's powerful Oldsmobile 442. The eye-catching '65 sedan turned heads at stoplights and got a few respectful salutes from yellow-vested cops on traffic detail. It was impossible to build up any real speed in morning traffic, but the dual exhausts still rumbled with authority.

Gripping the wheel, Poe was determined to shake off his worries about Helene and concentrate on the case. He needed to find out if the task force had anything new on the hospital or the school bus situations. He also knew the cops wouldn't hesitate to hold out on them—especially Duff, pompous prick that he was. Poe was happy to have Holmes along for support.

Poe pulled into a reserved space at the side of the building and brought a placard out from under his seat. OFFICIAL POLICE BUSI-NESS, it said. He tossed it onto the dashboard.

On their way to the task-force floor, Holmes and Poe shared the elevator with a couple of cops, one male, one female. They both stood as still and silent as mannequins. When the elevator door opened, Poe exited first and led the way down the hall to the war room.

They got as far as the door.

"Sorry," said the mountainous cop at the entrance. "Task force members only."

"That's us," said Poe. "We've been on this case from day one."

"They know us in there," added Holmes, reaching for the door handle. The cop bumped him back with his chest.

Poe peered around the guard into the glass-walled room where detectives and FBI agents sat at long tables, noses buried in their laptops. He could hear muffled conversations and the squawk of police radios through the glass. TV monitors showed rotating views of the St. Michael's parents' residences. Poe recognized the living room of the Cade penthouse as it flicked by.

Holmes pulled out his PI identification and held it an inch from the cop's face. "Private investigators," he said. "Open the door, please."

"Where'd you get that," the cop asked, "eBay?"

"Hold on," said Poe. "There's Duff!" He slipped past the cop and rapped on the glass. Duff was in the middle of a huddle at the far end of the room. At the sound, he looked up. The lanky captain extracted himself from his meeting and headed for the door. The huge cop stepped aside as the boss emerged.

"This oaf won't let us in," said Holmes.

"That's because he's familiar with the chain of command," said Captain Duff.

"What's going on in there?" asked Poe. "Any leads? New information?"

"Well," said Duff, "we know that three pissant PIs had a meeting with the St. Michael's parents the night before last and got them all riled up, telling them that their babies would never be found in this lifetime."

Poe shook his head. "That's not what we told them."

"The point is, you shouldn't be telling them anything," said Duff. "This is an official investigation, not some parlor game."

"Those parents are paying us to find the truth," said Holmes.

"Right," said Duff. "And the citizens of New York are paying *me* to do the same thing. So do me a favor. Get lost and let me earn my overtime."

"We have a right to be in there!" said Poe, making another move toward the door.

Duff stiffened his stance, blocking the way. The captain had about three inches on Poe and he was all lean muscle. He looked down his long nose with an unsettling sneer.

"Let's be clear," he said. "Your key to this room was your bed-mate, and I have it on good authority that she's left town. Maybe you should spend your time trying to track *her* down."

Poe balled his right hand into a fist and swung for Duff's prominent jaw. He felt a jolt to his upper arm, stopping his momentum. Holmes had Poe wrapped in a bear hug, pinning his arms to his sides and spinning him across the hall in an awkward dance. He looked back. The officer now had his Glock out, and two more cops were hustling in from either side, one tall and sinewy, the other built like a linebacker. They pried Holmes and Poe apart, then manhandled them separately toward the elevator. The door opened. The cops pulled Poe and Holmes inside. One of them pressed the L button.

"Okay, okay," said Poe, squirming against the linebacker. "Let go. We're good."

The cop tightened his grip. "I'll tell you when you're good." Sparks of pain shot down Poe's arm to his fingertips.

When the elevator reached the lobby, the cops shoved Poe and Holmes hard toward the exit. Harder than necessary. "Take the hint, assholes," the linebacker muttered.

Holmes paused to collect himself and rub the wrinkles out of his suit. "Some people haven't heard that violence is the last refuge of the incompetent," he said.

"Arthur Conan Doyle?" said Poe, still catching his breath.

"Isaac Asimov," said Holmes. "I'm branching out."

"Are you calling me incompetent for taking a swing at a police captain?"

"That's different," said Holmes. "You were defending the honor of a woman with child."

"Children," corrected Poe, holding up two fingers.

They were through the revolving doors now and standing on the sidewalk in front of Poe's car. A traffic citation was stuck under the windshield wiper. Poe swiped it up and read it. "A hundred and fifteen dollars?"

"Cost of doing business with cretins," said Holmes.

"What now?" asked Poe.

"I need a lift to Penn Station."

"Meeting a train?"

"No. Taking one."

"To where?"

"Delaware."

"To find what?"

"I'll let you know when I get there."

Poe pointed toward his illegally parked Oldsmobile. "If you pay the fine, you can take the car. I'll Uber back to Brooklyn."

"No, thanks," said Holmes. "I'm in the mood for a little nineteenth-century transportation."

"Make sure you take that new pocket watch," said Poe. "You'll fit right in."

CHAPTER 55

MARPLE HAD EXPECTED to end up at the iconic New Scotland Yard headquarters in Westminster. Instead, the car pulled up in front of a much smaller building a few blocks south along the Thames. The entrance was guarded by a single officer and a pair of stone gargoyles that looked like they might have survived from the reign of Henry VIII.

"Keeping your doula in a dungeon, are you?" asked Marple.

"It's an annex," said Dodgett as they exited the car. He patted the roof to signal the driver. The armored sedan pulled away, leaving Marple and the constable on the rain-soaked sidewalk. "We've been running the hospital case out of here," said Dodgett. "More privacy. Less press. Our own little black site."

"How have you managed to keep a lid on this?" asked Marple as they headed up the entry walk.

"The hospital is King's Grove in Kensington—small and exclusive. The four newborn babies who were taken were the only ones on the floor that night. We've closed the ward under the guise of equipment upgrades. So far, the staff have held. They don't want this kind of publicity any more than we do."

Marple remembered that one mother of the missing babies had an uncle in Parliament. "I suppose having an MP involved doesn't hurt when it comes to pulling strings."

"Doesn't help when it comes to pressure," said Dodgett. "Lord Essom is a backbencher with a big mouth, and he wants his little grandniece found. So far, we've convinced him that discretion is key to the investigation. But if he gets impatient, he could break."

Dodgett held the door for Marple as they entered. Inside, the classic stone building had been renovated in a generic office style. The austere lobby was lit with institutional fluorescents. A dour-looking female officer sat at a sturdy metal desk in front of an open staircase and a single elevator. She looked up as Dodgett approached.

"Did they bring her into L3?" he asked.

"Yes, sir," said the desk officer. "Soon as you rang."

"Working today?" He nodded toward the elevator.

"Questionable," said the officer. "I'd take the stairs."

Dodgett turned to Marple. "Right, then. Let's not get trapped in the lift." He led the way past the desk down the curved marble staircase. The treads were dished in the center from centuries of footfalls. Marple ran her palm down the curved walnut railing, worn and cracked by time. The lower they went, the older the place felt.

Two stories down, the air was dank and the marble gave way to rough stone. Clerks and uniformed officers moved quietly along corridors hardly wide enough for two people to pass without bumping elbows. Marple followed Dodgett single file. They stopped in front of an officer in a black vest. He had his back to a solid steel door.

"Anything from her yet?" Dodgett asked.

The officer shook his head. "Stroppy as hell."

"What's her name?" asked Marple.

"Jane Robinson," said Dodgett. "A real Scouser—born and raised in Liverpool."

He lifted the thick metal bar that held the door shut. As soon as the seal was broken, a loud shriek emerged from the room. Marple was startled. She'd been picturing a matronly British caregiver.

The voice from inside sounded more like a raving banshee.

CHAPTER 56

SNOW WAS FALLING in DC the night of the party, but not a single guest had cancelled. It wasn't every day a Georgetown department head got a five-hundred-thousand-dollar research grant. For the guest of honor, it was one of the biggest nights in an already distinguished medical career. His elegant townhome on P Street was the site of the celebration.

Nine-year-old Brendan was already in his pajamas, poking his head out of his upstairs bedroom door as guests circulated in the wood-paneled parlor below. He moved to watch and listen through the balcony rails.

As he tried to pick out and trace various conversations, the aromas from below practically knocked him back: seared meat and warm spices from the kitchen, colognes, liquor breath from the guests, hickory smoke from the fireplace.

When Brendan angled his head, he could see his father in the center of a cluster of people near the sofa. He was hard to miss. Not only tall and muscular but also the only Black man in the room. His ebony skin glowed in the firelight. He was smiling and talking more than usual tonight, bowing politely with each new flurry of congratulations. "Well done, Doctor!" "Edmond, you've done us proud!" "Will you be needing more lab assistants?"

The doctor replied with grace and good humor in his clear baritone voice. "Thank you so much!" "I couldn't have done it without all of you." "Yes, I believe we will need to bring a few more grad students on. Have any names for me?" He was surrounded by warmth and laughter.

Brendan could hear another voice, at the far end of the room, rise sporadically above the hum. He shifted his head and caught sight of his mother, Nina, in profile. She was pretty, with blond hair, delicate features, and a waist so narrow it could almost be encircled by her husband's broad hands. And she was young—younger than anybody in the room. She had stationed herself near the bar, methodically smoothing her dress and patting her hair. "Yes, I'm so very pleased and proud," she told everybody who came near. "So proud. I've worked hard for this moment too," she kept saying, tapping her finger on the bar to emphasize each point: contacting all those foundations, proofreading all those proposals, all while managing this big, old house...

Guests smiled and chatted with her as they stepped up to get their drinks. But Brendan could discern the difference in those smiles—the sort of smiles that lifted the edges of the lips but did not crinkle the corners of the eyes. Fake smiles that faded quickly as the guests, drinks in hand, drifted back to the eddy of excitement around his father.

For brief intervals, Brendan noticed, his mother was totally alone. In those awkward moments, he watched her pretend to be needed by straightening bottles on the bar or adjusting flowers in a vase. The sight of her stung him in his gut and burned in his cheeks. He wanted to rush downstairs and hug her. Hold her. Rescue her.

After a few minutes, she turned and headed upstairs, lifting the hem of her white silk dress as she went. Brendan quickly ducked back into his bedroom and closed the door before his mother could catch him. He pressed his ear against the inside of the door as she passed by in the hall. The scent of her perfume traveled under the door and blossomed in his nostrils. Brendan instinctively ticked off the notes: nothing floral, musky, or spicy, just sweet scents like honey, vanilla, caramel, chocolate.

He cracked open his door again as a fresh wave of guests arrived. The cold air from outside fanned the flames in the fireplace and wafted the room scents upward. By now, his father had moved to an armchair—the king surrounded by his court. The jabber, jokes, and laughter rose to a new level.

Brendan slipped out into the hall. Barefoot, he tiptoed past the hall bathroom, the guest bedrooms, and his father's office. The door to the master suite was closed. He turned the knob and peeked through into his parents' bedroom. "Mother?" he called out. No answer.

He slipped inside. The bed was covered with the guests' overcoats, and one window was open, letting in icy air and wafting the ivory-colored curtains inward. Through the window, Brendan could see snowflakes illuminated by the glow of streetlamps.

"Mother?" His heart was pounding now.

He heard a quick shuffling sound from the bathroom and noticed the sliver of light under the closed door. He walked over and knocked gently. More shuffling, then a soft sigh. He knocked and gripped the handle. "Mother? Can I come in?"

The door wasn't locked. He pushed open the door to see his mother sitting on the tile floor between the tub and the toilet, staring up at him. Nina's shoes were off, and the hem of her dress had ridden up over her knees. One leg of a pair of nylon stockings was wrapped around her skinny right biceps. The needle of a medical syringe poked into the crook of her elbow. Her thin fingers were slipping off the plunger.

"I'm fine, Brendan," she said. "Go to bed."

He watched as a gentle smile crossed his mother's face. He was frozen and confused. He'd never seen her like this. He knew something was very wrong. But she looked so happy.

Holmes woke with a jolt and sat straight up on the narrow vinyl seat. He could feel his heart thumping under his suit. The train wheels rumbled on the tracks below. Empty fields raced by the window.

Holmes shook off the memory, as he had many times before. Then, to distract himself, he engaged his left brain, pulling out his cell phone to plot the remainder of his course. The train would arrive in Wilmington in an hour. The address Oliver Paul had given him was about twenty miles south, near a town called Kirkwood, at the edge of a huge, forested preserve. He should have taken Poe up on the offer of the car. *I'll have to take a cab from the train station,* Holmes realized.

Google Maps offered no image of the property, which appeared to be hidden behind a row of trees. Public records showed that it last changed hands ten years ago, when it was sold to a Charlotte Drummond. According to Trulia.com, the house itself was small, only about eight hundred square feet—not much bigger than a trailer home.

Maybe the whole thing was a waste of time. Or some kind of test. Then his mind started spinning in another direction. Was there some reason that Oliver Paul wanted him out of town on a runaround?

Holmes felt his eyes watering. He dabbed his nose with his handkerchief. It felt like he was coming down with the flu, but he knew he was still in the throes of buprenorphine withdrawal. The mood swings and grogginess didn't help. Weary as he was, he pressed his back into the seat and forced himself to keep his eyes open.

He wasn't ready to have the same damn dream again.

CHAPTER 57

MARPLE SAT PATIENTLY on one side of a narrow steel table, waiting for the angry young doula to calm down. Jane Robinson was twenty-four years old, with hair that appeared to explode from her head in a blast of brown curls. She had huge, expressive eyes and full lips, frosted with pink gloss. She wore skin-tight black jeans and an equally confining T-shirt, sliced around the collar to reveal pink bra straps. Her iPhone sat on the table in front of her in a neon-orange case.

The doula ranted at length, her thick Scouse dialect nasal and lightning paced, with dropped g's and h's in every phrase. Spanish would have been easier to decipher.

Marple was able to pick out complaints about the temperature of the room, the quality of the tea, the odor in the loo, and the fact that Robinson had been called in at all, as she was probably the lowest of the low at the hospital—or, as she called it, the "ozzie."

Marple endured the tirade for a full five minutes.

"But what do you care?" Robinson concluded with a sneer, practically out of breath from her screed. "You so posh 'n' all."

"Finished?" asked Marple politely.

Robinson glared at her. "For now, yeah."

"I'm not posh," said Marple.

"You sound it," said Robinson, cocking her head. "You sound like Knightsbridge."

"That's a long story," said Marple. "I can show you my US passport."

"Why you in 'ere instead of the Ken doll, then?"

Marple had asked Dodgett to step out of the room. "Because I thought you might be more comfortable talking to a woman," she said.

She watched Robinson go from trying to stare her down to looking furtively around the room and then at her own fingernails. Marple started probing, with the accent as her opening.

"The woman you spoke to," she said, "was her accent posh like mine?"

"What woman?"

"The one who told you how to pick out the babies."

Marple was operating on jet lag, fueled only by a packet of stale biscuits passed out on the flight. But if there was a parallel to the lactation nurse in New York, she figured the brassy doula in front of her might be it. And she also sensed that beneath the tough facade, fear was setting in.

Robinson squirmed in her seat. "You can't arrest me for talking to somebody." She pronounced it *soomboody*.

"I can't arrest you at all, Jane. As I said, I'm from the US. I have no authority here. I just want to talk with you. Because I think you know more than what you're saying. In the States, we would call you a person of interest."

"Yeah?" said Robinson. "What makes me so interesting?"

"I think you know the answer to that," replied Marple.

Finally, Robinson lifted her head and stared Marple straight in the eye. "Look, I didn't know what would happen. With the babies."

"I didn't say you did," replied Marple. "But something did happen to the babies."

Marple could tell that Robinson was hiding something. She could feel it. And she knew that if she let it simmer, it would eventually come out. But she didn't have time to let things simmer. The long hand on the wall clock ticked another notch. Marple leaned forward in her chair.

"Jane, if you talk to me, I'll try to help. But you have to do it NOW!" On the last syllable, Marple slammed her hand down flat on the table, inches below the doula's chin. It sounded like a gunshot. Robinson bolted upright in her seat. Her eyes darted around the room as if looking for an escape route. She glanced at the red light on the security camera, then back at Marple.

"Now," Marple repeated, her voice soft and gentle again. Robinson was crumbling. Marple could read it in her darting eyes and in the almost imperceptible twitch in her upper lip.

"If I tell you something," said Robinson, "will you let me be?"

"Depends on what you tell me."

Robinson rubbed her hands together slowly and lowered her eyes. "I didn't talk to anybody but my sister."

"Your sister. What's her name?" asked Marple.

"Megan."

"Older? Younger?"

"Older. Two years."

"And Megan is where?"

"Somewhere in New York City," said Robinson. Her voice softened. "Maybe you can find her — keep her from trouble."

"What kind of trouble?"

"Like what happened here," said Robinson.

Marple leaned in even closer. "What hospital does Megan work for?"

Robinson shook her head and scoffed. "Megan doesn't have the noggin for that. She's just a fancy child minder, like a nanny."

"A nanny for whom?"

"She wouldn't tell me."

Marple tapped Robinson's cell phone. "Call her."

Robinson pulled the phone toward her but didn't pick it up. "She won't answer. Her mobile is off. She said no texting or chatting until the job is done."

CHAPTER 58

POE WAS LYING on his bed, a half-empty tumbler of Scotch resting on his chest. He was thinking about Helene and where she might have gone. As he'd predicted, she had disabled her cell phone. So, against his better judgment, he'd traced the car. He'd only caught the first three letters of the plate as she drove off, but it was enough. The car was a rental, turned in at midnight at a lot near Grove City, Pennsylvania. Beyond that, nothing. As he'd suspected, Helene had the skills to evaporate.

Poe's cell phone buzzed on the bedside table. He grabbed for it, heart pounding. He glanced at the ID.

It was Marple.

Poe exhaled slowly and put down his drink. "Hello, Margaret. How's London?"

"Auguste! Where are you right now?"

"In bed."

"It's not even noon there."

"I'm having a challenging day."

"Are you drunk?"

"Not legally."

Marple's voice was thin and broken slightly by static. "Listen to me," she said. "You need to get to Duff."

"Already saw him," said Poe. "We nearly came to blows."

"What about?"

"Never mind," said Poe. "But believe me. We are personae non gratae with the task force."

"Listen, Auguste. I have a lead that there may be another kidnapping about to happen in New York."

Poe swung his legs over the side of the bed. "Where?"

"I don't know. But take down this information."

Poe opened his side table drawer and pulled out a pen and notepad. "Ready."

"You need to track down a Megan Robinson. Age twenty-six. British. Possibly there on a work visa. May be working as an au pair, possibly under the table. All I know is that she's involved. Probably on the inside."

"I'll put Virginia on it," said Poe.

"No!" said Marple firmly. "Put *everybody* on it. You. Brendan. The task force."

"Brendan's not here," said Poe.

"Where is he?"

"He took off for Delaware."

"Oh, for God's sake. I *knew* it!"

"What's he looking for in Delaware? He wouldn't tell me."

Marple sighed. "He's looking for trouble, is what. All right, forget Brendan for the moment. Focus on the babies! Find the girl! Do it now!"

The line clicked off.

CHAPTER 59

HOLMES EXITED THE cab about twenty yards short of the address he was looking for. The street was narrow and lined with trees. Behind him, he could see the northern border of the state park. As the cab drove off, he started walking along the shoulder toward a weathered mailbox with the number 304.

Holmes stepped behind a hedge at the edge of the property and peeked through. There was a house visible at the end of a long gravel driveway. It was a downscale ranch with faded burgundy siding. The roof was patched, and the chimney was missing a few bricks near the cap. A dented RAV4 sat outside the closed garage.

Holmes walked along the far side of the hedge, scanning the yard for clues. No toys or playsets. Nothing to indicate the presence of a dog. No surveillance cameras poking out from under the eaves. The gravel near the car was worn down only on the driver side, indicating probably only one resident.

As he stared at the vehicle, making sure there was nobody inside, Holmes flashed on the last time he'd seen his mother. She'd been in the back seat of a large sedan, slumped to one side.

Holmes remembered tapping on the window to get her attention, but she had barely lifted her head to acknowledge him, as if she didn't even have enough life force to wave good-bye. He remembered the sensation of his father's large hands on his shoulders as the car pulled away.

Holmes remembered the burning in his throat and the sting in his eyes. He remembered walking back into the house and picking up the first book he laid his hands on, a mystery novel. He remembered slamming the door to his bedroom, ready to lose himself again in somebody else's problems. Problems that came with solutions.

By the time Holmes had reached the end of the hedge, he was only about fifteen yards from the rear of the house. He spotted a small, well-tended garden out back. He darted across a short patch of grass to the rear of the garage, then leaned his head out to peer through a kitchen window overlooking the backyard. Better to wait for dark, of course. But he couldn't wait.

Not if she was really here.

Holmes pulled the pair of folding opera glasses from his pocket and focused the lenses. He could detect movement behind the kitchen curtains. A single figure, short and slight but otherwise undecipherable—just a faint silhouette. He put the small opera glasses away and walked in a crouch toward the back entrance. As he passed by the window, his angle provided a glimpse between the curtains.

He froze mid-step.

There, reaching up into a cabinet, was a sixty-something woman with sharp features—features that Holmes remembered as delicate. He crossed to the back porch and leaned against one of the wooden posts. His mind was reeling. He couldn't catch his breath.

Oliver Paul was right. It *was* her.

Now what?

Holmes stood stock-still for a second. Then he felt himself backing away toward the garage. Nervous. Confused. Sweating. Coming here had been a bad idea. Maybe the worst idea ever. Better to leave the past in the past. The heel of his right shoe caught on the gravel. His left foot came down with a loud crunch. He heard the cupboard door slam. A second later, the back door opened. The woman leaned out, one hand on the doorknob, the other on the frame. "Hey!" she called out. "Who the hell are you?"

As Holmes turned, she stopped cold. Her chin poked forward. Her eyes narrowed. She slumped back against the doorjamb. "My God," she muttered. Holmes read no fear in her eyes. No confusion. Just resignation—as if she'd always known this day might come. He fixated on her scent as he started toward her. No sweet perfume. Just lemony deodorant and drugstore shampoo. Her hair was grey now, but it was still full and parted in the middle, an ashier version of the blond locks he remembered.

Now that he was facing her, a wave of emotions rose in his chest. Bitterness. Resentment. Anger. For a few seconds, for the first time in his adult life, Brendan Holmes was actually tongue-tied. Slowly, he reached into his pocket. He pulled out the letter he'd taken from his safe and held it up. The page unfolded and fluttered in the midday breeze.

"So tell me, Mother. Was this a lie too?"

CHAPTER 60

LIKE THE HEADQUARTERS of Holmes, Marple & Poe, Silvercup Studios in Queens had once been a thriving bakery. But the vast property had been converted to soundstages in the early 1980s, for movies and TV shows. In the offseason and on slow days, the smaller studios were often busy with more mundane productions. Corporate videos. Instructional films. Music videos.

And today, a diaper commercial.

In a dimly lit side room adjacent to one of the smaller soundstages, three beautiful baby girls were lined up in three identical cribs. The babies were almost perfect matches. Same pale skin. Same cherubic cheeks. Same rosebud lips.

The similarities were not coincidental. In fact, they had been a casting spec. Rose, the baby in the center crib, was the star of a new disposable diaper commercial. Her companions were her doubles.

The PA, a young woman described as "the baby wrangler," looked over her charges, all napping peacefully at the moment. The infants were all around nine months old, prime crawling age. The wrangler had helped the director assess their mobility, which had resulted in baby Rose winning the lead role. This was not Rose's first rodeo. She had been featured in a Gerber commercial at six months and had already earned enough in residuals to make a healthy start on her college tuition.

Through a small window in the soundproofed door, the baby wrangler could see the film crew moving cameras and lights into position around a nursery-room set with a colorful animal-themed rug. She looked up at the industrial clock on the wall. Almost time.

The mothers of the babies were in a separate room nearby in front of a bank of monitors and speakers nicknamed Video Village. From there, they could see the activity on the set. The wrangler was usually the person in charge of focusing the babies' attention while the cameras rolled, but if there were issues, the moms would be called in to encourage their children to move or smile on cue.

In the meantime, it was the wrangler's job to keep the babies safe, warm, and well rested. She moved from crib to crib, patting, rubbing, whispering calming words. She knew that one outburst could quickly spread to the whole bunch. Fortunately, the wrangler had a way with babies. Especially American babies.

Maybe it was her quirky Liverpool accent.

Of course, she had a special reason to be tense today. In exactly ten minutes, before one frame of the commercial was shot, she would help two accomplices spirit these beautiful girls into a waiting delivery truck.

The plan had taken months to set up — an enormous amount of effort for three babies. But these three were gems, well worth the wait.

Quality over quantity.

CHAPTER 61

HOLMES STARED AT his mother from across her sparsely furnished living room. Now that the initial shock was over, he was trying to sort out his feelings. So far, she hadn't said anything beyond inviting him in. Her voice was exactly as he remembered it—just deepened a bit by age.

"So you call yourself Holmes now," she said, assessing him from head to toe. "It suits you."

They sat in opposite armchairs, both frayed and faded. Holmes glanced around the room, finding it difficult to meet her gaze. The coffee table between them was marred by whitish cup rings. The pictures on the walls looked as if they had been lifted from a motel room. A faint whiff of mold emanated from behind the paneling.

"And you're calling yourself Charlotte Drummond?"

Nina's eyebrows went up.

"It's on the title to the house," Holmes said.

"Well, I suppose I needed to become somebody else. Cut ties to the past. You can understand that."

"Are you clean?" Holmes asked.

"Twenty years this week," said Nina. She gave him an appraising look. "You?"

"Work in progress."

"I had a suspicion. I'm sorry. I'm afraid you got that gene from me."

"Yes. Along with the one for disappearing without a trace."

Holmes was doing his best to tamp down his anger at the deception, the years lost. He loved his mother. Yet now he felt entirely betrayed by her.

She seemed to read his thoughts.

"It wasn't my choice," she said. "It was your father's. But I didn't disagree. We both thought you'd be better off without...me. After Edmond passed, it seemed best not to interfere with your life. I was still using. There was no point in my going back. For a long time, I didn't even know where you were."

Holmes still had the letter in his hand. He held it up again. "Tell me. Is this real?"

Nina took the page and unfolded it. Her eyes brightened slightly. "I haven't read this in decades."

"It's authentic?" Holmes said, pressing harder. "Not a forgery?"

Of course, he had long ago run his own detailed analysis on the penmanship, the ink, and the chemical composition of the paper. He knew the letter's origin story by heart. But he needed to hear it again. Directly from his mother.

"Sir Arthur Conan Doyle was quite the letter writer," she said, holding the letter in her lap. "He wrote thousands over his lifetime, mostly to his mother. As I'm sure you know, they were very close. But he wrote to a lot of other people too—friends, publishers, colleagues. One of those colleagues was my great-grandfather."

Holmes leaned forward, listening intently, watching for any tells of duplicity.

There were none.

"Lewis was a detective at Scotland Yard at the turn of the last century. A good one, apparently. Very clever. He gave Sir Arthur a lot of insights into the criminal mind. This letter has been in the family for generations. It was passed down to me by my father, who got it straight from his grandfather Lewis. When I saw how obsessed you were with mysteries, I gave it to you. On your tenth birthday, I think."

"Eleventh," said Holmes pointedly. "The last one you were at. Before you left."

His mother looked down at the letter again, then held it up a few inches from her face. She started reading it aloud. Holmes found himself mouthing the words as she spoke, like a memorized prayer.

My dear Inspector,

I cannot thank you enough for your help with the two novels. You have helped me bring Mr Holmes to life. He is beginning to find an audience here at home and even across the Pond. With all that you know about the evil men do, it's a wonder you're not a criminal yourself. I will owe you forever, and so will Sherlock. In many ways, he is your creation as much as mine.

Very cordially yours,
A. Conan Doyle

She handed him back the letter. "See? It's all there on the page. This is where it all started. I'm not surprised that you became a detective, Brendan. I'm not even surprised that you finally tracked me down. It's in your blood—that drive to run down every clue, wrap up every loose end. Even a loose end like me.

You have every right to call yourself Holmes if you want. I think it's your reason for living."

Holmes reached for the letter. He folded it and put it back into his pocket.

"Actually," he said, "I'm quitting before it kills me."

CHAPTER 62

AUGUSTE POE WAS tossed back and forth in the back of an NYPD patrol car as it sped through Brooklyn, lights flashing, siren wailing. The two cops in the front seat had pulled him out of Holmes, Marple & Poe headquarters with just three words: "Duff wants you."

"Did they locate the person I called about?" asked Poe, banging on the partition between the back and front seats. He'd contacted Duff's office earlier to relay the information Marple had given him, but all he'd gotten in response was a brusque brush-off. Until the knock on his door.

"Where are we going?" asked Poe. The cop behind the wheel turned around as they passed through Greenpoint, heading north.

"Silvercup Studios," he said. "Incident in progress."

A kidnapping! Poe thought. *Marple was right!*

As the car sped through traffic, Poe pulled out his phone and tapped the deerstalker hat icon on his favorites menu for the dozenth time. When the line clicked, he didn't even wait for Holmes to speak.

"Where the hell are you? Why was your phone off? I've been trying to reach you!"

"I'm on the train," Holmes replied. His voice was garbled by a weak connection. "Almost back to New York."

"Margaret got a lead on another abduction!" shouted Poe. "I think it's happening right now! I'm texting you the location." Poe looked up to see SILVERCUP in giant red letters looming over a pale brick edifice a few blocks away. "Get here fast!" he said, then clicked off.

The police car pulled up to the studio entrance, and a cop with an M4 carbine waved them through into a narrow parking area behind the studio complex. The driver pulled them to an abrupt stop in a cluster of other official vehicles—patrol cars, SWAT units, comms vans, ambulances. The lot was glowing with red, blue, and amber lights. A police helicopter hovered overhead. Poe spotted Captain Graham Duff barking orders to a couple of cops in tactical gear. The captain looked up and flicked his hand in a beckoning motion. The two cops grabbed Poe by the arms and hustled him over.

"What's going on?" Poe asked Duff, tugging his arms free. "They wouldn't tell me anything!"

"Three girl babies," said Duff. "Nine months old. Attempted kidnapping in the middle of a goddamn diaper commercial. Security guard spooked the perp and cornered her in a sound-stage over there." He pointed to a closed steel door, wide enough for a truck. Other ground-level openings had long ago been walled over. The place looked like a fortress.

"Was Marple's tip right?" asked Poe. "Is the suspect Megan Robinson?"

Duff nodded. "She came in on an H-2 visa six months ago. Started working here through a connection with some British producer. She was in charge of managing the kids."

"Where are the babies now?"

"In there with her." Duff took a step closer to Poe and tapped him on the chest. "How did you and your partners discover this information? What's your connection? Who's your source?"

Even in the midst of a tense situation, Poe couldn't help but take pleasure in Duff's consternation. "We've told you before, Captain, and I'll tell you again. We're very good at what we do."

They were interrupted by loud screams and wailing coming from a few yards away. Three crazed-looking women had burst out from behind a lighting equipment truck. They were being held back by uniformed cops. Duff glanced in their direction.

"The moms," he said. He shouted over to the cops. "Get those ladies back inside!" The cops half dragged the distraught women back down the sidewalk.

"Let me talk to them," said Poe, starting in their direction.

Duff planted himself firmly in his path. "Not a chance."

The roar of engines echoed off the building as another SWAT truck pulled up.

And behind it, a sedan with a single blue flasher on the dashboard. The car stopped, and a man stepped out.

"About damn time," growled Duff.

"Who's this?" asked Poe, eyeing the man's polo shirt and rumpled khakis.

"Hostage negotiator," said Duff. He turned to the two cops. "You guys have one job." He jabbed his finger at Poe. "Keep this jerk out of my way."

CHAPTER 63

"MOVE! COMING THROUGH!"

Holmes was running at top speed through Moynihan Train Hall at Penn Station, toward the Seventh Avenue exit, shoving slower-moving pedestrians aside. When he reached the plaza outside, he spotted a taxi queue at the curb. Travelers with backpacks and satchels were waiting in a ragged line. Holmes pulled his wallet from his pocket and waved his PI identification over his head as he ran. "Official business!" he shouted. He jumped into the first cab in line and slammed the door behind him.

The cabbie turned around and glared. "What the hell, buddy?"

"Silvercup Studios in Queens! Life or death! No questions! *Go!*"

The cabbie pulled away from the curb with a gut-twisting lurch, cutting off a city bus and getting a chorus of honks from other cars. Holmes pulled an assortment of bills from his wallet and waved them in front of the Plexiglas partition. "I'll pay you a hundred dollars for every ten miles over the speed limit you can go," he said.

"You're nuts if you think anyone's even moving as fast as the speed limit in this traffic, let alone ten miles over," the cabbie retorted. "Besides, I don't need another suspended license!"

Holmes fastened his seat belt. "Don't worry—I can fix that too! Let's move!"

The driver gave him a wary look in the rearview mirror. "I'm gonna hold you to that," he said. He made a hard turn on 34th Street and did his best to bull his way across town, making ample use of the bus lane and running two red lights along the way. He couldn't do much in the single-file flow of the Queens–Midtown Tunnel except curse and tap his horn, but he earned his money on the east side of the river, blasting up 21st Street through Long Island City and Hunters Point, then zigzagging through side streets to dodge the police barricades as they got close to the studio site.

A block away from the big red Silvercup sign, two patrol cars and a SWAT van blocked the street. Holmes pounded on the partition. "Close enough! Stop here!" He pushed a bunch of bills through the slot, including three crisp hundreds. "See? Big fat tip and not one speeding ticket."

"They got traffic cams, you know," said the cabbie. "I could still get nailed."

Holmes reached back into his pocket and stuffed a business card through the slot. "If they caught you, call me."

He shoved the back door of the cab open and started running. One of the cops at the barricade held up a hand to warn him off, but Holmes held up his PI identification again and vaulted over the far edge of the barricade, heading for the riot of lights ahead. He was gambling that nobody would give chase or shoot him in the back.

He was sweaty and out of breath when he rounded the corner into the parking lot. The scene was chaos. SWAT teams with automatic rifles were positioned behind vehicles and on top of the building. News vans were parked at the edge of the action, with reporters and cameramen competing for the best angle. All attention seemed to be focused on a single red steel door.

"Brendan!"

Poe's voice. Holmes spotted his partner at the edge of the scene, and Duff standing on the other side of a patrol car. Holmes pushed past a gaggle of plainclothes detectives, their badges dangling on lanyards over their street clothes, and made his way over to his partner.

"How was Delaware?" asked Poe.

"Clarifying," said Holmes. "What's going on?"

"Three baby girls. One female kidnapper." Poe pointed to the door. "They're holed up in that studio."

Holmes looked around. "Why here?" he asked. "What is this place?"

"Film studio," said Poe. "The babies were here to shoot a diaper commercial."

Holmes peered over the top of the patrol car. Duff was standing in the open a few yards away, his tall frame looming over a man with a bullhorn.

"Negotiator?" asked Holmes.

Poe nodded again. "He's been talking with her for the past half hour. No progress."

The negotiator's bullhorn was not currently in use. It was dangling by a strap over his shoulder. He was talking through a headset, wires hanging down his side. Duff had an earpiece too. Holmes started toward them. A cop grabbed him from behind. Holmes pounded his hand on the roof of the cop car. "Duff!" he shouted. The captain turned, yanked the earpiece out of his ear, and walked over.

He glared at Holmes. "Now you too?"

"What does she want?" asked Holmes.

"Not much," said Duff tersely. "Just free passage to JFK with the babies, plus a private jet and a pilot and enough fuel to get across the Atlantic."

"She's improvising," said Holmes. "This wasn't part of the plan."

"Well, there's no way in hell she's getting any of it."

"Any way to take her down?" asked Poe.

"We're trying to get a camera inside," said Duff. "But the place is built like a brick shithouse. Soundproofed and everything, for movies. We can't use teargas or flash-bangs because of the babies." He nodded toward the press vans. "Last thing we need on live TV is a bunch of stunned, deaf infants."

On the other side of the car, the negotiator pressed his hand tight to his earpiece. He turned toward the captain with a grim expression. Duff jerked his head to call him over.

"Any movement?" Duff asked as the man neared.

The negotiator clicked off his comms device. "She's giving us fifteen minutes to give them transport," he said. "Or she'll start killing the babies."

CHAPTER 64

IT WAS ALREADY 7 p.m. in London. Marple was pacing in a tiny office in the bowels of the task force annex. PC Dodgett was sitting at a small metal desk, drumming his fingers on the cover of a case binder. Marple was clutching her phone so hard her knuckles were white.

She'd heard from Poe when he'd arrived in Queens. He could only tell her what he knew, that it was a crime in progress. Beyond that, she was totally in the dark. And still nothing from Holmes. Was he lost in the wilds of Delaware or somewhere else off the grid? Marple was furious with him for picking today of all days to go off exploring his family history.

She dialed Poe again. The call connected, then dropped.

"Maybe the signals are jammed," said Dodgett. "From all the police activity."

Marple was exasperated. "This is Scotland Yard, for God's sake! You don't have boosters?"

"Main building, yes," said Dodgett, "but bare bones down here, I'm afraid."

"Well, then," said Marple, grabbing her coat, "let's get to head-quarters. I need to—"

The phone jittered in her hand. Dodgett sat up straight in his chair. Marple looked at the screen. It was an incoming FaceTime call—from Holmes. After a momentary glitch, his face filled the screen. Marple felt a flood of relief.

"Brendan! Where are you?"

Poe crowded into the frame, nudging Holmes partway out. "He's with me!" Marple could hear the crackle and buzz of police radios in the background. Emergency lights reflected off her partners' faces.

"Do they have her?" she shouted at the screen. "Do they have Megan Robinson in custody?"

Holmes shook his head, full-frame again. He flipped the phone around to show the massive police operation as he narrated the scene. "She's in that building, with three babies." The image flipped again to show Holmes in close-up. "Margaret, she's threatening to kill the babies if she doesn't get safe passage."

Marple felt her stomach drop. Her mouth went dry.

"The negotiator is trying to stall for time," said Holmes, "but the deadline is coming fast."

"Is Duff there?" asked Marple.

"Ten yards away," said Holmes. "He's pissed off that the lead came from us instead of from his precious task force."

"Take me to him," said Marple.

"On my way," said Holmes.

Marple turned to Dodgett. "Do you have a cell down here?"

"You mean a mobile?" He reached into his pocket.

"No, not a phone. A *cell*. A jail. A lockup."

"We have a secure cubicle. Tiny, but—"

"Perfect," said Marple. "Get the doula. Put her in there. Wait for me."

Dodgett jumped up from the desk and opened the door. Marple watched him hurry down the hall toward the interview room where they'd left Jane Robinson. She looked down at her phone. The screen image wiggled and flared out for a few seconds. Marple heard a few muffled male voices. The camera focused tight on an armored vest, then tilted up to Graham Duff's angular face.

"Marple?" he exclaimed. "What now?"

"I'm with somebody who can help," she said. "Get me in there."

"What do you mean?"

"I need to talk to Megan Robinson directly."

"Not easy," said Duff. "She's in a sealed building with a metal door. If we breach, she might kill the babies. Or *we* might, by accident."

While talking, Marple headed out of the room and down the hall behind Dodgett. "Listen to me. Tell your negotiator to inform Megan that I have a message from her sister, Jane." She could hear Jane Robinson down the hall, screaming like mad, spewing a fresh stream of Scouse curses. *Excellent.*

"Hold on," said Duff. Marple heard the rustle of the mic against fabric. The screen went black, except for a few flashes around the edges.

Marple rounded a corner. Dodgett was standing outside a small concrete cubicle with a clear door of ballistic plastic. There was barely room in it for a steel toilet and a concrete pedestal seat. Jane Robinson was inside. The door was thick, but her shouts pierced right through it. *What a pair of lungs on this girl,* Marple thought.

"Quiet down!" shouted Dodgett.

"No," said Marple. "Let her wail. The louder, the better."

She looked down at her phone. Holmes was on the screen again. She could tell from the jerky image he was on the move. "Okay," he said, his voice tight and low. "She's agreed to open the steel door just enough for us to slide in the phone."

The image jittered and went dark again. The mic picked up the sound of boots on pavement, along with the rattle of metal gear. Then the view was from flat on the ground, looking up at the sky as a police helicopter crossed the frame. The image spun out of focus and went dark again. Then the mic picked up a woman's voice.

"Got it. Now go! No fooking tricks."

Liverpool accent, no doubt about it.

CHAPTER 65

MARPLE STARED AT her screen and waited for the image to settle. She felt Dodgett leaning close over her shoulder. The first view was of a bare industrial ceiling, maybe thirty-five feet up, with movie lights rigged on horizontal black bars. Suddenly, a new face filled the frame.

Marple saw the sibling resemblance right away. Same pale English skin. Same curly brown hair. Megan's face was narrower than Jane's, her features more pinched. But the voice had the same timbre and intensity as her sister's—and the same attitude.

"Who the fook are you?" Megan asked, staring at the screen. "Where's Jane?"

"Show me the babies," said Marple, her voice calm.

"You FBI?" asked Megan. "Interpol?"

"I'm somebody you don't want to cross," said Marple firmly. "Show me the babies. I need proof of life. Or I promise you, nothing good will happen."

"Wait..." Megan's voice again, tight and low. The camera turned toward the center of a vast, empty space with a few black partitions. Thick cables wound across the floor like snakes.

The camera was moving again. It tipped and wobbled in the direction of three small duffel bags set close to a bare concrete wall. Marple could feel her heart pounding. She gripped the phone tighter. "Closer!" she said.

The camera moved in and did a shaky pan across the row of black bags, each with a tiny, perfect baby nestled inside. They looked as still and lovely as painted dolls.

"They're not moving," said Marple.

The camera whipped around again to show Megan's face. "Because they're bloody *sedated*!" she hissed. "I want to talk to Jane. Where is she?"

"I'll give you a hint," said Marple. She flicked the phone around toward the tiny enclosure as Jane gave out another ear-piercing shriek.

Marple turned the camera on herself again. "Your sister is in a very small cell. And unless you want to end up in an even smaller one, I suggest you listen to me."

She saw Megan's jaw tighten.

The rest took less than a minute.

At the end of the conversation, Marple heard a switch being thrown. The view from the phone camera showed a motorized metal door rising. Then a flood of men, an armory of guns, and loud shouts. *"Get down! Face down! Arms out!"* She heard Megan's voice crying, *"Jane!"* For a few moments, the phone got passed from hand to hand, flipping and jittering, until it lit up again with the smiling face of Brendan Holmes.

"Margaret! It's over!" he said. "You did it!"

"The babies! Are they okay?"

"They're putting them in ambulances now," said Holmes. "But the paramedics say their vitals are fine."

"Hold on a moment," said Marple. She put down her phone and nodded toward Jane Robinson, now slumped and silent on the floor of her cell. Marple looked at Dodgett. "I think we can take her out of your toy jail and put her in a real one now," she said. "I'd say you've got grounds for conspiracy."

"So it was Jane and her sister behind all this?" said Dodgett.

Marple shook her head. "Hardly. We haven't even scratched the surface."

CHAPTER 66

HER CONVERSATION WITH Holmes ended as Dodgett walked back into the office.

"Robinson's sorted," he said. "Moved to more spacious quarters."

Marple tucked her phone back into her bag. "Take me to the mothership."

"Beg pardon?" said Dodgett.

"We've gotten all from Jane that we're going to get. I doubt that her sister will be any more helpful. I need access to your Interpol team and your ICMEC liaison. And I need a proper desktop computer. Enough of your little underground lair. Get me to HQ."

"Absolutely, Margaret. At your service." Dodgett pulled out his phone and tapped out a short text. Marple didn't even wait for him to finish. She picked up her bag and coat and brushed right past him. He caught up with her halfway down the corridor.

"This way," he said, pressing the flat of his palm on her back to guide her to the left. An unnecessary gesture but not surprising. Marple had been observing PC Dodgett closely from the second she had spotted him in the airport. His expressions. His lingering glances. His way of positioning himself close to her.

There was nothing improper or forward in his actions; in fact, he retained a classic British reserve. But Marple was an expert at reading people—men especially. What she picked up from Dodgett was a slight but significant infatuation. And she intended to work it for all it was worth.

Once they were outside, Marple took a deep breath of cool night air, a relief from the dank atmosphere of the annex basement.

"It's only a few blocks," said Dodgett. "Shall we walk?" He pointed up the street past a pair of turreted brick buildings to a sturdy block of white stone peppered with small windows. The Thames was on their right, glimmering in the moonlight through a row of trees. Very romantic.

"No," said Marple. "Let's run."

Dodgett was in good shape, but Marple matched him stride for stride. When they reached the front entrance of New Scotland Yard HQ, he was actually panting harder than she was.

Unlike the sparsely populated annex, the pristine headquarters building was buzzing, even at this hour. And here, the lifts definitely worked. Dodgett escorted Marple into a nearby elevator and pressed 5.

"What happened to old Scotland Yard?" asked Marple as they glided upward. Christie's Marple would definitely have felt more at home there, in the ornate old brick building near Trafalgar Square.

"Converted to a Hyatt," said Dodgett. "Top suites go for a thousand pounds a night."

"I do hope you're getting a cut," said Marple.

Dodgett shook his head and chuckled. "Not even a mint on my pillow."

When the door opened, a welcoming committee of two was waiting. A stout middle-aged man in shirtsleeves stood next to a petite woman wearing glasses and a ponytail. As the elevator door closed, Dodgett made the introductions.

"Margaret Marple, private investigator, meet Chief Inspector Crouse, my superior officer, and one of our best criminal intelligence analysts, Rebecca Tran."

"Pleasure," said Marple, shaking each of their hands briskly. She turned to Dodgett with a frown. "Nobody from ICMEC?" She'd been hoping for a specialist from the international organization that dealt with missing and exploited children.

Chief Inspector Crouse stiffened slightly. "I think you'll find that Rebecca can access all the resources you need," he said.

Marple nodded toward Tran, who looked more like a grad student than a seasoned investigator.

"No offense meant," said Marple. "I just think that on a case like this, we need somebody with an expertise in this kind of crime."

Tran adjusted her eyeglasses and took a small step forward. "I was trafficked near Saigon when I was ten," she said softly. "Resold in Phuket at twelve. Escaped in Manila when I was thirteen." She paused, not blinking. "I'm familiar with the market."

Marple felt herself reddening. Crouse cleared his throat and extended his arm toward a corridor that led off the lobby. "Right, then," he said. "Shall we?"

Marple and Dodgett fell in behind Crouse and Tran as they led the way down the hall. Marple pinched the constable's arm beneath his uniform sleeve. Hard.

"You could have told me!" she whispered.

"Sorry," Dodgett whispered back. "I didn't know she'd been assigned to the case. Our good luck. She's bright as a bloody button."

The small procession came to a halt in front of a thick, windowless metal door. Crouse waved a plastic card over a panel. A loud click sounded. Tran pushed the door open to a large windowless room filled with rows of evenly spaced wood-topped tables. The space was lit mostly by the glow from a dozen computer screens and from a bright banner of images that ran in a moving mosaic above a world map at the front of the room. The images were of children—thousands of them—all ages, all colors, all nationalities, each captioned with an age and a DOD: date of disappearance.

Rebecca Tran pulled out a chair and sat down in front of one of the consoles. She looked directly at Marple, patting the next chair over.

"Have a seat, Miss Marple," she said. "Where would you like to start?"

CHAPTER 67

"OF *COURSE* YOU'RE on YouTube," said Virginia. "What did you expect?"

Back in the Bushwick neighborhood of Brooklyn, Holmes was bent over the screen at Virginia's desk with Poe crowded next to him. On a large TV in the background, the local news was showing a slow-motion loop of the police activity at Silvercup Studios earlier.

But the scene on Virginia's desktop was something else altogether. It was cell phone footage from the writers' convention four days ago. As Holmes moved closer, his feet collided with Baskerville, napping in his usual spot under Virginia's desk.

"Baskerville!" Holmes impatiently said to the dog. "Go chase a squirrel!"

Virginia snapped her fingers twice. With a loud groan, the huge mastiff rose to his feet and ambled out from under the desk.

The video's point of view was from the audience—the section to the right of the stage. After a blurry pan of the ceiling, the camera tipped down to show the dais where Holmes, Marple, and Poe were sitting. The moderator was in her chair at the far end. The discussion was already in progress, but the sound was garbled and barely audible.

"Who shot this mess?" asked Poe.

"Probably one of your devoted fans," said Virginia. "One who doesn't know how to work a volume control." She froze the image. "Look! Right there." She zoomed in. "That's your guy, right? Oliver Paul."

Holmes squinted, then picked out Paul's round face in the center of the audience, about ten rows back from the podium.

"Yes," said Holmes. "That's him."

Virginia tapped another key. Her screen shifted to a split image. The view on the right now showed surveillance footage from St. Michael's Hospital. The time stamp was from four days before the conference. "So what was he doing *here*—so soon before the kidnapping?"

Holmes pressed his finger against the screen. "I'll be damned."

Sure enough, there was the watchmaker amid the stream of medical personnel and patients passing under the maternity floor camera. He was only in the shot for 4.2 seconds but seemed clear and purposeful, not at all furtive, and appeared to be there alone.

"What reason would Oliver Paul have for being on the maternity floor at St. Michael's a week ago?" asked Poe.

"Maybe he was visiting a friend? Let me give him a call," said Holmes. He pulled out his phone and tapped Paul's number. The call went to voicemail. Holmes didn't bother to leave a message. "I'll go see him," he decided. "I've got some other questions anyway."

"Like how he found your supposedly dead mom alive and in Delaware after all these years?" asked Virginia.

"Exactly."

Holmes had filled Poe and Virginia in on his meeting with Nina. He trusted them both. But he was prickly about outsiders probing his past.

"I'll come with you," said Poe. "I love Harlem in the evening."

Virginia pushed back from her desk. "Take me too!" she blurted. It seemed to come out of nowhere, and it sounded more like a command than a request. Holmes blinked. He looked at Poe, then back at Virginia. She was already putting on her denim jacket and brushing a few strands of her tinted hair back behind her ears.

"Virginia," said Holmes. "It's late. Take Baskerville and go home."

Virginia immediately switched her attention to Poe. "Mr. Poe, when you hired me, you said that I'd be involved in exciting, important work. Remember?"

"And you *are*," said Poe, pointing to her computer. "Look what you just dug up!"

"Right," said Virginia. "From here at my desk—while Miss Marple is flying off to London and you two are running around movie studios rescuing babies." She leaned closer. "Do you know what I did today? Most of the day? I itemized your expenses, cleaned the espresso machine, ordered ink for the printer, and baked a dozen apple turnovers."

"Which were excellent," said Holmes. The sweet aroma of the pastry still hung in the air.

"Gentlemen," said Virginia firmly, "I'm underutilized."

Holmes glanced at Poe as Baskerville walked closer to them, panting loudly. Virginia snapped her fingers again. The dog promptly flopped down onto his belly. "Besides," she said, "with Detective Grey and Miss Marple gone, you two need a female perspective." She pushed her desk chair out of the way. "Shall we go?"

Holmes stood up as Virginia walked past him on her way to the front door. "You're just coming to observe!" he called out. "Nothing more."

"Of course," Virginia called back. "'It is a capital mistake to theorize before one has data.'"

Poe nudged Holmes in the arm. "See that? Now she's quoting Arthur Conan Doyle to you."

"She's found my weak spot," said Holmes.

"Right," said Poe. "One of many."

CHAPTER 68

"IT'S NO USE. They're not here," said Marple.

She was exhausted and discouraged in equal measure. Her lack of sleep was catching up with her and her eyes were starting to go blurry. She had spent hours sitting next to Rebecca Tran, scrolling through images of missing infants and children, without a single match.

It was just the two of them now. Crouse had gone back to his office, and Dodgett had been called away to help with Jane Robinson's processing.

Marple had had Tran upload fresh scans of the six missing St. Michael's newborns and the five missing third graders from Putnam County.

"Two completely different age sets," said Tran. "Unusual."

"Any theories?" asked Marple.

Tran toggled back and forth among the faces. "For illegal adoption, the demand is highest for infants. Especially newborns. But some people will pay a premium for an older child. No diapers or bottles to mess with. Easier to transport. If kids are taken before age nine, they'll easily pick up new languages.

Over time, I've seen older children totally erase their own pasts. A survival mechanism."

Tran's facial recognition software was finely tuned, the best Marple had ever seen. Built into the system was a sophisticated tool that could instantly project what a child would look like from any angle, at any age, with a range of complexions and an endless matrix of hairstyles and shades.

"Who coded this?" asked Marple. "It's fantastic."

"I did," said Tran.

Marple was impressed. She was embarrassed about her earlier assumptions, and quickly coming to realize that Tran was one of the most intuitive and patient investigators she'd ever met.

But there were still no matches.

"Babies are hard," said Tran. "With their indistinct features. And it may be too soon for the older kids to show up. They could still be in transit."

"To where?"

"None of them are Asian," said Tran, "so I'd rule out China and India. The demand there is for indigenous or at least a reasonable facsimile. But for Caucasian children? Bulgaria, Germany, Russia, the Netherlands. Adoption cartels are working in all of those countries." She hesitated, then added, "Sex traffickers too."

Marple felt woozy. She stood to stretch her legs and take deep breaths. She walked over to a screen on the back wall showing rotating portraits of adult faces—men and women in their forties. Some smiling, some with defiant stares.

"Who are they?" asked Marple.

"An ongoing project," said Tran. *"Hijos de los Desaparecidos."*

"Children of the Disappeared?"

Tran nodded. "When the junta in Argentina was secretly executing leftists in the late '70s and early '80s, they often gave the orphaned babies to right-wing families—sometimes politicians or military officers. Those babies are adults now, with kids of their own. And most don't even know their own pasts. It's delicate work. We don't always have DNA as a tool."

"How many?" asked Marple.

"Hundreds, maybe thousands," said Tran. "Some we'll never identify. They'll go to their graves not knowing that the parents they grew up knowing had their real parents murdered."

Marple blinked as something clicked in her brain. Something about right-wing politics. She turned to Tran. "Do you have a database on Brexit?" she asked. "Not mainstream. Extremists. Fanatics."

"Political intelligence? Not my area," said Tran. "But I'll bet I can access it."

"Do it," said Marple, hurrying over to take her seat at the console again. "We're looking for racists. White supremacists. People who like their citizens on the pale side."

Tran cocked her head. "That's a big category. Can you narrow it down?"

"Maybe," said Marple. "Look for a woman."

CHAPTER 69

IT WAS 8 p.m. by the time Holmes, Virginia, and Poe pulled up in front of the Paul house. Poe, as usual, had wanted to drive, but Holmes insisted on an Uber Black. After hours in a stiff seat on the train to and from Delaware, he craved a touch of luxury.

When the big Suburban pulled away, he bounded up the town-house steps and rang the doorbell. Virginia and Poe stepped up behind him. No answer. Holmes felt a quick shiver pass through him. He pulled out his phone and tried Paul's number again. This time, there was no voicemail prompt. Instead he got a message that the number was no longer in service.

Poe looked up at the facade of the four-story building. "No lights," he said. He stepped forward and pulled a thin metal tool from his pocket.

"Watch closely, Virginia," said Holmes. "You're about to witness a property crime."

Poe leaned in close to the door and worked his tool into the keyway of the lock. It took only a few seconds before he pushed the outer door open. Holmes and Virginia followed him into the entryway. The interior lock took a little longer. But not much.

Holmes led the way up the stairs. He had his hand on the butt of his pistol under his jacket but didn't pull it out. Not yet.

The door to Paul's apartment was slightly ajar. "Oliver?" Holmes called out. "Irene?" No answer.

Poe pulled Virginia behind him, then unholstered his own gun and stepped up next to Holmes.

Holmes pushed the door open with one hand, holding his pistol up with the other. He stepped inside. Poe followed him. Virginia followed Poe.

The apartment was dark, except for a few night-lights plugged into outlets near the floor.

"Stay back," Holmes whispered to Virginia as he and Poe split up to search the parlor, kitchen, and downstairs bath. "Clear," they each stated as they emerged from one room after another.

Holmes moved toward the staircase and started up, heart pounding, with Poe and Virginia close behind him. As the treads creaked, Holmes tightened the grip on his pistol. If somebody was waiting at the top of the stairs, the element of surprise was certainly gone. He felt stupid for having allowed Virginia to come along. This could be dangerous. For a second, he considered turning around and taking her back downstairs. But then he felt Poe behind him, pressing him forward.

On the upstairs landing, Holmes and Poe quickly split up again. Holmes moved down the narrow hall and into the master bedroom at the end, one with bow windows looking out over the street. Empty. So was the luxurious attached bathroom.

When Holmes came back into the hallway, Poe had finished with the second bedroom on the floor. He shook his head and tucked his pistol back under his jacket.

Holmes looked down the staircase.

Where is Virginia?

Suddenly, he heard a thud from the bathroom at the end of the hall. Through the half-open door he could see the edge of a claw-foot tub. He moved quickly down the hall and pushed the door all the way open.

Virginia was slumped on the tile floor, unconscious.

"Poe!" Holmes shouted.

As his partner burst through the door, Holmes slid his arm behind Virginia's shoulders and lifted her gently. He saw her eyelids flicker, then open slowly.

"What happened?" asked Holmes.

"Not sure," Virginia mumbled. "Something about this room." Suddenly, her eyes burst open. *"Kids!* You said kids lived here?"

"Right," said Holmes. "Oliver Paul's little girls."

"What about the boy?" asked Virginia.

"No boy. Only the girls."

Virginia pushed Holmes away and lunged toward the huge porcelain tub. "Not now," she said. "Years ago. A teenager. A teenage boy."

Poe stepped over, listening intently. It wasn't the first time Virginia had sensed things that nobody had told her about.

"What about the boy?" Poe asked.

Virginia's normally pale skin went a shade whiter. She gripped the edge of the tub. "He killed somebody," she said. "Right here. A woman."

Now Holmes blanched. The mother. The drowning. The boy. *Oliver Paul!* He helped Virginia to her feet, knocking the bathroom door partway shut behind him.

Holmes looked up. On the back of the door was a calendar turned to September. A thick red circle was scrawled around one date. September 30. The anniversary of Oliver Paul's mother's death. Just over a day away.

Holmes grabbed the calendar from the door. "Dammit!" How could he have been so stupid? How could he have been so stuck in the details of the case that he didn't see the plain truth? But he saw it now.

Somewhere, another mother was about to die. Accidentally on purpose. With the help of Oliver Paul.

CHAPTER 70

MARPLE WAS IMPRESSED again. It had taken Rebecca Tran only a few minutes to hack into a cache of Brexit surveillance files that MI5 had apparently been collecting for the past twenty years. Top secret cases. Eyes-only files.

"Will you get into trouble for this?" Marple asked.

Tran turned to her with a stern expression. "No. *You* will." She held the look for a second, then broke into a conspiratorial smile. "Just kidding. Dodgett will probably get you diplomatic immunity."

Marple was really starting to like this woman. She pulled her chair close as the analyst skimmed through grainy videos of edgy skinheads, fringe politicians, and eccentric billionaires. The speeches had been captured over the years in public squares, conference centers, and dingy meeting rooms. The common themes of the diatribes were "pushing back the wave" of immigrants and "saving British tradition." The tone was universally belligerent, often ominous.

On a panel alongside the videos, Marple noticed an audio

visualizer, showing a running graph of sound levels, often spiking into the red zone. The Brexit radicals were a high-decibel bunch. Mostly, but not exclusively, men. Marple found herself shifting her eyes from the images of the speakers to the electronic dance of the audio signals.

"Can you filter by frequency?" asked Marple. She had an idea.

"Frequency of appearance?"

"Audio frequency. Can you isolate higher-pitched speakers?"

"Not sure," said Tran. "I'll try." She tapped out a new set of instructions on the keyboard. After a few seconds, she leaned forward in her chair. "Okay. That helps."

Now, instead of hundreds of speakers in the video queue, there were only three.

Three women. Tran clicked the isolated links one by one.

The first showed Ellie Babitch, a wealthy pot-stirrer from the fringe of the Conservative Party. Marple recognized her from the tabloids. Babitch's Brexit garden parties had been famous but relatively innocuous. Most guests had come for the free drinks, and for a chance to rub shoulders with Babitch's much-younger husband, a retired striker for the Arsenal football team.

Next up was a lithe, foul-mouthed woman with a German accent speaking in a deserted factory. She delivered her profanity-laced speech beneath a painted symbol that evoked the Reichsadler, the imperial eagle symbol from Hitler's era.

"Who's the storm trooper?" asked Marple.

Tran quickly pulled up a profile on another screen. "Else Schmidt. Deported three years ago." She scrolled down. "Serving a ten-year sentence in Stadelheim Prison on a weapons charge. I'd count her out of the picture."

One left. The last video in the queue had been captured by a cell phone in some kind of club. More like an underground bunker. Low ceilings. Dim light. Graffiti-scrawled walls. The crowd was scruffy and frantic, chanting a single word over and over again: *"Regal! Regal! Regal!"* Most of them were women.

The camera tipped toward the front of the room as a slight figure emerged from behind a makeshift curtain. The shape was waifish but clearly female. There was no ID available on the face, even in close-up. The woman's entire head was covered in stocking material stenciled with the Union Jack.

As she started to speak, a banner unfurled behind her. Spelled out in large letters was the word "REGAL," in bold, widely spaced capitals.

"An acronym?" Marple theorized.

Tran typed it into the system. The response took less than a second.

"REGAL," she read out loud. "Restore English Glory and Language."

"Pithy," said Marple.

Tran scanned the highlights from the accompanying intelligence report. "Small group. No more than fifty at their peak. On a watch list for a couple years in the late twenty teens. Maybe disbanded or inactive. No social media tracks for years."

"Maybe they've moved on to other activities," said Marple.

"Here's one of their old posts," said Tran. She enlarged the image and sharpened it. Beneath a close-up of the fine-boned woman in the flag mask, the text read, "Make Britain White Again."

Marple heard her phone vibrating in her bag. She reached in and pulled it out.

On her screen was a text. All caps.

COME BACK. SOMEONE'S ABOUT TO BE MURDERED.

It was from Holmes.

He always knew exactly how to get her attention.

CHAPTER 71

MARPLE CAUGHT A few hours of rest and a quick shower at headquarters before the next available flight back to New York—and slept throughout that as well, for once—but it was still nearly noon the next day before she landed at JFK. PC Dodgett had driven Marple to Heathrow himself. He had proven to be as solid as his literary namesake—hardworking and loyal—but Marple couldn't wait to reunite with her true partners.

"Miss Marple! Over here!" a voice called out from the throng in the waiting area as she exited Terminal 4 at JFK. "Welcome back!"

It was Virginia. Black leggings. Denim jacket. Tinted hair.

Marple waved. "Where's Holmes?" she asked as she neared. "And Poe?"

"Downtown at police headquarters," said Virginia. "New development."

"Take me there," said Marple.

"That's the plan," said Virginia.

As they pushed through the door to the loading zone, Marple spotted a rakish two-door parked at the curb. Poe's treasured

Trans Am. A uniformed baggage attendant was sitting in the driver's seat.

"Fantastic ride," said Virginia. "I can't believe Mr. Poe let me borrow it." She moved quickly around to the driver side. She pressed a folded bill into the baggage handler's palm as they traded places. Marple slid in on the passenger side.

"Strap in, Miss Marple," said Virginia, wrapping her fingers around the shift knob. "This thing's got balls."

The tires screeched as Virginia pulled the car away from the curb. She quickly wound her way down the access road and onto the Belt Parkway. In no time, she had the Pontiac up to 75. Margaret realized this was the first time she'd ever seen Virginia behind the wheel.

"Is this how they drive in rural Pennsylvania?" Marple asked as Virginia swung past a delivery van, missing its bumper by inches. She wondered if Poe would approve.

"Can I tell you a secret?" said Virginia, eyes firmly on the road. "I did a little street racing in high school."

"I see," said Marple. "It shows." She grabbed the armrest and held on tight, bringing her focus back to the message from Holmes. "What's going on, Virginia?" she asked. "Holmes said somebody was about to be killed."

"Oliver Paul," said Virginia, her voice rising over the engine roar.

"Who would want to kill Oliver Paul?" asked Marple.

"No. Sorry," said Virginia, banking into a turn. "He's the *killer*. Mr. Holmes says Oliver Paul is going to kill somebody. And it's going to happen tomorrow!"

The little watchmaker? A killer?

"Mr. Holmes says he's sure of it. But he doesn't know who the victim will be. Not yet."

Marple's mind was spinning. London. New York. Kidnappings.

Murder. For a moment, her usually sharp multitasking faculties were slightly overwhelmed. She closed her eyes, losing track of time and distance as the Pontiac blasted past signs for Brighton Beach and Luna Park. The next thing she felt was a jolt from the transmission. Virginia downshifted as they approached the entrance to the Battery Park tunnel. A few minutes later, as they glided through the long tube under the East River toward the Manhattan side, Virginia glanced over at Marple. "He missed the hell out of you," she said.

"Who did?"

"Mr. Holmes."

Marple felt a slight burn in her cheeks. "Did he tell you that?"

Virginia sped up as she spotted the end of the tunnel. "He didn't have to," she said. "I pick up things."

Marple heard a buzz near her feet. She looked down. Her purse had toppled off the seat and into the footwell. She reached down and pulled her phone out of the side pouch. She glanced at the screen. International call.

"Hello?"

"Margaret, it's Ben. Ben Dodgett."

Marple smiled. Apparently, the lovestruck PC was going to be a hard man to shake.

"It's Rebecca Tran," said Dodgett. "She's dead."

CHAPTER 72

MARPLE CRACKED OPEN her door even before Virginia came to a full stop in front of One Police Plaza.

"Thanks for the lift," Marple said as she jumped out.

"Any time," said Virginia, revving the engine loudly.

Marple heard the car peel away as she headed into the lobby. She half expected to be stopped or asked for ID, but instead the cop in front of the elevator pressed the Up button for her.

"Your buddies are with the task force," he said.

Marple nodded. Her head was still spinning with the news about Rebecca Tran.

According to Dodgett, Tran was found dead in her Fulham apartment, mere hours after Marple had left. No blunt-force trauma. No penetration wounds. No strangulation marks. Dodgett suspected poison, but the full tox report wouldn't be in for another twenty-four hours. Margaret wondered if they'd made a fatal mistake by hacking into MI5 files. Maybe she and Tran had turned over the wrong stone.

When the elevator door opened, Marple could see right through the glass wall into the war room. Holmes and Poe were standing with Captain Duff, who was gesturing emphatically toward a screen at the front of the room. At the long tables, detectives and FBI agents were tapping furiously on laptops and shouting into their phones. The energy seemed through the roof. As Marple reached for the handle of the glass door, Holmes spotted her and rushed over.

"Margaret!" As soon as he caught the look on her face, he put a hand on her shoulder and stooped slightly to bring his eyes even with hers. "What's wrong?" he asked. "What happened?"

"Not now," said Marple, brushing his hand away. "Tell me what's going on here. Who is Oliver Paul about to kill?"

Holmes waved an arm toward where Poe and Duff were standing. "Impossible to know," he said. "We need to find him before it happens. I got Duff to put out an APB on an of-interest basis. Like pulling teeth. In the meantime, we've finally got some insights on the kidnappings upstate."

"Such as . . . ?"

"The school bus driver."

"Bill Barnes?" Marple noticed the commercial driver's license enlarged in a rectangle at the top of the screen.

Holmes nodded. "Closet alcoholic with money problems."

Marple pursed her lips. "You think a drunk bus driver masterminded a flawless kidnapping?" She glared at Duff. Her frustration was showing. "If he'd only allowed us to talk to the parents up there . . ."

"Hold on," said Holmes. "Auguste has a theory."

As they reached the center of the room, Marple noticed that the screen everybody was staring at was crisscrossed with fluorescent-green lines.

"Aircraft tracking patterns?" she asked.

Poe turned, noticing her for the first time. "Margaret! Welcome home." He nodded toward the screen. "After our little visit to the cornfield, I did some checking with a friend at the FAA. This is every recorded helicopter flight over Putnam County on the day the bus disappeared."

Duff scowled. "And like I've been saying, every single pass has been accounted for." He thrust a finger toward the screen, where the borders of Putnam County were outlined in red. "Two traffic units, two local news crews, one training flight, three state police flyovers, and an Army formation from Camp Smith. That's it!"

"Doesn't prove anything," said Poe. "A chopper doing under 86 knots 15 meters above ground level wouldn't throw off a detectable signal."

"How the hell would you know that?" asked Duff.

"Because I do my research," said Poe. "The only plausible explanation for their supposed disappearance is that those kids were airlifted out by helicopter, then carried off at low altitude to a transfer point. Farm country. No witnesses."

Across the room, a detective slammed down a phone headset. "The baby wrangler from the TV studio!" he called out. "She wants to talk!"

"Megan Robinson? Where is she?" asked Marple.

"Downstairs in holding," said Duff.

She started for the door. "I'll talk to her."

"Are you nuts?" bellowed Duff. The room went quiet. Marple turned around. Duff lowered his voice. "You really think I'm letting a PI interview a prime suspect?"

Marple walked up to him until her chest practically bumped his bony torso. "Look, Captain," she said, "I'm hungry. I'm dehydrated. I'm jet-lagged. A colleague of mine in London was just found dead, probably murdered for investigating this case on the UK side. We've still got a total of fifteen missing children that we know about, and this girl could be the link. Without me on that FaceTime call, you might still be in a standoff at Silvercup, and you wouldn't have her to interview in the first place. And you'd have three more babies gone. Megan Robinson won't talk to you. But I guarantee she'll talk to me."

Holmes leaned in. "Margaret was just with Megan's sister in London."

"That's right," said Marple, her eyes fixed on Duff. "I'm practically family."

CHAPTER 73

HOLMES WATCHED FROM behind the one-way glass with Poe, Duff, and a cluster of other task force members as Marple walked into the small room where Megan Robinson was sitting. The sound came through on a pair of speakers mounted below the window. Holmes stuffed his hands into his pockets and rocked back and forth on his heels. He desperately wanted to be in there himself. On the other hand, he knew this kind of work was Marple's forte.

"Hello, Megan," said Marple. "Recognize me?"

The young woman with wavy brown hair sat slouched at a stainless-steel table. She looked tired. She stared at Marple's face for a few seconds before the connection clicked.

"You were with Jane," said Megan, her back stiffening. "Is this some kind of scam?" Her Scouse accent was thick and nasal. "Some" had come out as *soom*.

"No scam," said Marple. "That was me in London with your sister. I just got back."

She slid onto the seat across from Megan. "I think you know that Jane is in big trouble. So are you. And the people you're working for couldn't care less. In fact, whether you go to prison or beat the system, you will never be safe from them. *Never.* Not unless you help me catch them."

Megan's eyes were red and her face was drawn. Her cheeks were hollow below high cheekbones. Her nails tapped a jittery pattern on the steel tabletop. She tensed her jaw but said nothing.

"You were a good nanny, Megan," Marple said. "We checked with the parents you used to work for in England. And you clearly have a way with babies. They trust you." She paused again, for a long time. Letting her words sink in.

Holmes watched as Megan shifted in her seat and brushed the hair back from her face. He admired Marple's restraint. He might have gone in hard, like the police had done earlier, scaring her out of talking to a lawyer. But Marple was clearly taking a gentler approach. More conversational. More empathetic.

"The children you took are safe, Megan. Healthy and sound. No worse for the experience. And that's a very good thing. But there are others still missing. This is part of a bigger plan. You know that. We've searched every site. We've used the most sophisticated software on Earth. But we can't find the other children. Where are they? Who has them?"

For a few seconds, Megan stared down at the table. Then she looked up. "What can you do for me and my sister?" she asked.

"Megan," said Marple, leaning across the table, "I'm not a police officer. I'm not a lawyer. I'm not a prosecutor."

"Then who the fook *are* you?" hissed Megan. "Why are you here? What is the point?"

Marple turned around and pointed to the back of the room. "See that mirror? If you help, the people behind it will know that you did the right thing." Marple turned back toward Megan. "I know you don't have names," she said, her voice barely above a whisper. "I don't need names. I just need a little guidance."

Nothing from Megan but a dull stare and a long stretch of silence. And then, a flurry of words, tumbling out fast and hard. "You won't find the kids on those black-market sites. That's old-school. Too much exposure. Too easy to trace. And this is not about sex trafficking." Megan lowered her eyes. "I would never have anything to do with that."

Holmes glanced at Poe with a small smile. Marple was a master. He watched her reach across the table to rest her hand on Megan's. "I believe you," she said. "So what's this about?"

"Adoption," said Megan. "And money. *Loads* of it."

"Adoption. Where? By whom?"

Holmes had his nose pressed up against the glass. He could always read the moment before someone broke. And he could see that Megan Robinson was right at the edge. He knew that Marple was letting the silence hang, waiting for the truth to slip out. He admired her patience. Envied it.

"Staten Island," Megan blurted suddenly. "Some old farm. There's going to be an auction. Live-streamed. One-time event. I don't know when exactly. The kids are going to be sold to the highest bidders around the world. As long as the bidders are rich and..." Megan was running out of steam, clearly exhausted. She swallowed hard.

"Rich and *what*?" pressed Marple.

Behind the glass, Holmes mumbled, "Say it..."

Megan looked up as she spoke. She was staring directly at Holmes, as if she could see straight through the glass. "Rich and bloody *white*!"

CHAPTER 74

AN HOUR LATER, Marple fell into bed with her clothes still on. She barely had enough energy left to flick off her shoes. As her second sole hit the carpet, her cell phone rang. She groped the phone off the side table and looked at the screen. Dodgett again.

"Hello, Constable."

"Any progress there?"

"The police are staking out a location on Staten Island," said Marple. "By morning we'll know more. Anything on Rebecca yet?"

"I'm still betting on a needle spike," he said, "but nothing definitive yet. Rebecca was a diabetic. Used insulin. She had multiple injection sites."

"And whoever killed her knew that," said Marple.

"I have something else," said Dodgett. "I pulled the last session Tran was working on after you left. She was doing some high-level voice analysis."

"Right," said Marple. "She was looking for a match for a woman we'd picked out. Needle in a haystack. But I'd asked her to keep trying."

"The woman in the Union Jack mask," said Dodgett.

"That's right." Marple rolled over. "Did she locate any information on her?"

"Yes. Her name is Agnes Matts. Originally from Yorkshire. Dropped out of school and more or less disappeared from society years ago, but she has family money from a string of right-wing tabloids and a medical device company."

"Medical devices?" said Marple, sitting up. *The malfunctioning ID bracelets?* She switched tacks. "Do you have a picture of Matts?"

"Nothing current," said Dodgett. "Just this." The screen lit up with a photo of a young woman with long brown hair and a bright smile. She was wearing an open-necked shirt under a blue sweater and an orange-trimmed blazer.

"Looks like a school photo," said Marple.

"Precisely," said Dodgett. "St. Swithun's, 2004. Not long after that, she lost contact with family and friends. Then a few years ago, she started showing up at fringe meetings with other Brexit nutters. That's when she first started speaking. Hasn't been seen without the mask since 2019."

The screen clicked to a grainy video of the Union Jack speaker. This was different from the one Marple had watched with Tran, but the message was the same: homogeneity over diversity, tradition over change, English over bilingualism. *"Don't let this be the last generation of true Brits!"* the masked woman shouted from the tiny stage as members of the audience waved homemade REGAL banners.

"Send me the link to this," said Marple.

"Done," said Dodgett. An email with the link pinged her inbox moments later.

"Nice work, Constable," said Marple, rubbing her eyes. "I'm going to sleep now."

"Right, then," said Dodgett. "Sleep well."

Fat chance, thought Marple.

As soon as Dodgett clicked off, Marple tapped the link he'd sent through. The video file was twenty minutes long. Marple stuck in her earbuds and sunk her head into a down pillow, as the voice of Agnes Matts bored even deeper into her brain.

CHAPTER 75

BEFORE SUNRISE THE next morning, Poe eased his growling Dodge Shelby Charger into the NYPD staging area north of Staten Island's Latourette Park. In the predawn mist, his head-light beams swept across police cars, SWAT trucks, and FBI vehicles, arrayed like a military squadron at the border of the New York City Farm Colony, a long-abandoned poorhouse and sanitarium.

"This is the place," said Poe. "No question."

"Bleak," muttered Holmes from the passenger seat.

"It looks like a lost civilization," said Marple, leaning forward from the back seat.

Poe pulled to a stop and turned off the ignition. They were both right. The last residents had left or died off fifty years ago. Through a cluster of trees, Poe could make out the faint outlines of century-old structures and walkways, now laced with vines and covered in faded graffiti. The scene was as grim and fore-boding as anything from his namesake's imagination.

Suddenly, a fist banged on the driver side. Poe jumped in his seat and lowered the window. It was Duff, a thick ballistic vest hanging off his narrow shoulders. "Get this thing out of the way!" he growled. "This isn't a goddamn car show."

Poe waited for Holmes and Marple to exit, then put the car in reverse and swung it behind a huge flat-black SWAT transport, totally out of Duff's view. He shut down the engine and walked back to where his partners and the tall captain were standing. A phalanx of SWAT officers had formed to their right. Poe could hear the crunch of boots and the crisp sound of gun chambers being checked. Dozens of uniformed cops hung back by their idling SUVs. A squad of boxy ambulances waited one row behind.

"We did drone surveillance on the place all night," said Duff. "Looked livelier than usual. Could be something going on."

"Livelier than usual? Who the hell normally comes here?" asked Holmes.

"Kids mostly. Or ghost hunters," said Duff. "And devil worshippers." He nodded toward the underbrush and the crumbling complex beyond. "There are lots of shallow graves out here from years back."

Poe felt a cold shiver.

"Grab your vests," said Duff, pointing to the open trunk of an unmarked car. "And don't leave my goddamn sight."

Poe walked over to the trunk and lifted out a piece of NYPD-stenciled body armor. He dropped the vest over his head and tightened the Velcro straps. The vest was heavy on his shoulders, but there was something else. A dark weight inside his chest. He looked across the compound. The SWAT team was already moving in assault formation through the trees.

There was evil here. *Fresh* evil. Poe could feel it.

CHAPTER 76

POE MOVED IN a low crouch alongside his partners, a few steps behind Duff, who held his service pistol at his side. Ahead, past the sparse tree line and a tangle of vines and brush, the SWAT team had already reached the first building, or what was left of it. At this point, the colony structures were no more than shells—walls crumbled, roofs caved in, elevator shafts gaping.

The cops swept in, one ruin at a time. Shouts of "Clear!" echoed in succession across the eerie compound.

"Dammit!" muttered Duff. "There's nothing here."

"What about other farms on the island?" asked Marple.

"We checked them too last night," said Duff. "Mostly small family operations and pumpkin patches. Maybe Robinson lied to us."

"No. This is it," said Poe. He faltered slightly, then leaned back against a crumbling concrete post.

Marple stepped over and grabbed his arm. "Auguste! Are you okay?"

Poe waved her off. "I'm fine." But he wasn't. He felt lightheaded and queasy.

The image from Helene's sonogram flashed into his head. Two tiny shapes floating in a void. Then Helene's face. Worried.

"Auguste!" Marple again.

Poe took a deep breath and snapped to. "I'm here," he said. "Ready."

The next building in line was a large stone structure with an arched entrance. It looked like it had once been the centerpiece of the compound. There was nothing farmlike about it. It was built like a nineteenth-century factory.

"Wait here," said Duff, holding his arm out as a barrier.

Poe watched with Holmes and Marple as a SWAT team moved through the entryway under a large stone arch. Poe was out of patience. Especially with Duff.

"Wait, my ass," he muttered.

Poe started running toward the building. He heard a shout, then footsteps.

He glanced back to see Marple and Holmes right behind him. Duff was in the distance, shouting into his portable radio.

Poe and his partners reached the entrance at the same time. SWAT teams were already moving through the first floor. Poe looked up. The second story was totally gone, no structure left. A staircase from the ground level ended in midair.

A massive SWAT sergeant stepped forward and planted himself in their path. "You guys can't be in here," he said.

"And yet we are," said Marple.

"Sarge!" a young SWAT officer called out from the top of another stone staircase. "Down here!"

Poe got to the staircase before any of the other cops. But they jammed him up against the wall and forced their way past. He followed them down, with Marple and Poe close behind.

The stairs led to a square landing, then took a turn to the left for a drop to the basement level. The air was dank and musty.

Poe saw Holmes pull out a handkerchief and hold it over his nose.

The corridor at the bottom led to a single door, partway open. A portable generator sat idle in the corridor outside. A SWAT officer kicked open the door and stepped through. He clicked on his flashlight.

"Holy shit!" he called out.

Poe rushed to the entrance, bumping shoulders with the cop. The flashlight raked the room with a wide, bright beam. The space was huge, with its stone floor swept clean. Filling one side of the room was a large curve of blue seamless paper. In front of it was a wooden chair and a table covered in thick padding. Mounted on stands on either side were banks of lights, with cords dangling. A few portable fans sat in the corners. In the center of the room, a sturdy tripod held a top-of-the-line Canon video camera.

"Porn set?" muttered one of the cops.

"Online auction house," said Poe.

"We're too late," said Holmes, sniffing the air tentatively. "There hasn't been anyone here for hours. The kids are gone. Sold and shipped off. Just like Megan said."

Two cops moved in with emergency scene lights. They switched them on, flooding every corner of the room. Duff stepped through the door and did a slow 360.

"What in the name of God . . . ?"

Holmes took a few steps deeper into the space. Took in a few more breaths. "Sodium polyacrylate," he mumbled. "And ammonia."

"Baby diapers," said Marple.

In the fresh glare, Poe noticed a row of black equipment cases against the back wall. They were professional grade, with rounded metal edge guards and heavy-duty handles.

Poe reached into his pocket and pulled on a pair of latex gloves. He walked to the wall and stood over the cases. Some were battered and worn from use. Others looked brand-new.

He bent down and flicked the latch on the first case in the row. He lifted the lid.

Inside was a tangle of cords and adapters. He moved to the next case, filled with heavy-duty black cables. The third box looked like a camera case, big enough to hold the Canon and a few backup batteries. Probably a set of extra lenses too.

Poe flicked the latch and opened the lid. The interior was cavernous and lined in maroon-colored velvet. Poe bent low, one hand braced against the side of the open case. He reached down, then recoiled, gasping.

He looked down again. Just to be sure.

Nestled in the fabric at the bottom of the case was a tiny baby, barely a week old.

Eyes open. Still warm. Dead.

CHAPTER 77

AS POE STOOD over the case, heart thumping, Holmes and Marple crowded in beside him. Marple looked down, then quickly turned to face the opposite wall. Holmes dropped to his knees and started to reach gently into the case. Suddenly, Duff was behind him, roughly yanking him away by the shoulder. "What the hell do you think you're doing?" he shouted. "Back the hell off!"

Holmes stood as Duff looked down into the case. "Jesus Christ!" The captain spun on his heels and clenched his fists. He lowered his head for a few seconds, then looked up and locked eyes with the nearest cop. "Call the ME."

Poe looked up. Suddenly, a row of bricks near the top of the foundation began to shake loose. Dirt spilled from cracks in the mortar. There was a loud roar and vibration from outside, behind the wall.

Poe and Holmes raced out of the room and up the stairs, beating the heavily armored cops to an open doorframe at the rear of the structure. A large box truck roared past, banging into low-hanging limbs as it barreled toward the near end of the police perimeter. Two SWAT officers burst through the doorway right behind Poe, rifles aimed toward the fleeing truck.

"No!" shouted Holmes, knocking one of the gun barrels aside. "There might be kids in there!"

Poe watched, eyes wide. The truck swerved through a gap between two NYPD vehicles, scraping a deep furrow in the side of an SUV. Poe grabbed Holmes by the sleeve and yanked him forward. "Let's go!"

As police radios crackled, Poe and Holmes broke into a dead run, shrugging off their heavy vests. They split up to pass on either side of the creased police vehicle and ended up together behind a SWAT transport. The front end of the Charger was already pointed toward the street.

Poe slid into the driver's seat. Holmes jumped in from the other side.

"What about Margaret?" asked Holmes.

"No time! We'll catch up later!"

A half dozen police vehicles were already revving up and pulling out in pursuit. But Poe put the Dodge in low gear and muscled his way toward the front of the pack along the dirt path leading out of the compound. Once his tires gripped hard pavement, he shot out ahead. The truck was already out of sight around a turn.

Poe blasted through two intersections, then made a hard left, speeding through a quiet suburban neighborhood with police cars single file behind him.

"*There!*" shouted Holmes.

The truck was already about fifty yards ahead, turning onto the expressway. Poe closed the distance, ignoring stop signs and red lights. He turned left and accelerated onto the ramp.

The truck was now a rectangle in the distance, speeding in the direction of the Goethals Bridge. "He's headed for Jersey!"

shouted Holmes. The emergency lights from the pack of police cars reflected off the Pontiac's interior. Sirens split the air from behind, along with a squawk from a PA speaker. *"Charger driver! Pull over!"*

"I think they're calling your name," said Holmes, turning his head for a quick glance at the posse.

"Who, me?" Poe replied, cupping a hand around his ear. "You know I can't hear anything over this engine."

With that, he floored the pedal, expanding his lead over the cops and gaining on the truck. They were now rocketing down Route 278 at nearly 90 miles an hour, shooting past other civilians in a blur. Poe's tires whined against the pavement.

"Blockade!" shouted Holmes, pointing through the windshield.

"I see it!" Poe shouted back.

Two police SUVs were angled at the entry ramp to the metal-framed bridge.

But the truck wasn't stopping. It blew through the barricade, spinning the police vehicles like toys, fenders smashed, windshields shattered. Poe downshifted and blasted through the gap a few seconds behind. The bridge ahead was clear, except for the truck.

"Don't crowd him!" shouted Holmes. The truck picked up speed again, widening its lead. Suddenly, it began to wobble to the right.

"Tire!" shouted Poe, swinging hard into the other lane.

Shreds of a blown retread spun out from the right rear of the truck and hit the side of the bridge. One rubber scrap bounced cleanly over Poe's hood. The truck tipped hard to the left, and then physics took over. In the next instant, the whole vehicle crabbed sideways and crashed onto its side, sliding along the bridge roadway, shedding sparks and shards of metal.

Holmes braced himself as Poe downshifted and hit the brakes.

The Dodge went into a controlled skid. The next second felt like a slow-motion eternity. The car stopped broadside about three inches from the truck's still-spinning tires.

Police cars pulled up behind the Dodge as Poe jumped out. He could hear the blare of radios and strident shouts from the cops, but he ignored them all. He saw Holmes running toward the rear door of the cargo box. One side was open, lying flat on the pavement, hinges torn off.

Poe headed for the cab, using a now-horizontal front wheel as a step. He pulled himself up until his head was almost level with the shattered window on the driver side. Chest heaving, he looked inside.

The driver was hanging toward the opposite door, his large body still tethered by the seat belt and peppered with pellets of glass. His forehead was bloodied by a large, oozing gash and his right shoulder was jerked out of its socket. His mouth hung open and his chest was still. The odor of scorched oil from the engine mixed with the distinct smell of alcohol.

Even with all the blood and the bad light, Poe recognized the dead man as the school bus driver. He jumped down onto the roadway. Cops were barking into their shoulder mics and spraying foam on a spreading stream of diesel fuel.

Holmes crawled out of the cargo box and stood up, pinching a hospital receiving blanket between his thumb and forefinger. "Nothing," he said. "Except for this."

"The driver was Bill Barnes," said Poe.

"Past tense?" asked Holmes.

Poe nodded. "He probably came back to the farm, intending to pick up the equipment, but got spooked," he said, lightly touching the baby blanket as it waved in the air. "Right after he delivered the goods."

CHAPTER 78

MARPLE WALKED SLOWLY alongside a young officer who held the deceased infant's body in her arms. As they approached the ambulance, the rookie's jaw was set and her eyes were glistening. She looked like a teenager. Marple suspected this was one of the first dead bodies the officer had ever encountered. Definitely the tiniest.

The baby was Edwin Cade, son of Sterling and Christine. Marple had ID'd the body herself from her stash of hospital pictures. She knew that within the hour, a pair of NYPD detectives would be standing in the doorway of the Cades' spectacular Upper West Side apartment, informing them that their only child would not be coming home. Marple resisted the urge to race there first and take the brunt of their pain and outrage herself. In her mind, that's exactly what she deserved.

"Some investigator I am," Marple mumbled to herself. She felt more like an undertaker. Behind the trees, the team was completing its sweep of the compound. After the ambulance doors slammed shut, Marple said silent prayers for Edwin and his parents—and that no other bodies would be found.

Her phone vibrated beneath her bulletproof vest. She ripped the Velcro straps apart and let the vest drop to the ground, then pulled the phone from her pocket.

It was Poe. In the background, she heard a rumble of engines and the whine of approaching sirens.

"Bill Barnes was driving the truck!" Poe shouted above the noise. "The school bus driver from upstate! It's all one operation!"

"Where *are* you?" asked Marple, pressing the phone against her ear.

"On the Goethals Bridge. We were right behind him. He was headed for New Jersey."

Marple took a few steps away from two nearby cops. She lowered her voice. "Is he talking? Has anybody questioned him yet?"

A long pause.

"The truck flipped, Margaret. He's dead."

Marple's mouth went dry. Another dead end. Another dead body. "What was in the truck? What was he carrying? Please tell me it wasn't the children."

"No," said Poe. "He'd already delivered the kids. I'm sure of it. The only thing left in the truck was a baby blanket from St. Michael's."

Margaret gripped the phone. Her throat tensed up too. "So maybe we should have followed from a distance instead of chasing him to death. He could have given us a location! He could have given us a *lot!*" She was getting more frustrated by the second, and her tone became more biting. "If there had been babies in the back of that truck, the crash could have killed them along with Barnes. Did you consider that? And we'd all be to blame."

"Margaret, we had to—"

Marple cut him off. "*Enough!* You and your machines. Not everything can be solved by a bunch of men in fast cars."

She ended the call.

CHAPTER 79

HOLMES PACED BACK and forth near the carnage on the bridge. The adrenaline had mostly drained from his system, but his mind was burning with anger and guilt. He knew Marple was right. They could have handled the situation with more finesse. But the sight of that dead infant had fired him—and Poe—up so much he doubted anything could have stopped them.

Holmes was actually surprised that he and Poe weren't under arrest for obstructing a police chase, or worse. Maybe because the cops on the scene were too busy picking truck parts off the roadway and redirecting a mile-long backup of drivers.

The late Bill Barnes had already been loaded into an ambulance and carted off to a local morgue. Now the wrecker was pulling the heavy truck upright for a tow to the police garage.

Poe was on the far side of the Charger, running his hand over the hood and fender panels. Amazingly, there didn't appear to be a scratch anywhere, just a few streaks of fire-retardant foam.

Holmes felt his phone buzz. He hoped it was Margaret.

It was Virginia.

Holmes put the phone on speaker as Poe came around the

front of the Charger. "Virginia! Are you at the office?" The hour was early, even for her.

"No, I'm not," came the reply. "I'm at SmallTime. Oliver Paul's watch shop."

"Hold on!" said Holmes, his adrenaline spiking again. "Is Paul there?"

"No," said Virginia. "I'm alone."

"Who let you in?"

"Nobody," said Virginia. "I broke in all by myself. You need to come right now!"

CHAPTER 80

"*THERE!* RIGHT THERE!" Holmes pointed to Paul's store sign as Poe pulled up to the curb. They'd both been talking to Virginia nonstop as she described what she'd uncovered inside the clock shop. Travel records going back two decades. Proof that Oliver Paul had been all over the country during the period of the mysterious deaths. The Charger was still rolling when Holmes unclipped his seat belt and jumped out. He raced across the sidewalk and yanked on the door.

Locked!

A second later, the buzzer sounded.

Poe was right behind him now. They burst through the door in quick succession.

"Virginia!" Holmes shouted.

"Back here!" she answered.

The interior was dim, but Holmes caught a flash of pink-hued hair behind the counter. He heard panting. He reached over and turned on a ceiling light. Virginia was bent over the glass, dressed in black from head to toe, with a magnifying glass in one hand. Baskerville was sitting on his haunches at the end of the counter.

"You broke in?" said Poe *"How?"*

Virginia held up a small, thin metal tool. "I watch, I learn, Mr. Poe."

Spread out in front of her were thick piles of documents in an assortment of white and pastels. Holmes stepped around the counter and ran his fingers lightly over the paperwork. At a glance, he could pick out motel invoices and restaurant receipts running back to the early 2000s. From towns that linked up with his research.

To the side, Virginia had stacked handwritten tickets from two decades' worth of purchases—antique clocks, jeweled watches, entire timepiece collections. There were piles of marked-up auction catalogues, estate listings, even circled classified ads and yard-sale flyers.

"Where did you find all this?" asked Holmes.

"If you cracked a safe," said Poe, "we'll have to promote you."

"It was all back there," said Virginia, "in his office files."

Holmes turned and looked through the curtain that separated the office from the main floor of the shop. The office was tiny, with a grey metal desk and shelves overflowing with dismantled clocks and parts catalogues. A metal file cabinet sat in the corner, both drawers now open.

Had all this evidence been mere yards away the first time he visited the shop? Had it been here the whole time? Was Oliver Paul that careless? That bold? That *insane*? Or had he purposefully left it here for Holmes to discover?

"Look!" said Poe. Holmes ducked out of the office. Poe was tapping one invoice after another. "Indiana, Minnesota, Vermont, Louisiana..."

"He was everywhere," said Virginia.

"Hold on!" said Holmes, remembering something. He bent down behind the counter, feeling his way along the underside of the shelving unit. He slid open a compartment at the bottom and felt inside.

"It's still here!" said Holmes.

He pulled out a cardboard bankers box and set it on the counter.

"What's this?" asked Poe.

"Oliver Paul's notes on the case. He offered to show them to me the first day I visited."

"And...?" said Virginia.

"I turned him down."

"You never looked?" asked Poe.

"I hadn't committed to the case," said Holmes. "And I considered him an amateur."

He lifted the cover. Inside the box was a loose stack of eight-by-ten prints. Photo enlargements. Virginia and Poe leaned over to look as Holmes shuffled through them. Each print was a picture of a young woman.

"The victims," said Virginia with a shiver.

Holmes started laying the photos out on top of the counter. Some shots looked like profile pictures, scanned from Facebook or Instagram pages. Some looked like blowups from driver's licenses. Others looked like enlargements from snapshots. From the quality of the images and the hairstyles on the women, they seemed to be in chronological order, the most recent on top.

Holmes spread out the photos and counted. Twenty-three. He picked up the photo at the end of the line. The earliest one. It was a head-and-shoulders shot of a young woman in a colorful tracksuit.

The woman looked straight at the camera with a pleasant smile. But something was off. Unsettling. Holmes leaned in closer. Then he saw it. The pupil of her left eye was aimed just slightly off center.

His phone rang. Unknown caller.

"Brendan Holmes. Who's this?"

"I knew you were weak, Sherlock. I just didn't know how far you'd fallen."

Oliver Paul's voice.

Holmes felt his entire body tense. He put the call on speaker and set his phone on the counter. "So you've found my little collection," Paul's voice continued. "In the old days, you would have figured this out already, without any extra help."

"Where are you?" asked Holmes, his jaw tight.

"Close enough that I could have killed young Virginia the moment she arrived. I would have made it look like an accident, of course. But as you know by now, she's not my type."

Virginia huddled closer to Poe. Holmes looked at the ceiling and into corners of the shop for cameras, then swept his gaze across the faces of the hundreds of clocks on display.

"Don't embarrass yourself, Sherlock," said Paul. "Don't you think a master watchmaker would know where to hide a lens?"

Holmes pointed to the array of photos. "What do you have against all these innocent women?" asked Holmes. He picked up the last one in the line. "What did you have against your own mother? And if you did kill her, would you kill your wife too?"

"We all have our quirks," said Paul. "Speaking of which, by midnight another mom will die."

Then silence.

CHAPTER 81

ON STATEN ISLAND, Marple watched the rear guard of the search team walk out of the brush and back into the staging area as bright streaks of sunlight broke through the trees at the edge of the compound. Stopping in pairs and small clusters, the officers shed their vests and slung their rifles casually over their shoulders.

The equipment had been hauled out and laid on a canvas tarp behind one of the SWAT vehicles. Paper scraps and loose parts had been placed in clear evidence bags. One by one, the bags were being logged and loaded into cartons in the back of a black NYPD van.

Marple saw Duff emerge from between two camo-patterned trucks. He paused mid-step and looked over. "I guess you'll need a lift back to the city," he said.

"Unless you'd prefer that I hitchhike," Marple replied.

Duff pointed at a patrol car idling near the van. Marple saw the rookie from earlier behind the wheel, talking on her radio. "That car right there," said Duff. "Officer Amy Polacco will take you." Duff rapped his knuckles on the hood. Polacco looked up. Duff pointed at Marple, then toward the exit road. Polacco got the message. She nodded and lifted a bag off the passenger seat to make room.

Marple walked over. As she passed the evidence van, an officer started to put yet another bag inside. "Wait. Stop," said Marple, grabbing the officer's arm. As the bag hung suspended from his glove, Marple leaned forward and lifted the clear plastic toward her face. Inside was a coil of narrow-gauge connector cable with gold-plated jacks at both ends.

What had caught Marple's eye was a strip about one inch from the end of the cable, where the manufacturing specs were often inscribed. It was an adhesive label. Same bright leaf green as the baby ankle bands. She looked closer. There was lettering on the label, small and faded, barely legible.

Novartis...? NovaTech...?

NovaGen!

Marple yanked out her phone and googled "NovaGen" and "New Jersey." She whirled around and spotted Duff standing in a cluster of detectives. "Captain!" she shouted. "I know where to look! I know where they took the kids!"

Duff broke from the group. Marple ran over to meet him, pointing at the Google map on her screen. "The baby-band company," she said. "They have a warehouse in Elizabeth. I think that's where the truck was headed."

For a second, Duff just looked at her. Then she saw a tiny shift in his expression to something vaguely resembling trust. He turned and started shouting orders. Marple texted Poe and Holmes the address. **MEET ME HERE.**

As she slid into the front seat of the patrol car next to Officer Polacco, Marple's heart was pounding. She realized that her attitude toward speed had evolved quickly over just the past few minutes. She fastened her shoulder harness and looked over.

"I know where the other babies are," she said. "How fast can this car go?"

In seconds, Polacco had the Ford Interceptor in gear, pulling away, lights flashing. "Let's find out," she said.

CHAPTER 82

MARPLE AND POLACCO were among the first of the Staten Island contingent to arrive at the Elizabeth location. It helped that the Goethals Bridge had been blocked and placed under police control. By the time they pulled up at the warehouse, dozens of Jersey police and FBI vehicles were already parked around the perimeter. Five New York State Police SWAT trucks were staged in the parking lot. Camo-suited snipers were sighting from adjacent rooftops. It looked like a battle zone.

Marple looked over at Polacco as they pushed their car doors open. "Nice driving," she said.

Polacco nodded, then hustled over to an NYPD van and started strapping on armor.

Marple walked to the front of the car and scanned the scene. The target was one of five warehouses stretched along a huge lot near the waterfront. The main building was two stories high. Steel sides. Flat roof. Loading dock running along the entire back end with four corrugated metal doors—all closed.

To the left of the warehouse, Marple saw an attached one-story office building with a bright green stripe across the top. On the pavement about twenty yards from the office was a platform about thirty feet square, with a faded white circle at the center.

"Margaret!"

Marple turned to see Holmes and Poe hurrying toward her from the other side of the parking lot.

"We were in Manhattan when we got your message," said Holmes, slightly winded.

"At Oliver Paul's shop," said Poe. "With Virginia."

Marple glanced behind them. "Tell me you did *not* bring that girl here!"

"We sent her back to the office," said Holmes. He leaned in close. "But she found a gold mine—all the evidence we need to tie Paul to the Mother Murders crime scenes."

"Without a search warrant?" said Marple. "Have you lost your minds?"

"Margaret," said Poe. "He called while we were there. We heard him. He's going to kill another woman by midnight tonight!"

"Unless we find him and stop him," said Holmes.

"We should have poisoned his lunch when we had the chance," said Marple.

"Police action! Move back!" A cop in tactical gear was moving toward them from across the parking lot. Marple realized that they probably looked like local curiosity seekers.

Holmes pulled out his identification and stepped forward to intercept the cop. "We're private investigators," he said. "We've been on this case from the start."

The cop poked his nose toward the ID. "That a New York license?" he asked.

Holmes nodded. "It is."

"Well, you're in New Jersey now," said the cop. "Step behind the barricade."

He punctuated his command with a nudge of his rifle butt. *"Now!"*

Marple could tell that Poe was ready to snap. As he cocked his shoulders, she stepped in front of him, glancing at the cop's name tag. "Officer Neal, who's your scene commander?"

Neal narrowed his eyes suspiciously before answering. "Quinn," he said. "Captain Quinn."

Marple scanned the staging area behind him and picked out a barrel-chested, crew-cut guy in a suit, weaving quickly between vehicles, followed by a posse of Jersey uniforms. He carried himself like a Marine.

"That him?" Marple asked.

The cop quickly glanced around to look. "Yeah. That's Quinn. You know him?"

Marple shook her head. "Not yet."

Just then, the crew-cut guy turned his gaze their way and started moving in their direction, palms straight out and thrusting forward. He shouted at Neal. "I told you, get those people back! This is a live-fire zone. No goddamn spectators!"

When Quinn was ten feet away, the dust in the parking lot began to swirl. Marple felt pellets of gravel stinging her ankles as her hair whipped around her neck and face.

A loud pounding sound vibrated the air. She tipped forward, nearly blown off her feet.

Holmes grabbed her around the shoulders and curled forward to shield her from the debris being kicked up by a sleek black-and-white helicopter with NYPD markings. It crossed the parking lot about twenty feet overhead and landed cleanly on the pad near the office building.

The skids had barely touched the surface when Graham Duff jumped out. He started trotting toward where Holmes, Marple, and Poe were standing, his suit jacket flapping around his narrow torso.

Quinn turned as he approached. "You Duff?" he asked.

Duff nodded. The two officers shook hands.

"Welcome to the Garden State," said Quinn. He turned to Neal. "Why are these people not gone?"

"Hold on," said Duff. "They're with me." He pointed at each of them in turn. "He's Holmes. That's Poe. And this is Marple. She's the reason we're here."

Marple brushed her hair back into place. Quinn was staring straight at her. Behind him, about fifty militarized cops, troopers, and agents stood ready for his command.

"Well, Miss Marple, let's see if you're right."

CHAPTER 83

"GO! GO! GO!"

The SWAT team leader pressed his men forward with hard shoulder slaps. Holmes was crouched in front of Poe and Marple—all in fresh armored vests—a few feet behind the four-man team. In seconds, they were facing one of the warehouse's side doors.

A single blow from a sledgehammer demolished the padlock. An officer with a ballistic shield breached the doorway first. His squad-mates followed, rifles pointing left, right, up, down. *"Police!"* the lead officer shouted. His voice echoed as if he were shouting into a canyon.

Holmes listened for gunfire or voices. He heard nothing but the sound of shuffling boots and rattling gear. The air inside reeked of construction dust, warm metal, and human sweat. He slipped inside.

The vast space was lit by hanging banks of fluorescent lights. Industrial shelving rose two stories into the air, packed with cardboard cartons. A massive cargo container was lined up in front of one of the cargo bay doors. Thirty feet up, a metal cat-walk ran across the entire width of the warehouse.

"Stay the hell back!" One of the cops shoved Holmes, who knocked into Poe, who almost toppled Marple. As Holmes reached back to steady her, a two-inch hole blasted through the wall right behind her ear. Marple's hands flew to her head. Then three more shots. Like hammer blows on metal.

"Contact left!" shouted the cops, firing off a flurry of single shots in return.

Holmes grabbed Poe and Marple by the backs of their vests and pulled them behind the nearest shelf. They ended up flattened side by side, faces pressed against the battleship-grey floor.

Then the whole place erupted.

Gunfire came in rapid-fire bursts from at least two directions. The noise was stunning, disorienting, deafening. Holmes pulled his pistol out of its holster and peered through a gap in the cartons on the lowest shelf. On the catwalk above, he could see muzzle flashes silhouetting black-suited shapes. Oily smoke hung in the air.

"AR-15s," Holmes shouted. He could smell the factory grease from the chambers and the ammonia from the ammo. He turned to Marple. *"Margaret! Do not move! Do you hear me?"* She looked stunned from the concussion of the first shots. When Holmes looked up, Poe was gesturing with his pistol. "I'll go right," he shouted, starting off down the long aisle between the first shelving row and the outside wall.

Holmes waited for another burst of gunfire to end. The length of a single clip. Then he dashed across the gap in front of the door and moved down the long row of shelving on the opposite side. He could see SWAT teams pouring in from another door on the far side of the building. One cop swung his rifle toward the catwalk as a blast from above kicked up chunks of the floor. The cop fired back with two quick shots.

Holmes saw a blur in the air, then heard the sickening crack of a body hitting concrete.

A second later, another officer spun around as if he'd been struck with a pipe. Rolling onto his back, he returned fire, blasting a stack of boxes to shreds. From behind the stack, another body fell.

Holmes rounded the corner of the shelving row, his gun held straight out. Suddenly, a figure in a black mask whipped around to face him. A blur, then a flash. The round banged into a metal shelf behind him. The figure stepped forward, then crumpled as if hit by an invisible punch. Holmes looked to the side, ears ringing. He saw Poe, pistol raised, advancing toward him.

In seconds, the aisle was full of cops, shoving them both back, surrounding the still figure on the floor, as a dark pool of blood spread underneath. One of the cops looked up at Poe. "Clean kill," he said. "Center mass." He leaned forward and yanked the black mask off.

It was a woman.

Holmes leaned down. Dark hair. Late twenties. He recognized her face from the hospital surveillance video. "Haven-Care," he muttered. He looked over at Poe. Poe nodded. They were staring at one of the women who'd posed as a HavenCare executive.

"*Runner!*" The shout had come from a few aisles over. Holmes heard hard panting and the pounding of feet. Then he saw the flicker of a shape racing past the cartons in the next aisle, heading toward where he'd left Marple.

"Margaret!" Holmes shouted. As he shoved past the cops, he heard a fierce, high-pitched scream, then caught an acrid smell.

He rounded the shelf unit and started running, Poe at his heels. At the far end, a masked figure was on the floor, writhing and wailing, a gun at her side. Margaret was standing over the figure with her feet planted, one arm extended.

In her hand was a purse-sized canister of pepper spray.

CHAPTER 84

"MARGARET! ARE YOU hurt?" Poe saw Holmes dodge the squirming masked figure on the ground and grab Marple by the shoulders.

"I'm fine," said Marple, lowering the canister and twisting out of Holmes's grasp. "I told you," she said. "I'm fine."

Poe's heart was thudding, and his ears were still ringing. He looked around. It took him a second to grasp that the shooting had stopped.

In the aisle behind him, about ten yards away, the perp was lying on the concrete floor, still oozing blood. Same with the two dead shooters at the other side of the warehouse. Unmasked now. Both women. Off to the side, a SWAT cop barked into his shoulder mic. "Target secure. Three KIA. One in custody."

"Who are the KIAs? Any IDs?" It was Quinn, pushing his way through the ring of cops. Duff was two steps behind him. Holmes tucked his pistol back into its holster.

"Three women," said Holmes.

"All women?" said Duff.

"These are just acolytes," said Marple. "We're nowhere near

the mastermind. But based on a lead from Scotland Yard, I think the mastermind is also female."

Poe knelt down to yank the mask off the contorted figure on the ground. Another woman. She was clawing at her eyes, her teeth clenched in pain.

Marple grabbed a water bottle from a SWAT officer's pack and splashed it over the woman's face. The captive flinched and spat. *"You bitch!"* she screamed. *"I'll kill you!"* The voice was shrill, the accent British. Poe stepped between her and Marple. When the woman turned her face toward him, he had another flash of recognition. The second fake HavenCare exec.

As a cop pulled the prisoner's arms behind her, Marple bent down toward her face. "Where are they?" she asked. "Where are the children?"

The woman was blinking hard, eyes red, water dripping off her chin.

"I swear to God," said Marple, brandishing her canister, "I will spray you again."

Poe grabbed Marple by the arm, pulling her back. It took most of his strength. Marple's whole body was tense, straining against him. He could feel the fury radiating from her. The captive sat back, her chest heaving under her black jersey. Poe saw fear flash across her face, then resignation. The woman glanced over her shoulder.

"The box," she said.

Holmes leaned in. *"What* box?"

Marple dropped her canister on the floor. "She means the big one."

Poe and Holmes followed Marple as she walked to the rusted green cargo container in the center of the warehouse. A cop with a massive bolt cutter hustled into the lead, then banged on the side of the metal box.

"Police!"

No response.

Quinn nodded to the officer with the heavy-duty clippers. Two cops stood on either side, rifles ready. With a loud *ching,* the lock fell open. Two more cops moved forward to muscle the hatch open. Flashlight beams pierced the interior. A pungent ammonia odor—the smell of human sweat and human waste—flooded out.

"Jesus Christ!" muttered Duff.

Poe blinked and swallowed hard. He held his breath and looked in. The hairs on the back of his neck bristled. The container was lined with cargo blankets and plastic sheeting. At the far end, five young children were slumped with their backs against the metal wall, as still as corpses. Holmes recognized them instantly from their photos: the missing children from the school bus.

He looked closer, stunned by what he saw next. The St. Michael's infants were cradled in the arms of the third graders.

"Medic!" shouted Quinn.

Marple pushed past the men with guns and stepped into the container first. She rushed to the children, moving quickly from one to the other. A moment later, she called out, "They're alive! They're sedated, but they're all alive!"

As Marple knelt on the thin mattress pads, Poe saw some of the older kids begin to stir, raising their hands against the glare of the lights. He watched as Marple touched their heads gently and called them by name, one by one. *Olivia. Ava. Lucas. Grace. Logan.*

"You're safe now," said Marple softly. "You're all going home."

Poe turned as the rattle of gurneys echoed through the warehouse. In seconds, the cargo container was jammed with uniforms. They took the babies first—all pale and impossibly tiny—then the eight-year-olds, each one hanging limply. Ambulances were already backed up to the doorways. Within minutes, all ten children were loaded in, wrapped in blankets, with oxygen masks over their faces. One by one, the ambulances headed off, lights flashing, sirens wailing.

Quinn and Duff came up. "Looks like you were right, Marple," said Quinn.

"About this?" said Marple, looking back at the box. "Yes. We got here in time, this time. But four babies are still missing in London. And I guarantee there are more children being taken and held in places we don't even know about. I think these children were bound for overseas. This was only a way station—and we just disappointed some very dangerous people."

Suddenly, a raspy voice crackled from somewhere on the upper level of the warehouse, so loud it made Holmes cover his ears.

"Hello again, Sherlock..."

CHAPTER 85

DOZENS OF RIFLES came up as cops spun toward the sound. Holmes stepped forward, his adrenaline pumping. Poe jerked Marple back behind the cargo container.

"Who the hell is Sherlock?" asked Duff. He looked at Holmes. "*You?*"

Holmes scanned the upper level, staring in the direction of the sound. "It's a nickname," he muttered. "Unsolicited."

"*Look how well things turned out today, Sherlock.*" Oliver Paul's voice boomed from above. "*All those young lives saved, thanks to your partner's intuition. Good for her. Remember the days when you solved mysteries on your own?*"

One of the cops jabbed his finger toward the catwalk. Holmes peered into the shadows on the second level. All he could see was a long stretch of metal grating leading to a boxy structure at one end.

A SWAT sergeant made a quick circling gesture with his hand. A squad of five gathered behind him. At his signal, they all began moving in a crouch toward a rusted metal staircase on the far side of the building.

Holmes turned to Poe. "You and Margaret stay here," he said. "Do not move from that spot!" He pulled out his pistol again and followed the SWAT team toward the stairs.

"Holmes!" Quinn shouted. "Get your ass back here!"

Holmes didn't answer, and didn't stop. This was his fight. His right foot was already on the bottom tread of the staircase. As the cops moved up, he pressed in tight behind them. He was still wearing his body armor, but he felt completely exposed. He was beginning to realize that Oliver Paul could see him anywhere, hear him anywhere, get to him anywhere. Always one step ahead.

Holmes looked up to see red sight beams crisscrossing the darkness at the top of the staircase, tracing the length of the catwalk and bouncing along the metal wall behind it. In another couple of seconds, his shoes were on the metal grate. He glanced down to see cops and agents crouched behind shelving and cartons, weapons pointed up. From this height they looked like toy soldiers.

"You'd better hurry, Sherlock," said the voice, even louder now. "Time is running out." With each step, Holmes felt his fury building, overwhelming the fear.

The small squad turned left toward the small rectangular structure at the end of the catwalk. It looked like a pillbox. Holmes peered into the shadows. The structure had no windows, just a single door made of solid steel. A triangular sign to the side read, DANGER! HIGH VOLTAGE!

"All those officers," Paul's voice called out. "All that firepower." His tone was mocking now. "What a waste, Sherlock. Remember when all you needed was your ingenuity — your impressive powers of deduction?" The sound was coming from inside the box.

Red beams danced across the doorway. The squad leader held up one arm with a closed fist. "Hold right here," he ordered. "Wait for the bomb squad."

Holmes felt a bitter taste in his mouth as bile pumped up from his gut. *God! Not now!* He held his stomach and lurched forward, shoving his way past two SWAT cops. He grabbed the heavy door handle.

"Yo!" the commander shouted. "Go back!"

"No!" Holmes yelled in return. *"Take cover!"* He wrapped both hands tightly around the vertical handle grip. "If I blow up, find Oliver Paul!" He braced himself and yanked the door open, eyes closed, waiting for the blast that would end his misery. Maybe hoping for it.

Nothing.

Holmes opened his eyes. The space was bare except for a metal worktable. On top sat a large Bluetooth speaker and an antique clock with a gold-plated second hand. The time read 12:30.

The cops were crowding in behind him now, laser sight beams tracing the outlines of the tiny room. The speaker crackled to life one more time.

"Less than twelve hours left, Sherlock. Remember, accidents happen. No mother is safe today. Not even yours."

CHAPTER 86

"AUGUSTE! MARGARET!"

Poe kept Marple pressed behind him and peeked out around the edge of the cargo container. He saw Holmes bolting down the metal staircase two steps at a time, his hands barely touching the railing. The SWAT team was still circulating upstairs on the catwalk. Quinn held up his walkie. "What's going on up there?"

"All clear," came the reply. "Nobody home."

Poe saw Holmes come around the side of the cargo container, eyes wide, forehead glistening with sweat. "I know who the next victim is!" Holmes whispered hoarsely. "We need to get to Delaware! *Now!*"

Marple grabbed his arm. "Your mother?"

Poe stared at Holmes for a second, then made an executive decision. "Follow me!" He led the way to the loading dock at the rear of the building, where one of the massive doors had been forced open. Poe and his partners were now blocked from the main group by the cargo container. "Keep going!" said Poe. "Trust me!"

It was a five-foot drop from the loading dock to the ground.

Poe jumped first. Marple next. Then Holmes. Poe led the way around the corner of the warehouse. For a second, he stopped and looked both ways. Then he stared into the middle distance.

There it was.

A concrete platform with an NYPD Bell 206 helicopter sitting on it.

No guards. No pilot.

Holmes was at his side, gripping his shoulder. "Can you fly it?" he asked.

"Absolutely," said Poe. In his head, he was a lot less confident. He hoped Bell hadn't updated the controls too radically. He hoped his muscle memory was intact. It had been fifteen years since his last sortie.

Poe shook off his nerves and sprinted toward the platform. He could hear Holmes and Marple right behind him. He vaulted onto the pad and climbed into the right forward seat. The chopper was out of the sight line of most of the assault force, but Poe knew that would only buy him a minute. Maybe less. He strapped in.

Holmes settled into the left-hand seat. Marple slipped onto a cramped bench behind her partners. Poe flicked the battery switch. The cockpit filled with a chorus of loud beeps. The controls lit up. "Full disclosure," Poe called out above the noise. "I'm skipping some steps here."

He rolled the throttle to idle and started the engine. The blades started to spin overhead, first in a lazy circle, then in an increasingly fast blur. He looked back toward the staging area. A few officers were paying attention. Some were pointing in his direction.

"Why aren't we moving?" shouted Holmes as the engine built to a loud whine.

"It's not an Uber," Poe shouted back. "It takes a minute."

His eyes darted across the gauges. He ran through a rudimentary preflight checklist. Generator switch. Hydraulics. Pedal resistance. Altimeter. Fuel level. Good enough. *Jesus.* He would have been kicked out of flight school for this.

He rolled the throttle to the fly position.

He turned to see a few cops moving in the direction of the pad. He saw arms waving and mouths moving, but he couldn't hear anything over the sound of the engine. He clamped his headphones on and signaled Holmes and Marple to do the same. He looked back to make sure the tail rotor was clear. He checked the gauges again. All green. Now or never. He pulled back gently on the stick and feathered the left pedal.

"Go, dammit!" shouted Holmes. "Paul could be there already!"

The aircraft jittered. A few of the cops were running toward the pad now, getting closer and closer. The chopper slid forward, then lifted free, hovering a few yards off the ground.

Poe looked back as the prop wash hit the cops. The next instant, he saw Duff rounding the corner of the warehouse, walkie in his hand, suit jacket flapping. Poe pulled up about fifty feet, turned in a tight circle, and made a pass directly over his head.

He watched as Duff spun and hurled his radio against the warehouse wall.

Poe heard Marple's voice crackle through his headset. "Too bad," she said. "We were getting along so well."

A few seconds later, Poe straightened out and headed south, skirting power lines and rooftops. It was all coming back to him now. He poured on more power and felt the machine come to life. Then he flicked off the transponder.

"How long?" asked Holmes, shifting anxiously in his seat.

Poe checked his gauges again. "About an hour," he said. "Or until somebody shoots us down."

CHAPTER 87

LESS THAN AN hour later, the chopper touched ground at the edge of a grassy dog run in Lums Pond State Park, a few hundred yards from the street Holmes had pointed out.

Holmes yanked off his headset. He was already out of his seat by the time Poe shut the power off. The blades were still whirring, whipping the leaves on the nearby trees. Holmes dialed his mother's number again, for probably the hundredth time since leaving Jersey. Still no answer.

As he put his phone in his pocket, he spotted a couple of curious dog walkers strolling toward them with their pooches. Poe pulled out his ID and waved them off.

"Police business!" he called out. "Stay clear." Overhead, the blades were winding to a stop.

"Let's go!" said Holmes. He took off at a run in the direction of his mother's house.

By the time his partners caught up with him, he was already crouched by the hedge at the end of the driveway. The RAV4 still sat in front of the closed garage, as it had yesterday.

"The car?" asked Poe. "Maybe he cut the brake lines?"

Holmes shook his head. "Too mafioso. Paul is more refined than that." Paul was a master craftsman of ingenious mishaps. In his hands, anything seemed possible.

Suddenly, Holmes spotted movement between the house and the garage. A hand reaching for a rake.

"There!" he whispered.

Holmes led the way down the length of hedge to the back of the garage. Poe and Marple stayed tight on his heels. Holmes saw a thin figure in a sun hat heading for the backyard garden.

"Thank God!" he muttered.

"That's her?" Poe asked. "The mysterious Nina?"

"*Stop!*" Holmes called out. "*Mother!*" He ran toward her.

Nina stopped with her hand on the gate latch. She turned and squinted in the afternoon sun. "Brendan?" She tipped her sun hat back from her face. "Back for more closure?" She pulled a spade from the pocket of her overalls.

Holmes stepped through the gate, scanning the yard. "Mother, you need to come with me."

Nina lowered herself carefully to her knees in front of a row of lavender mums. "Come where? Why?"

"You're not safe here."

Holmes turned as Poe and Marple walked up behind him.

"Mother, these are my partners," said Holmes. "Auguste Poe and Margaret Marple."

"Your son is right," said Marple. "We need to get you out of here."

Nina turned and squinted at both of them. She looked back at Holmes. "You mean the partners you're quitting on?" She showed no signs of moving.

"Please," said Marple. "We're here to protect you."

"Protect me? From who? From what?" Nina put down her spade and opened a burlap mulch bag. Suddenly, a thick ribbon shot out of the sack and whipped hard against her right forearm. *Snake!* Nina fell back in shock. "Christ Almighty!"

Holmes lunged and grabbed the coiling shape with one hand. When he jerked it away, he saw a small mark on his mother's pale skin. Nina sat on the ground, stunned and breathing fast, holding her right arm up in front of her face.

The snake was about three feet long, thick in the middle and crossed with brown bands. Holmes dangled it by the tail and let the head drop down onto the dirt. He pressed his foot on the neck as the coils undulated furiously. Poe grabbed the spade and raised it for the kill.

"Stop!" Marple grabbed Poe's hand. "It's only a water snake." She knelt next to Nina and touched her forearm gently. "Harmless," said Marple. "Nonvenomous. Just aggressive when cornered."

She reached into her bag and pulled out a small packet, ripped it open with her teeth, and rubbed an alcohol wipe over Nina's forearm.

"See? Didn't even break the skin."

"You're sure?" asked Holmes, still pressing the writhing snake beneath the sole of his shoe.

Marple nodded. "The only venomous snake in Delaware is the copperhead. It has hourglass bands." She nodded toward the squirming reptile. "Look for yourself. These bands are wide, then tapered. *Nerodia sipedon.* Trust me, I'm a gardener. I know my serpents—and this one is only a threat to frogs and fish."

Holmes lifted his toe and held the snake off the ground. He carried it across the garden and dropped it into the dirt, where it quickly slithered off. As he walked back, he saw Poe poking the burlap sack with the spade. He lifted it gingerly by the bottom and tipped it upside down. A thick pile of mulch fell out onto the ground—along with a white envelope with lettering on the front. Poe plucked it from the pile and handed it to Holmes.

The lettering on the envelope said: *To Sherlock.*

Holmes felt his mouth turn sour. He opened the flap and pulled out a single handwritten page. He scanned it quickly, his jaw tightening. Then he read it aloud.

> *Forgive the speckled band reference, Sherlock. Rudimentary, I know. A bit of misdirection. Your mother was never the target. She's suffered enough by having you as a son. No, I've decided that my next crime needs to be much, much closer to the heart. Who says you can't go home again?*

Poe and Marple helped Nina to her feet. She brushed the dirt off her clothes. "Who wrote that?" she asked. "What does it mean?"

Holmes looked at his partners. "We need to go now," he said. He stuffed the note into his pocket. "Oliver Paul is about to kill his own wife!"

CHAPTER 88

IT FELT LIKE threading a series of needles at 190 knots per hour.

Poe had been skirting bridges and treetops the whole way from Delaware, monitoring the chatter on the police frequencies the entire time. He knew they couldn't stay undetected much longer—not at this speed, and definitely not in New York airspace.

He eased back to 130 knots as he flew up the center of the Hudson River, barely twenty feet above the choppy surface. He checked the fuel gauge. It was moving toward empty. Only a few minutes left.

"Hold on!" Poe called out through the intercom. He rose and banked hard over the rooftops of the Upper West Side.

"Land this thing, dammit!" shouted Holmes, tilted sideways in the cramped bubble of the cockpit.

"Working on it," said Poe. He wasn't about to crash land after all this effort. Not in uptown Manhattan. There! He spotted the green spread of Central Park below and headed for the North Meadow, touching down in a grassy corner about two blocks south of Harlem. Joggers and families paused to gawk as the skids hit the ground. A few people whipped out their cell phones.

"So much for stealth mode," said Marple, unclipping her harness. Holmes was already on the ground and racing toward the street. Poe and Marple reached the curb just as he flagged a boxy yellow cab to a stop.

"Marcus Garvey Park!" shouted Holmes, sliding into the back seat. Poe squeezed in with Marple and pulled the door shut.

Four minutes later, they were standing at the entrance of Oliver Paul's town house.

"We should call Duff," said Marple, "get some backup."

"No!" said Holmes. "Cops would spook him. We need to see this through."

"Brendan's right," said Poe. "This is on us now. *Our* collar. I didn't steal a two-million-dollar helicopter for nothing."

Holmes tested the door handle. It turned easily. Unlocked. Same with the inside door. The staircase was dark, but there was light coming from a sconce on the landing above. Poe drew his gun. So did Holmes. Marple crouched between them as they moved slowly up the stairs. One flight. A turn. Then another few steps to Paul's apartment. Holmes opened the unlocked door.

The living room was dark, but Holmes reached for a wall switch and clicked it on. A ceiling fixture lit up. The room was empty.

There was a glow coming from a room at the end of the hallway, right past the kitchen.

"*Sherlock! Is that you?*" The watchmaker's rasp.

Poe pressed against one wall, with Marple right behind him. Holmes took the opposite side. They inched toward the doorway, pistols raised.

"Don't be afraid. The hallway's clean," Paul called out. "No wildlife, I promise."

Five feet. Then three. Then two...

Poe looked at Holmes. Holmes nodded. They burst through the doorway together, pistols up—and froze.

Poe's breath stuck in his throat.

Oliver Paul was standing in the center of the room, with a gun to Helene Grey's head.

CHAPTER 89

"HELENE!" POE GASPED.

Grey was dressed in black jeans and a sweatshirt. Her hair was rumpled and her face was pale. A fat strip of silver duct tape covered her mouth.

"Surprised, Mr. Poe?" said Paul. "You probably thought she was gone forever. But I know my way around small towns. There's hardly one I haven't visited. It wasn't that hard to track her down once I put my mind to it." He lowered his voice to a hoarse whisper. "Or maybe I just cared a little bit more than you do."

Grey flinched and twisted, but her hands were obviously tied behind her back. She stared directly at Poe. Her eyes were burning fiercely and her nostrils flared with each breath.

Poe felt his body vibrating with fear and anger. He took a quick step forward but stopped when Paul pressed the gun tighter against Helene's temple.

"Helene, are you hurt?" asked Holmes.

Grey gave a tight shake of her head.

"Of course not," said Paul. "Not yet. I've been waiting for all of you."

Poe had his pistol aimed directly at Paul's mouth. One clean shot through the brain stem. That's all it would take. But he couldn't chance it. Not with Paul's finger on the trigger. Not with Helene so close. Out of the corner of his eye, he saw Holmes shift right, looking for a better angle. Paul noticed it too.

"Look at the two of you," he said with mock approval, "working as a team." He cocked his head toward Holmes. With his one unfocused eye, it was hard to get a bead on exactly where he was looking. "But not for long—right, Sherlock?" Then he turned back toward Marple. "How about you, Miss Marple? No gun today? All out of pepper spray?"

"What's this about, Oliver?" asked Holmes. "What do you want with her? She doesn't fit your profile. She's not a mother."

"No," said Paul, "but close enough." He reached over with his free hand and stroked Grey's belly. "Mother to be. A variation on my theme." Grey tried to twist away. Paul yanked her back.

"Goddamnit!" Poe shouted. "Don't touch her!" He grimaced and tightened his grip on his pistol.

Paul ignored him. "I haven't figured out the right accident yet. Or the right venue. It has to be perfect for Helene. Someplace special." He flicked his wrist to look at his watch. "But no worries. I have a few hours left."

"And you think we're going to just let that happen?" said Holmes. "Let you walk out of this room with her?"

"Actually, he does." A woman's voice. "He's a bit mad that way."

CHAPTER 90

MARPLE FLINCHED AS she felt the cold metal against her neck.

"Perfect, my dear," said Paul. "Like clockwork."

Glancing down, Marple saw the barrel flick toward Holmes and Poe. "Guns down, please." The woman's voice was in her ear. British accent.

Across the room, Paul had a sick, satisfied smile on his face. "Miss Marple. Mr. Poe. I don't believe you've met my wife, Irene."

Marple felt warm breath on her neck. "I said, *guns down!*" Marple watched as Poe and Holmes laid their pistols carefully on the floor. "Kick them away!" Irene ordered. They did.

"Now," she said, "you will both stand aside so that Oliver and Helene can leave without interference. Otherwise, Miss Marple will be as dead as her London girlfriend." Marple felt a hand tighten around her upper arm. "Sorry about Rebecca Tran, Margaret. She was getting too close."

The voice. The accent. The Yorkshire dialect. Marple recognized it now. She'd listened to the same voice last night—for hours.

"I'm sorry too, Agnes," she said.

Holmes glanced at Marple. "What's going on?"

"This is not Irene Paul," said Marple. "Her name is Agnes Matts. She's behind all the kidnappings, and at least one murder. She believes in making the world safe for white people, and to hell with everybody else."

"Oliver has his passions," said Matts. "I have mine. We're lucky we found each other."

Something else clicked for Marple. "Right. Because you needed someone who could decipher a security band for you. And make exact replicas."

"Oliver is very good with small objects," said Matts.

Marple looked at Holmes. "That's why he was at St. Michael's. For a test."

Paul grinned. "See that, Sherlock? Another mystery solved without your help. Maybe you were right. Maybe you never had the magic. Maybe all you inherited was a dog-eared letter."

Holmes was shaken. Confused. Marple could see it. His face paled. He glanced past Matts into the hallway. "Your daughters! Brenda! Lily! Where are they?"

"Sold," said Paul curtly.

For a second Marple thought Paul was making a cruel joke. But then she realized that he was dead serious.

"We were just holding them temporarily," said Paul. "They're both in new homes now. Superior homes. With excellent values."

"You can't put a price on family," said Matts. "And I was never cut out for motherhood." She pulled Marple back against the wall, clearing a path to the doorway.

"Time to go, Helene," said Paul. He jerked her by the arm and pulled her toward the door, pistol firmly against her head. He glanced at Matts. "Where's the car?"

Matts slipped a key fob into Paul's pocket. "Two spaces to the right of the door."

"Hold on," said Paul. He paused for a moment and placed two fingers at the edge of the tape across Grey's mouth. "We need to be presentable for the drive." He ripped off the tape. Grey flinched in pain. The tape left an angry red stripe. Marple could see Poe's body tensing, ready to lunge.

Grey gave a small shake of her head. "No," she said softly. "Don't."

"Listen to your girlfriend," said Paul, moving toward the door. "Sorry. *Ex*-girlfriend."

Paul backed out of the room using Helene's body as a shield. Once they were through the doorway, he jerked her around and hustled her ahead of him. Marple listened to the sound of their footsteps receding down the staircase.

Matts glared at Holmes and Poe. "Step back against the wall." She leaned in, her lips brushing Marple's ear. "You know, I wish I could have more respect for you, Margaret. But you can't even keep your own firm pure."

She pulled Marple around to face Holmes squarely. "If you want, we can eliminate your half-blood partner Holmes right now." She flicked her pistol. "Say the word. One bullet and it's over. He said he's done with you anyway. Why not be done with him?"

Marple could feel her whole body trembling. She closed her eyes, took a deep breath, and held it for a moment. Then she let out a piercing cry and drove her elbow straight back into flesh and bone. The pistol fired, punching a hole in the floor. Marple whipped around and knocked the gun free. She grabbed Matts by the wrist and twisted. Something snapped. Matts screamed and dropped to the floor. Marple dropped right on top of her, knee on her spine. She grabbed the gun and jammed the barrel against the base of Agnes's skull. It all happened in less than five seconds.

Holmes and Poe jumped to retrieve their guns.

"I've got her," Marple shouted. "Go!"

CHAPTER 91

POE GOT TO the top of the staircase first. His heart was pounding and his throat was tight. He pointed his pistol through a gap in the banister and looked down toward the tile floor in the entryway. No movement. He started down the staircase, hugging the railing. Holmes followed, his back pressed against the opposite wall.

There was no sound from below. No footsteps. No breathing.

Then, a heavy thud.

Poe raced the rest of the way down and took the last four steps in a single leap. At the bottom of the staircase, he stopped cold.

On the right side of the foyer, a figure lay crumpled on the floor.

"Helene!"

Poe holstered his gun and dropped to his knees. He rolled Grey over gently by the shoulders. Her hands were still tied behind her back. She looked stunned and groggy. "Helene! What happened?"

"I think he got me in the head with his pistol butt," said Grey. She blinked and shook her head. "I'm okay. Just a little blurry."

Poe looked up. Holmes flipped him a penknife. Poe sliced through the ties around Grey's wrists and ran his hand gently over her scalp. When he looked back, Holmes was moving toward a half-open service hatch behind the stairs. Barely large enough for a child. Or a very small man.

"He must've taken off through there," said Grey.

Poe turned toward the front of the foyer. He heard a flurry of footsteps outside — then a loud bang.

The front door flew open.

"Police! Nobody move!"

Poe pulled Grey tight against him. He saw Graham Duff step through the entryway, gun raised, with a half dozen heavily armed cops behind him. Duff looked over. His eyebrows shot up.

"Grey?"

"She's hurt!" shouted Poe. "Call an ambulance!"

"I'm fine, Captain," Grey mumbled. "Only a bump."

"Duff!" shouted Holmes. "Oliver Paul just went out through the back! Set a perimeter! *Now!*"

Duff holstered his pistol under his suit jacket. "Oliver Paul? You mean your theoretical cold-case serial killer?"

"It's not a theory, Duff!" shouted Holmes. "We have proof."

"Don't bother. You'll never find him." The voice came from the staircase. Poe looked up. It was Agnes Matts. Marple was walking her down, gun in her back. "Oliver can smell police," said Matts. She looked directly at Duff. "He obviously smelled *you.*"

Duff stared at Marple. "We got your 911. Who the hell is this?"

"She's the boss, Captain," said Marple. "I told you a woman was behind it. St. Michael's, the school bus, Silvercup, London. Everything. This is Agnes Matts, alias Irene Paul. She's wanted in the UK on suspicion of kidnapping, conspiracy, and murder."

"I want a solicitor," said Matts calmly. "And a representative from the British embassy."

"Right," said Duff. "Let's call the king while we're at it." He turned to the cops in the foyer and barked off a series of orders. "Get Grey to a hospital, whether she wants it or not. Escort her majesty here downtown for questioning. Start a door-to-door for Oliver Paul. And as for *you* three..." He looked pointedly from Holmes to Marple to Poe and twirled his fingers in the air like a propeller. "Where's my goddamn bird?"

CHAPTER 92

IN SPITE OF her protests, paramedics wheeled Helene Grey into the ER at St. Michael's. There were closer hospitals, but Poe had insisted on taking Grey to a place he knew—even if it was a place he'd almost been tossed out of.

He walked alongside the rolling gurney, squeezing Grey's hand. "How are you feeling?" he asked over and over. "Are you in pain? Does anything hurt?"

Grey turned her head toward him. "You look worse than I do," she said.

He knew it was true, and it was all from worrying about her. If Oliver Paul hadn't sensed the police outside his town house and taken off, Helene could be dead by now.

As soon as Grey was lifted from the gurney onto the ER bed, three sturdy nurses crowded Poe to the side. A few seconds later, a doctor in scrubs entered the cramped room and whipped the curtain shut behind him.

"What have we got?" he asked curtly.

One of the paramedics recited the bullet points. "Pregnant patient, thirty-eight. Blunt force contusion to the left parietal.

Probable pistol butt. Mild ecchymosis and second-degree abrasion. No loss of consciousness. Pulse 80 and steady. BP 130 over 80."

"What's your name?" asked the doctor. He walked to the head of the bed as the paramedics backed out with their gurney.

"Helene. Helene Grey."

"Helene, I'm Dr. Farnham. I'm going to check a few things, okay?"

"She's having twins!" said Poe, his voice cracking.

Farnham leaned over and looked into Helene's pupils with a penlight. "Is that true, Helene?"

Grey nodded. "Yes, it is."

"How far along?"

"Thirteen weeks."

He glanced over at Poe. "Is this your husband?"

Grey rolled her head from side to side. "Absolutely not."

"I'm the father," said Poe.

"Hold still, please," said Farnham.

The curtains parted again. Poe looked up. It took a second for the face to register. "Dr. Revell Schulte!"

"Mr. Poe." Dr. Schulte stepped up next to Farnham, almost bumping him aside. "Is she stable?"

Poe could see that Farnham was intimidated. The young doctor cleared his throat and tugged on the stethoscope around his neck. "Stable and responsive. But we need a CT, and I think we—"

"Unit 4," said Schulte. "*Now.*"

The young doctor blinked, then nodded. He stepped back and barked at the nurses. "You heard her."

Schulte leaned in. "Helene, I'm Dr. Revell Schulte, remember? I'm chief of maternity. We met the night of the kidnappings. You're with me now."

In seconds, two nurses started pushing the bed out of the ER bay and down the hall, with Dr. Schulte leading the way. Poe followed alongside as the wheels hummed across the smooth linoleum floor. They passed through a set of metal hospital doors, then another.

Poe was getting frantic. Unit 4? What the hell was that? Operating room? Intensive care? Had Schulte noticed something the others had missed?

At the end of the next corridor, Schulte held up a key card. Another door opened, this one sliding cleanly into the wall. Schulte turned to the nurses and put her hands on the back of the bed. "I've got her." She wheeled Grey through the entrance herself. The door glided shut behind them with a cushioned whoosh.

And suddenly everything was quiet.

Poe looked around. They were in a high-ceilinged reception area with elegant potted palms and expensive art on the walls. There was no frantic activity here. No raised voices. Just soft light and gentle beeps in the background. The air was scented with sandalwood. It was as if they had left the ER and rolled into the lobby of a Four Seasons Hotel.

A nurse appeared out of nowhere. She looked like a spa attendant. "Welcome to Unit 4, Helene," she said. "We're going to take very good care of you."

"What's happening?" asked Grey. "Did I die and go to heaven?"

"What is this?" asked Poe. "Where are we?"

"It's our special-patient wing," said Schulte. "Every hospital has one." She dipped her voice to a whisper. "Ours is just a little *more* special."

CHAPTER 93

POE WATCHED IN amazement as Unit 4 spun into motion, like an impeccably rehearsed ballet. Grey was wheeled into a spacious wood-paneled suite, changed into a soft cotton gown, then transferred gently onto an oversized hospital bed.

Then, so she wouldn't need to be wheeled off again for tests, advanced diagnostic equipment started coming to her. First, a team with a portable CT scanner. Next, a technician with a small x-ray machine.

Within minutes, Grey was examined by the head of the emergency department, then by the chief of neurology. Her scalp bruise was cleaned and bandaged by an attentive resident. By the time Dr. Schulte herself wheeled in a sleek white sonogram cart, she already had all the other results.

"The images of your head look good, Helene," she said. "No fractures. No swelling. No internal bleeding. You're lucky you have such thick hair. Good cushion."

"Thick hair or thick head?" asked Grey with a wan smile.

Schulte tapped a few keys on the console. "Now let's check on those babies." Schulte slid Grey's gown up and applied warm gel to her belly, then picked up the wand and moved it slowly across her abdomen. Poe leaned in close to the monitor as the images came into focus.

"There they are," said Schulte, pointing to the two tiny bean shapes on the screen. "Safe and sound." She tapped another key. The room filled with the sound of a tiny heartbeat—then another.

Grey looked over at Poe and patted his hand. "See? I told you I was fine."

Poe dropped his head and let out a loud exhale. It felt like he'd been holding his breath for an hour. "Thank God."

Schulte wiped the gel from Grey's abdomen with a warm towel, then lowered her gown and covered her with a soft blanket. "You're going to be fine, Helene. Just get some rest, okay?"

Grey nodded and settled back on the pillow. She looked relieved but exhausted.

"Be right back," said Poe, squeezing her hand. He followed Dr. Schulte out of the suite and back into the serene reception area. "I want to thank you," he said, catching up to her. "For the celebrity treatment, I mean."

"Happy to do it," said Schulte. "I'm glad Helene's okay." She stopped and turned to face him. "But actually, Mr. Poe, this is partly to thank *you*. You and your partners. For everything you've done."

Poe's throat tightened. He stared at the floor. For a second, he flashed to the image of that tiny corpse in the camera box in that cold, deserted building. "We didn't get them all back, you know," he said. "We lost one."

"I know. I heard," said Schulte. "And that's a tragedy. For you. For us. For the parents. But you rescued the other five. And five more from the school bus. And the three from the TV studio. That's thirteen lives." Schulte gave Poe's shoulder a gentle squeeze. "That's a very good outcome."

Dr. Schulte turned and waved her key card. The door parted, then closed behind her. Poe walked back into Grey's suite. Her eyes were closed. Her chest rose and fell in a gentle rhythm. Poe stood by the bed for a minute, just staring at her face.

He pulled his gun out of its holster and ejected the clip. He opened the top drawer in the bedside stand and put the weapon and ammo inside. Then he gently lowered the rail on the bed and kicked off his shoes. He slid one knee onto the mattress, then the other, trying not to jostle Grey too much as he nestled in beside her. He rested his cheek on the edge of her pillow and placed one hand on her arm.

His body was exhausted, but his brain was spinning. He had so many questions to ask her. About where she'd disappeared to. And if she planned to disappear again. But none of that now. Helene's eyelids fluttered and her eyes opened for a couple of seconds.

"Sorry," Poe whispered. "Is there room for two?"

Grey reached for his hand. She pulled it down until it rested on the blanket over her belly. Then she closed her eyes again.

"Four," she said softly. "Did you forget how to count?"

CHAPTER 94

ELEVEN P.M. MARPLE put down her phone after checking in with Poe one last time. The hospital was keeping Helene Grey overnight, and Poe was staying with her. As it should be.

"Auguste," said Marple before she hung up, "don't let that woman go again. Not tonight. Not *ever.*"

Marple was exhausted, emotionally drained. Earlier, she'd made some other calls. She'd woken Constable Ben Dodgett in the middle of the night, London time, to tell him that Agnes Matts was in custody. Then came the emotional calls with the parents of the rescued children.

She'd tried to call Sterling and Christine Cade first. But they weren't answering, and she couldn't blame them. Their son's funeral was tomorrow. Though Marple would attend, it was possible they wouldn't talk to her then either. The firm had already received word through the Cades' attorney that they requested Holmes, Marple, and Poe donate their investigative fee to St. Michael's neonatal intensive care unit. Marple was happy to turn over every penny.

As Marple sat on the edge of her bed, Annabel purred in her

lap. At the moment, they were the only two beings in the building. Virginia had left with Baskerville hours ago, and Holmes was apparently still out searching for Oliver Paul. Waste of time, in Marple's opinion.

In the wake of his near miss, she had no doubt that Paul had gone to ground, or maybe even scooted out of the country, using his fake wife's contacts. Paul had clearly been dancing around the authorities with no problem for twenty-three years, Marple realized. Even with the evidence from his shop, he might *never* be found.

She briefly considered waking Dodgett again to rehash the status of his investigation, in the unlikely event he'd forgotten to share an important development. The four London babies were still nowhere to be found, and it was getting harder and harder to keep the kidnapping quiet. Marple checked the clock. It was now 4 a.m. in London. *No. Let the constable sleep.*

Annabel's ears perked up, and she jumped to the floor, striking an attentive pose. *A mouse?* Then Marple heard it too.

A scratching noise. But not from an animal. Like metal on glass.

It was coming from downstairs.

Marple reached into her drawer and pulled out her pistol. She wasn't about to be caught without a sidearm twice in the same day. She moved out of her bedroom, through her living room, and out the front door of her apartment.

She was in her bare feet, stalking quietly along the hardwood floor. At the edge of the balcony, she looked down. Nothing moved in the kitchen below, or in the office space beyond. She quickly padded down the staircase to the first floor.

She heard it again.

The sound was coming from outside the front door.

Marple clicked the safety off her pistol and went into a low crouch, moving through their open office space, then toward the entryway.

The sound was like nails on a chalkboard. Small, unsettling scrapes. Was somebody picking the lock? Trying to disarm the security system? Duff had offered to post a squad car across the street for the night, just to be safe. Now Marple wished she hadn't turned him down.

As she reached the door, she peeked up at the security screen and checked the image from the entry camera. There *was* somebody outside! She looked closer, then exhaled slowly and lowered her pistol. She could only see the side of the figure's head, but that was enough.

Brendan.

Marple opened the door. Holmes had one hand on the frosted glass panel to the side. He seemed to be working intently at something.

"Hello, Margaret," he said without looking up.

"What are you doing?" asked Marple. She looked closer. Holmes was holding a single-edged razor blade between the thumb and two fingers of his right hand, using it to scratch his name off the company decal. As Marple watched, flakes of gilt lettering fluttered to the ground, until HOLMES was totally obliterated.

All that remained was MARPLE & POE.

"I told you I was serious," Holmes said, stepping back to admire his minor work of vandalism.

Marple swallowed hard. In spite of everything Holmes had said since returning from rehab, she hadn't believed this day would really come. She slid her gun into her side pocket. "Are you finished?" she asked.

"I am," he said.

"Good," said Marple. "Because there's something I need you to know."

"What's that?" he asked.

"It's a company personnel matter," she said. "I've always had a firm policy against relationships between coworkers."

Holmes looked puzzled. Marple stepped out onto the stone front step. Holmes lowered the hand holding the razor blade and let it fall to the ground with a light click. Marple moved in close. Very close. She slipped her arms around his neck and stood on her bare tiptoes to bring her face close to his.

"I thought you'd *never* quit," she said.

Then she tugged his head down, parted her lips, and kissed him.

Marple felt Holmes tense, then tremble. Then, slowly, he began to kiss her back. His arms went around her, pulling her tight against him, so tight that the breath went out of her. She could feel his heart pounding through his shirt. Then he pulled back.

"Margaret, what...?"

She put two fingers against his lips. "Stop. No questions. Not everything is a mystery, Brendan. Sometimes the truth is staring you right in the face."

Holmes exhaled slowly and brushed her hair back from her forehead. "I've loved you since the day we met, Margaret," he said.

Marple smiled. "See how simple that was?" She wrapped her hands around her ex-partner's back and pressed her cheek against his chest. "I love you too."

She couldn't believe it had taken her so long to realize it.

CHAPTER 95

"WE COMMEND THIS child into the hands of God. Now let us take him to his place of rest."

The bishop's final commendation rang out as sunlight speared through the stained glass of St. Patrick's Cathedral. Marple stood next to Holmes in a back pew, her shoulder brushing his.

Across the aisle, Poe stood close to Helene Grey, a small mourning veil hiding her injuries. Virginia was in the pew just behind them, her streaked hair covered by a sheer black scarf.

Near the main altar, the exit procession was forming. From the loft above, a children's choir sang "Kyrie Eleison," their piercing voices resounding through the massive marble nave.

The service had been magnificent and heartbreaking—the Mass of the Angels, a Catholic ritual reserved only for the young and innocent. Now the procession was moving slowly down the center aisle, led by the bishop and a contingent of priests and deacons. The coffin was tiny and gleaming white, draped with delicate flowers.

Marple looked directly at Sterling Cade and his wife, Christine, walking a few paces behind their lost child. They stared straight ahead. Marple could see Christine's mascara streaking under her sheer black veil.

After the coffin passed, the congregants stepped out of the pews and followed the procession onto the steps.

The morning air was crisp and the sky was bright blue. The pallbearers carried baby Edwin Cade carefully down steps lined with New York City police officers. Marple spotted Officer Amy Polacco at the far end of the row, standing at attention in her dress blues, her white-gloved hand rigid in salute.

Captain Graham Duff waited alongside the police escort at the bottom of the steps. Dr. Revell Schulte was there too, with a team of nurses from St. Michael's. Across the street, TV crews aimed cameras from a respectful distance.

As the pallbearers slid the tiny coffin into the white Mercedes hearse, Holmes leaned in toward Marple's ear. "This is why," he whispered.

"Why *what*?" Marple whispered back.

"Why I can't do this anymore."

Marple nodded. "I understand." At least she tried to. But as she heard the sharp echo of the hearse doors closing, *she* felt more determined than ever. She could not — *would* not — let this death defeat her.

She felt a vibration from the phone in her bag. It was Dodgett, calling from London. Marple thought about letting it go to message, but then she eased her way past the police honor guard and stepped behind a column next to one of the cathedral's massive side doors.

"Hello? Ben?"

"Margaret, I have fantastic news."

Marple closed her eyes and exhaled slowly. "You found them."

"We did indeed. All four babies. They were in a medical supply warehouse in Southampton, drugged and ready for transport, just like the ones on your side. They're all fine, heading home today."

"I'm *so* glad," said Marple. "Glad for you. Glad for the parents." She took a small pause and cleared her throat. "Glad for Rebecca."

"Same here," said Dodgett softly. "Her service is this afternoon."

"I'm sorry I'm not there," said Marple.

"I am too."

An awkward pause.

Marple could sense that Dodgett had more to say but didn't know quite how to say it. She glanced over at Holmes, standing alone at the top of the steps.

"I have to go," said Marple. "Take care, Constable."

"Right," said Dodgett. "Be well, Miss Marple."

Marple put her phone away and glanced up at the spires rising twenty-four stories into the sky. Four more children saved. That was something. She touched the thick wall of the cathedral and whispered her final prayer of the day.

A prayer of thanks.

CHAPTER 96

TWELVE HOURS LATER.

For Brendan Holmes, like for most people in the city, the morning had been incredibly poignant and sad. It was amazing how far his emotions had turned in the course of a single day. Because, at this particular moment, sadness was the last thing on his mind.

In fact, he had never been happier.

Right now Holmes was in a place he had only dreamed of being—in a bed, under flower-patterned sheets, with his arms around Margaret Marple. Margaret looked happy too—a smile on her lips, a flush across her cheeks. Exhausted but in a very good way.

"Was that all right?" Holmes asked. After all the years of anticipation and longing, he was concerned that he'd been too anxious, too selfish, too quick.

Marple pulled his head down and kissed him softly. "It was excellent, Mr. Holmes," she said, still catching her breath. "You're exactly what this apartment has been missing."

She rolled over to face him. He curled himself around her,

absorbing the warmth of her body, the scent of her perfume, her hair, her skin.

It had been overwhelming at first—the sheer sensory impact of being so close to her. Making love with her. But his senses adapted, then quieted. Now he felt like he was floating on a wave of gentle energy. It was a new feeling for him. Better than drugs. And he wanted desperately to make it last. He closed his eyes and...

BOOM!

A deafening explosion rocked the walls.

Holmes hit the floor in his pajama bottoms. He was covered in plaster dust and his ears were ringing. Smoke filled the room. Flower vases lay shattered by the bed. The fire alarm was screeching.

He shouted over the din of the alarm. *"Margaret!"*

She was on her knees a few yards away, covering herself with a robe. *"What happened?"* she shouted back.

"Bomb!" No doubt in his mind. He smelled calcium hypochlorite, nitrobenzene, sulfur... *"Goddamnit!"* The smoke was getting thicker.

Holmes stood up and pulled Marple to her feet, then out of the bedroom and through the living room. He placed his palm against the apartment door, feeling for heat. The frame was cracked and tilted. He braced one foot against the molding and pulled hard on the knob. The door flew open. More smoke poured in.

Outside the apartment, the balcony was tipped at an angle. Emergency strobes blasted through the haze. Two doors down, Poe burst out into the hallway in briefs and a T-shirt, a rifle at his hip. Helene was right behind him, wrapped in a blanket.

"Can you see anybody?" Poe shouted, pointing his gun over the railing.

"Cut the alarm!" Holmes shouted back.

Poe ran to the far end of the balcony and opened a metal panel. A second later, the screeching stopped. Marple ran to wrap her arms around Helene.

Holmes looked down. The explosion had leveled the entire first floor with surgical precision. Windows were shattered, woodwork splintered. The bottom of the staircase had been blasted off its supports. Flames licked at laptops and file cabinets. The office was destroyed.

The work of a master technician.

Behind him, he heard a bright ding, then another. He thought his eardrums were still ringing.

No. The sound was coming from Marple's living room.

His cell phone.

Holmes lurched back through the doorway and saw the screen glowing on the floor. He reached down through the smoke and picked up the phone. Coughing, he stumbled back out onto the balcony. Poe was leading Margaret and Helene down the broken staircase with his rifle in one hand and a fire extinguisher in the other.

Holmes blinked the sting out of his eyes and looked down at his phone. Texts were scrolling onto his screen—one sentence at a time, like a bizarre digital poem.

THE PAST IS GONE, YOURS AND MINE.

NOW THERE'S NOTHING BUT THE FUTURE.

AND EVENTUALLY, I'LL BE THE CAUSE OF YOUR DEATH.

I'M COUNTING THE DAYS, SHERLOCK.

THINK OF ME AS YOUR VERY OWN PROFESSOR MORIARTY.

ABOUT THE AUTHORS

JAMES PATTERSON is the most popular storyteller of our time. He is the creator of unforgettable characters and series, including Alex Cross, the Women's Murder Club, Jane Smith, and Maximum Ride, and of breathtaking true stories about the Kennedys, John Lennon, and Tiger Woods, as well as our military heroes, police officers, and ER nurses. Patterson has coauthored #1 bestselling novels with Bill Clinton and Dolly Parton, and collaborated most recently with Michael Crichton on the blockbuster *Eruption*. He has told the story of his own life in *James Patterson by James Patterson* and received an Edgar Award, ten Emmy Awards, the Literarian Award from the National Book Foundation, and the National Humanities Medal.

BRIAN SITTS is an award-winning advertising creative director and television writer. He has collaborated with James Patterson on books for adults and children. He and his wife, Jody, live in Peekskill, New York.

For a sneak peek at an intriguing New York City detective case, turn the page.

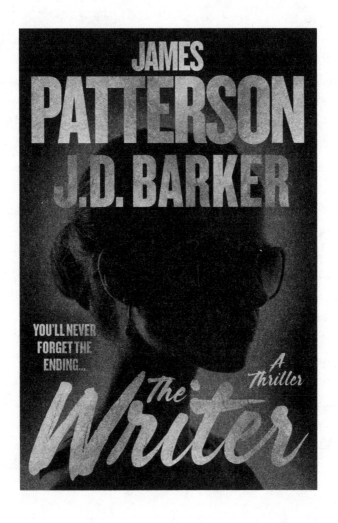

STUDYING THE SMALL observation monitor two doors down from the precinct interview room, assistant district attorney Carmen Saffi taps the end of her pen against her lips. Declan, next to her, nurses a cup of tar-black coffee from the break room. On the screen, Denise Morrow is sitting at the aluminum table, her hands in her lap; her attorney is in the chair beside her. He keeps looking up at the camera. When he speaks to her, he does so in whispers.

"Geller Hoffman just happened to show up?" ADA Saffi asks Declan.

Although it's approaching midnight, Saffi looks as sharp as she does in the courtroom—gray pantsuit, hair and makeup perfect. She's the same as Cordova, married to the job. It's like the two of them sleep standing up in their Sunday best, ready to roll at a moment's notice. Like they wait for it. Unlike Declan, who knows he still stinks of subway and despair. "The Morrows' alarm was tripped. He said the monitoring company called him," he tells her.

"Seems odd to have a defense attorney on the call list, doesn't it?"

"Said he's a family friend."

"What do you make of their body language?" she asks. "Something seem off to you?"

Declan has picked up on that too.

Denise Morrow is an attractive woman—a bit on the odd side, but attractive. She has that mousy thing going on. With the black-rimmed glasses and her hair swept up, she makes you think of a sexy librarian or a teacher from some '90s rock video. It's like she knows she's attractive and purposely tries to dial it back. Even now, sitting in an interrogation room wearing borrowed scrubs, she's striking. Every guy who passed her in the precinct hallway

2

turned to get a second look. Declan flashes back to Geller walking in on Denise Morrow naked when she was being processed—*he didn't give her a second look. He didn't give her a first look. He went out of his way not to,* Declan thinks. *Not out of respect—that squirrelly fucker doesn't know from respect. It was something else.* Declan got the feeling that seeing Denise Morrow naked was nothing new to Geller. He got the feeling that Geller and Morrow were intimate and going out of their way to conceal it. Her husband was just found dead. *She's traumatized,* Geller said, yet he didn't do a damn thing to comfort her. For her part, Morrow gave no indication she needed or wanted comforting. None of this was typical. While it might mean nothing, it also might mean something.

Cordova knocks twice on the door frame and steps into the small room; he's clutching a computer printout. "We've got life insurance, but not exactly what I was expecting."

ADA Saffi frowns. "What does it say?"

"Joint policy. They took it out three years ago. Pays out five million for natural death, eight million for accidental."

Declan whistles. "There's your motive."

"I agree. It would have been a fantastic motive if Denise Morrow hadn't canceled the payouts on David six weeks ago. Would have been one hell of a motive."

"What?" Declan snatches the paper from him and scans the text. "Says here she terminated all coverage related to David but left hers."

"That's what I just said."

Saffi's frown deepens. "So she dies in a home invasion, he gets eight million, but he dies, she gets zero?"

Cordova nods.

"And she changed that six weeks back?"

"When she paid the premiums for the year."

"You saw that apartment," Declan says. "She doesn't need the insurance money. This woman is smart. She knows we'd see insurance as motive, so she took it off the board. Don't forget, she writes about this sort of thing for a living."

"Oh, I didn't forget." Cordova smirks. "I've been looking at that too. There's something I want you to watch, an interview she did for her second book, *A Mother's Burden*. The book's about Michelle Bacot. Remember that case?"

Saffi does. "Bacot killed her husband when she learned he was molesting their thirteen-year-old daughter. Made it look like an accident—pulled the ladder out from under him when he was cleaning gutters around the house. Jersey City, right?"

Cordova nods. "I found this interview on YouTube. I'm skipping the preamble nonsense and starting at the eight-minute mark." Holding his phone between them, he plays the video.

> *"The jury didn't take any pity on her, though, right? I mean, Bacot is serving twelve years. Hardly the perfect crime," the interviewer says.*
>
> *The camera flashes to Denise Morrow. She looks a little younger, and her hair is longer, but she's otherwise the same. "She didn't get caught; she turned herself in. It wasn't the police that got her, it was the guilt. She had saved her daughter, but she couldn't live with what she'd done. Even with the understanding her daughter would be raised by someone other than her if she surrendered, the guilt ate her up until it outweighed everything else."*
>
> *"So you take guilt out of the equation, and Bacot is a free woman today."*
>
> *"Exactly."*
>
> *"The perfect crime," says the interviewer.*
>
> *"There were no witnesses. People fall from ladders all the time."*

"Not once did she report her husband's activity to the police. That's why the jury convicted. Maybe if she'd filed a complaint, gone on the record, and proved the system failed her, the jury would have shown some leniency."

"If she had filed a report, created that paper trail, the police would have had reason to suspect her when her husband died. The fact that she didn't report the crime is the reason she would have gotten away with it," Denise says.

"If not for the guilt."

"If not for the guilt."

"Why do I get the feeling that if you were in Michelle Bacot's shoes, you'd be a free woman today?" the interviewer says.

"If I had been in Michelle Bacot's shoes, not only would I be free, my daughter would be sitting here next to me, not an ounce of guilt between us."

Cordova stops the video, and a heavy silence falls over the room. He slips his phone into the breast pocket of his jacket. "I checked with Murdock at CSU. They covered every inch of that apartment and found no sign of an intruder. The only prints on the main bedroom's terrace door belong to the Morrows. No unknowns in or out on security footage. Neighbors and doorman saw nothing. Break-in appears staged. Sometimes you gotta call it what it is."

Saffi's gaze goes back to the monitor as she takes this all in. Finally she says to Declan, "Remember how I told you to handle this with kid gloves?"

"Yeah."

"Be ready to take the gloves off."

DECLAN AND ADA Saffi go in; Cordova stays in the observation room. He's got a few more calls to make and doesn't want to crowd the room. Backed into a corner, Morrow is liable to clam up, and that won't do anyone any good.

Declan doesn't expect the truth—they never tell the truth—but he and Saffi know she'll feed them a story, and once they have her on record with a story, they can punch holes in it.

Declan closes the interview room's door and holds up his half-empty coffee cup. "Are either of you thirsty?"

Hoffman glares at him for several seconds, then turns to Saffi. "Do you have any idea how many civil rights your detective has violated in the past two hours? Before we leave here, I want to see him up on disciplinary or my first stop tomorrow morning will be a filing against this precinct!"

Hoffman has actually found time to change. He's in a fresh Armani suit, a pale blue shirt with a white collar, and a sleek dark tie perfectly knotted.

Saffi brings in several folders, including the one containing the insurance information. She drops them on the table and sits. "Calm down, Geller, your nostrils are flaring. It's not a good look for you."

Carmen Saffi is anything but a pushover.

Holding back the smirk that desperately wants to come out, Declan tells Hoffman, "I'm doing you a damn favor. I'm here because your client asked for me. I've been off the clock since six. Saffi or my LT want someone else on this, I got no problem going home and getting some sleep."

"Sit, Declan." Saffi waves at the empty chair beside her. "It's a little too late at night for a pissing match. Both of you need to put it to rest so we can get to the bottom of all this."

Geller's frowning. "My client didn't ask for you."

Declan takes out his phone and scrolls through his texts with Cordova until he finds the 911 call. He hasn't heard it yet but presses Play anyway. Denise Morrow's whispered voice fills the room:

"My...my husband...somebody stabbed him! God, he's... somebody stabbed him. I think they might still be here!"

"Ma'am, can you confirm your location? I have two eleven Central Park West."

"Yes."

"What apartment?"

"Tower number two."

"I've got officers en route. Is your husband responsive?"

"Responsive?"

"Awake? Breathing?"

"I think they're still here!"

"If you feel you're in danger, you should exit the apartment immediately and wait in the lobby or on the street for officers to arrive."

"No! I can't leave my husband."

"Is he responsive?"

"I have a gun. I can't leave him."

"Ma'am, if you're in danger, you need to get out."

Sudden intake of breath. "Detective Declan Shaw."

"Excuse me?"

"Declan Shaw! Detective Declan Shaw!"

Declan's not sure what to make of that. When he looks up from the phone, Denise Morrow is staring at him; the others are too. Before he can say anything, Morrow speaks in a low voice:

"I don't even remember making that call."

And this is where ADA Saffi shines—in the disarm. She reaches across the table and places her hand on Morrow's. "Of course not. Who could expect you to in a situation like that? I can't imagine what that must have been like. Let's just take this one step at a time, okay? We're right here with you. You found your husband when you came home?"

Denise Morrow nods.

"Where were you prior to that?"

"Tribeca. I was giving a talk at a bookstore."

"Which bookstore?"

"Mysterious Bookshop on Warren Street. If you call Otto, he can confirm."

"Otto?"

"He owns the store."

Hoffman says, "Otto says there were sixty people in attendance, not including employees. I confirmed with him about twenty minutes ago."

"You called him? This late?"

"With good reason."

Declan can tell Saffi doesn't like that. The last thing they need is Hoffman getting ahead of potential witnesses. Sixty percent of any good prosecution is controlling the narrative, and the other forty is dumb luck. She lets it go for now and asks Morrow, "What time did you leave for the bookstore?"

"Seven fifteen."

"Did you drive?"

"No, I took a cab."

"And your husband was..."

8

Morrow purses her lips. "David was in the kitchen making a sandwich when I left."

"Did you lock the door when you left?"

"Always."

"In a building like that?"

"Especially in a building like that. The Andersons in fourteen C were broken into last year. Two years before that, there was a home invasion in eight A. I love the Beresford, it's an incredible place to live, but it makes you a target. And I've had fans appear out of nowhere too. They just show up on my doorstep. So we always keep the door locked."

"Anyone recently just show up?"

Morrow considers this, then shakes her head. "The last one was about four months ago. A sweet senior lady. About six months before that, there was a young guy. They were harmless. I signed their books, let them take a few photos, and they left, so—"

Hoffman interrupts. "My client's talk was widely advertised. There's a good chance whoever broke in knew she'd be out and expected the apartment to be empty. David... David surprised them."

Saffi doesn't acknowledge that, most likely because she knows it's bullshit and doesn't want to go down that rabbit hole. She returns her attention to Morrow. "You caught a cab to the book-store at seven fifteen p.m. What time did you arrive there?"

"About twenty minutes to eight."

"Did you keep the receipt?"

"I don't keep paper. I used my credit card, though. Easy enough to confirm."

Hoffman raises a hand. "For the record, we're not authorizing you to check credit card records. You want that, you'll need a warrant."

Morrow frowns at him. "Geller, don't be difficult. I have nothing to hide. Let them check it if they want to."

"Yeah, Geller," Declan says. "Why make it hard for us? She has nothing to hide."

Saffi clears her throat, keeps her focus on Morrow. "What time did your talk begin?"

"Eight o'clock. I was up there for about thirty minutes, and I signed books and answered questions until nine. I didn't want to be out too late, so I left right after that."

"Another cab?"

She nods. "I was home in maybe fifteen or twenty minutes."

"Anyone see you?"

"Hank, our doorman. I went up and..." She goes quiet, closes her eyes, and draws in a deep breath. Nearly twenty seconds slip by before she speaks again. "Sorry...I just...until just now, I couldn't really recall this."

"It's okay, take your time," Saffi tells her. "Let it come back."

Morrow licks her lips and slowly continues. "When I went to unlock the door, my key didn't work right. It got stuck. Then I saw the scratch marks around the lock and realized something was wrong. I...I twisted my key a few times until it finally grabbed and I opened the door. Something felt...wrong. I don't know how to explain it. The air just felt heavy. I knew David was home, but the space felt unoccupied. That's crazy, right? It sounds crazy when I say it out loud. And listen, I don't go in for that supernatural nonsense. That's not what I'm saying. There was just something wrong—that's the only way to put it. David is...was...cautious, and he kept a gun in his nightstand and another near the front door, hidden in the bottom of a vase of silk flowers. I dumped the flowers from that vase and grabbed the gun the moment I came through the door. I didn't see David, not right away."

"We found blood on the door frame. Was that there when you went in?"

Morrow's gaze drops to the table. Her brow furrows slightly as she struggles to recall. "Not that I remember, but everything is very...hazy. At that point, I was so worried about David, I didn't notice much of anything." She shakes her head. "I should have been paying more attention."

"It's okay," Saffi says quietly, then prompts the woman to continue: "So you entered the apartment..."

Morrow nods. "I found David at the end of the hall leading off our foyer. He wasn't moving. I...I went to him and...he was covered in blood. Blood was everywhere. Then I remember I heard a sound deeper in the apartment, a thump. Like someone was walking in the dark and hit something." She raps the table with her knuckles. "I think that's when I called 911."

"You think you did or you know you did?"

"I don't remember."

"Did you check David for a pulse? See if he was breathing?"

"I don't remember."

The room goes quiet for a long moment. Saffi reaches across the table, lines up the corners of the folders in a neat stack. Pulls them closer. She opens the top folder and reads something, shielding the text with her hand, then closes it. When she leans back to Morrow, the concern that filled her eyes earlier is gone, replaced with a flash of ice. Declan has seen that look before and never wants to be on the receiving end of it. It's go time. "Mrs. Morrow, security footage has you arriving home at nine twenty p.m. You didn't dial 911 until nine thirty-one. That's eleven minutes. It takes a minute or two to get to your apartment from the lobby. The actions you just described account for maybe another minute. What were you doing for the remainder of that time?"

Morrow says nothing.

"What aren't you telling me?" Saffi says.

"Nothing. I told you everything I remember. I'm sorry. I don't remember."

Saffi leans closer to her. "I think we need to cut the bullshit, so I'm going to ask you a very simple question: Did you kill your husband?"

The latest from New York City's top cop

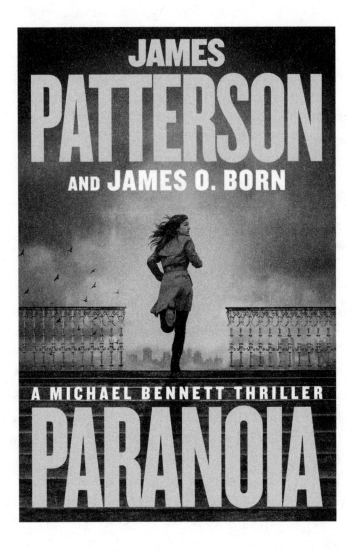

AFTER THE SHORT, official reception at the parish house of the church, I dragged Trilling to the Irish Rose, one of Lou's favorite pubs. As soon as we stepped through the old wooden doorway, it was like entering another universe. The place was absolutely packed. Most of the people who'd attended the funeral were there, plus a bunch of cops just getting off shift, some still in uniform. There was a certain subdued rowdiness that Lou would've appreciated. The Saturday afternoon atmosphere magnified the emotions.

I nodded to half a dozen people as we walked through the crowded pub. Somehow we found a couple of stools at the far end of the bar. Without even asking, a stout bartender with a fancy curled mustache set down two Guinnesses in front of us.

A short, balding Black man with thick glasses crawled up onto a table and started banging a metal tray with a serving spoon. I turned toward Trilling and said, "That's Dave Sharp. One of the truly great guys in the NYPD."

Sharp waited for everyone's attention. "I'll let you get back to drinking soon enough. I just wanted to remind everyone why we're here. Lou Sanvos will never be forgotten in this town. His support for youth centers is unparalleled. Lou's wife, Margaret, tells me she's fine financially and that any money people might want to donate should go to Lou's favorite cause: helping young people.

"I'm going to pass around the bucket, and anyone who feels like it can throw in a few bucks. We'll split it between the two youth centers in the Bronx Lou worked so hard to build."

Someone came up and tugged on Dave Sharp's sleeve. He leaned down, then turned to the crowd and said, "And even though it's not official, let's not forget our own Celeste Cantor, who'll be retiring soon and running for New York City Council. We're hoping that's just a stepping stone to bigger and better things." That comment got a loud round of applause as Inspector Celeste Cantor—an attractive fiftysomething woman dressed in a dark-blue pantsuit and not her usual uniform with more ribbons and medals than a nineteenth-century Bavarian count—stood up and waved to everyone in the bar.

Trilling said, "Cops can run for political office?"

"You have to retire first. If she's half as good a City Council member as she is a cop, we'll all be in better shape soon."

Cantor smiled when she noticed me at the corner of the bar. She pointed directly at me and started marching in my direction, fending off a few people trying to corner her as she approached.

After she gave me a hug, I introduced her to Rob Trilling. Cantor smiled and said, "We've both come a long way from patrol work in the Bronx, haven't we, Mike?"

I turned to Trilling and said, "Inspector Cantor was part of a narcotics squad when she was a lowly sergeant. They called themselves the Land Sharks, after an old *Saturday Night Live* skit. It only took a couple of months before every dealer in the city took notice and worried about 'the Sharks' coming onto their turf. Even the commissioner referred to them as 'the Sharks' during a news conference."

"And now I'm about to be cast out to sea."

"If you're running for City Council, I call that *catching a wave.*"

Cantor laughed. "As tough and dangerous as police work can be, I think I still prefer it to politics."

I raised my glass of Guinness and said, "Hear, hear."

Trilling turned and stared at me, so I quickly said, "Sorry—the

Irish pub got in my brain." I turned back to Cantor. "Let me know if there's anything I can do for you."

A crooked smile, the result of a broken jaw from a protester, spread across her face. "As a matter of fact, I do have something you could help me with."

I already regretted making the offer.

CELESTE CANTOR MOVED through the crowd like a great white shark. No pun intended. She was graceful and smooth, and anyone who noticed her got out of the way immediately.

I left Trilling at the bar and followed behind her like a remora. She certainly wasn't cold or menacing. She stopped and talked to a couple of people as we worked our way to an empty table in a corner.

An old-time narcotics detective gave Cantor a hug. He said, "Did you hear about Tabitha Arnold? She died from carbon monoxide after she got drunk and passed out in her kitchen with her car running in the garage."

Cantor nodded. "And I just heard Ralph Stein and Gary Halverson both committed suicide down in Florida."

The retired narcotics detective shook his head and looked down at the floor. "I heard. I knew Gary had advanced lung cancer. I just can't believe they'd use propane tanks to blow themselves up."

It was a shock to hear from a credible source about the retired detectives, longtime associates who'd started as patrol partners. Police suicides were becoming an epidemic.

Cantor continued to make her way through the crowded pub, graciously accepting congratulations from a half dozen people on her imminent retirement. A few people also wished her luck in her campaign.

It felt like forever, but we finally reached a quiet table in the corner. Cantor sat right next to me and leaned in close so no one would overhear our conversation.

She said, "You heard about Ralph Stein and Gary Halverson. And poor Tabitha Arnold. Now we have Lou Sanvos. We all know the statistics on police deaths. But for four retired cops to die this close together…makes me a little nervous. They were all members of the Land Sharks. Sooner or later, you start to see a pattern." She reached over and squeezed my arm. "I was hoping you'd come to the wake, Mike. You're one of the few people I really trust."

I saw where she was going but kept my mouth shut. No way I wanted to volunteer for something. I was going to make her say it out loud.

She looked me in the eye and said, "I want you to look at these deaths. But quietly. Just you on it for now. I don't want to start a panic. I can get you a special assignment. You can report only to me. What do you think?"

I didn't want to speak too quickly. I considered several options. Then I said, "I'm not sure why we need to keep it quiet. A little coverage might help flush out information, if there's anything to it."

"That's where personal and public interests overlap. Obviously, it's no secret I'm running for City Council. If these deaths turn out to be something other than what they appear, it'll look bad for me on the campaign trail that I didn't catch it. This is the sort of thing that falls directly under me as an inspector. But if I have you look into things, and if it turns out to be more than random deaths, I look proactive in having recruited you to solve them. You're the best homicide detective out there. Hands down. No one will question me about these deaths if they know I assigned you the investigation."

I appreciated her honesty about how this could affect her campaign. She was also right. These deaths alarmed me and deserved to be investigated.

I slowly nodded. "I've got some time. But I don't need to be reassigned to you. Harry Grissom is on vacation. I'm the acting supervisor on the squad. I should be able to cover this without drawing too much attention."

Cantor patted me on the arm. "I knew I could count on you. As I get closer to my retirement date, I find I have less and less time for real police work. As I said, you're one of the few people I trust to do it for me. I'll get you some reports to read over the weekend so you can get a head start."

Just as I was about to temper her expectations, Cantor stood up to greet a well-wisher. Whether it was official or not, she was already on the campaign trail.

I GOT HOME a little earlier than usual, but I now had on my iPad copies of police reports from White Plains and Hollywood, Florida, along with a report from the Westchester County Medical Examiner. My initial look through the details of these retired cops' deaths told me that the investigating detectives hadn't suspected anything beyond either suicide or accidental causes.

I made it all the way to the kitchen before any of my kids even noticed I was home. Chrissy jumped up from her homework to give me a hug. Jane, who was walking out of the kitchen, gave me a gentle pat on the belly. At least it was better than the stern look my teenager often threw my way these days.

Trent sat at the opposite end of the dining room table, doing his own homework. I leaned in as a concerned parent, willing to offer assistance.

"Whatcha working on?"

"Algebra."

I tried not to recoil too violently. I patted my son on his shoulder, mumbled, "Good luck," and eased my way into the living room. Ricky and Eddie played a video game from the couch. The rest of the kids had to be around here somewhere.

I took notice of my wife, Mary Catherine, sitting on a lounge chair on our balcony. She wasn't typically one for "lounging" during the day. In fact, I could easily imagine Mary Catherine calling an Army general too soft for giving his soldiers an hour off during a combat tour. Maybe that's an exaggeration. But maybe it's not.

The flip side was that, as exacting as her standards could be,

Mary Catherine was also the kindest and most loving wife and mother imaginable. Though we were technically still newly-weds, for the better part of a decade now she'd been acting as mother to the ten children I'd adopted with my late first wife. And now we were embarking on a brand-new experience for the both of us, being in the early months of expecting an eleventh child after a grueling IVF process.

The more I thought about a new baby around the house, the more terrifying it became. I'd never considered having ten kids a huge challenge. We had fun. We worked well together. And now that a couple of the kids were older, life had gotten a lot easier for me. I didn't know why I kept thinking adding one more would drive me over the edge. I calmed myself down and tried looking at it from a different perspective.

I had to admit the idea of a smiling infant held a lot of appeal. I loved a baby's laughter. I wanted this baby every bit as much as Mary Catherine did. The kids were on board as well.

I went to the balcony and leaned down to kiss her hello, taking a moment to look at her. "Are you feeling okay?"

"Just a little tired. I thought I should get off my feet for a few moments. What about you? How was the funeral?"

I shrugged. That's like asking how someone enjoyed their visit to the dentist. Most people don't like funerals. Unless you're Rob Trilling, who was a little odd. I said, "I might've agreed to do something for Celeste Cantor."

"Something like an investigation, or something like mainte-nance around her apartment?"

Mary Catherine's Irish accent made most things sound cheerful and funny. Basically, any time she told a joke, I laughed out loud. This time was no exception. I shook my head. "It's not a big deal. I should be able to clear it up before Harry gets back from vacation."

Mary Catherine smiled. "It's hard to think of Lieutenant Harry

Grissom actually leaving the job for a few weeks to visit a beach in the Caribbean. I'm glad *you've* always recognized there is a whole world outside of the NYPD. Of course, Harry never had any kids, so he doesn't understand how much time a real family can take."

"He knows how much time a wife can take. He's already experimented with those three times," I said. Then I added, "This vacation might have something to do with Lois Frang, the *Brooklyn Democrat* reporter he met during the sniper investigation. She seems nice."

Mary Catherine giggled and sat up in the lounger. I gave her a hand, helping her to her feet. She used the opportunity to give me a hug. We walked into the living room together.

I saw both Ricky and Eddie immediately set down their video-game controllers. They never did anything like that when I walked into a room. Mary Catherine was definitely influencing these kids.

As we started toward the dining room, I noticed a hitch in Mary Catherine's step. Then she started to sag. I reached to support her at the elbow, guiding her toward the recliner. Just as Mary Catherine plopped into the chair, she was out. I mean full-out unconscious.

Commotion brewed around me. Jane stepped in from the dining room to see what was going on. She immediately took control of the other children and started barking orders like a Marine Corps gunnery sergeant.

I wasn't sure I'd ever experienced panic like this before.

I had to get Mary Catherine to a hospital. Now.

For a complete list of books by
JAMES PATTERSON

VISIT
JamesPatterson.com

 Follow James Patterson on Facebook
@JamesPatterson

 Follow James Patterson on X
@JP_Books

 Follow James Patterson on Instagram
@jamespattersonbooks